Harper,

Happy reu

K. M.

CLUB

X

SURRENDER

SURRENDER

CLUB X #2

NEW YORK TIMES BESTSELLING AUTHOR

K.M. Scott

2014 Copper Key Media, LLC

Published in the United States

ISBN-10: 1941594050
ISBN-13: 978-1-941594-05-6

Cover Design: Cover Me, Darling
Interior designed and formatted by E.M. Tippetts Book Designs

ABOUT THIS BOOK

Stefan March lives for a good time. Born into wealth, he sees everything in terms of what he can have, especially women. So far, life has denied him nothing and no one. When he meets his newest bartender, he instantly knows who his next conquest will be, but Shay's not like the usual women he collects. To get her, he'll have to be more than just the player he's always been.

Shay Callahan is beautiful, determined, and intelligent. She's got plans for her life, and they don't include getting sidetracked by a man, and certainly not her wealthy player boss. Her job at Club X is for one thing—money to fund her education—but if she can make Stefan March see he's not God's gift to women, all the better. She never expects to find out there's more to him than meets the eye.

As different as day and night, can these two see past who they think they are to find love?

Sometimes it's the ones you're sure you won't like who turn out to be your favorites. You're one of those souls for me. May others see in you what I see.

ONE

❀ SHAY

Elliot lay still half asleep, spread-eagled and taking up three-quarters of the bed as I sat down on the edge of the mattress to slip on my stockings. I turned to look at his naked body barely covered by the sheet and nudged him back over to his side, but he grumbled some words to let me know he didn't like me waking him so early. The man didn't seem to recognize any time before noon.

"I have a job interview today, El. It might be nice if you woke up to have some breakfast with me before I go. Maybe a little pep talk?"

He waved his hand in the air and gave me the thumbs up sign, mumbling, "You'll be great, Shay. Don't worry."

Standing up, I straightened my black pencil skirt and shook my head. "Let's hope my potential new bosses think the way you do."

Elliot rolled over and slid his hand up my leg and under my skirt to where the top of my stockings sat on my thigh. Looking up at me with his sexy hazel eyes, he chuckled. "Baby, if these men don't want to hire you to bartend, then they're fucking crazy. You're hotter than any other bartender I've ever seen. Just be yourself and you and I will be celebrating tonight."

"And you've seen how many bartenders? You aren't even legal to drink, El."

He looked up at me and winked. "I don't have to know any bartenders to know you're sexier than fuck. Now get that gorgeous ass back in bed so I can show you how sexy I think you are."

I nudged his hand down my leg, but he fought me, pushing against my hand to feel the cotton of my panties. "El, I have to go. I'll see you when I get back."

"I like the idea of you lifting that skirt and riding some morning wood a whole lot better. You have time. You said you wanted me to have breakfast." Inching his fingers up underneath my panties, he slid a fingertip over my clit, sending a jolt of pleasure straight through me. "I want this for breakfast."

"I can't," I protested, wishing I could. We'd spent most of the night making love, but that's what a new relationship was all about. I couldn't or didn't want to see his negatives, such as the fact that he didn't seem to be much of a worker if the number of hours he spent in bed with me and by himself was any indication. Or that he had little money. I didn't care about that yet. What I enjoyed about Elliot was that he was good in bed and like most guys of twenty, he could fuck for hours. Being twenty-four, I appreciated his youthful enthusiasm.

"Baby, you can do whatever you want. They won't care if you're late for this interview. It's a bar."

Shaking my head, I tried to push him away again, but he was insistent. This was what I got for hanging out with a twenty-year-old guy. "Elliot, stop. I need this job."

"So serious all the time." He pulled the covers down

to show me his rock hard cock ready to go, as he always was. "Thank God one of us keeps us off the straight and narrow. Now come here."

I couldn't help but lick my lips as I stared at his body ready to go. His dark brown hair, too long for my usual taste, hung in his eyes, but even lying there as a disheveled mess he still made me wet just looking at him. Not an ounce of fat marred his perfect body, although in two months I'd never seen him do even a single push up. Maybe he didn't just lie around the apartment when I worked, after all?

This thing between us was basic biology. I knew this. He was a hot, young guy in his prime, and I liked that. Nothing more. Not that it had to be anything more. We'd gotten into this knowing neither one of us wanted a serious relationship. I knew I'd be leaving in a few months and likely never see him again, and he was a typical twenty-year-old nearly grown up boy whose only mastery of anything was shirking responsibility.

We were an odd couple everywhere but in bed. My goals included earning my Ph.D., and Elliot had not one goal. None. He had no job, and as far as I could tell in the whole time we'd been together, he had no plans to get one. Where he got money was a mystery to me, but the truth was if I cared about him—truly cared—I'd want to know.

I'd never asked, and he'd never offered the information. I only knew he had money but no job. And I was the exact opposite. I always had a job, even with attending school full time, and never had enough money.

"Shay, you worry about things for nothing. If you don't get this job, you'll get another. No big deal. Now come here so I can bury myself balls deep inside you."

"This means a lot to me, El. I have to save up for my

trip. I can make a lot of money at Club X."

Elliot laced his hands behind his head. "Club X isn't really your style, though. What's wrong with your current job?"

"I don't make enough money, and what do you mean it's not really my style? As long as they pay in good old American dollars, it's my style."

"I've heard things. It's not like a usual bar."

I lowered my head and stared down at him. "And you'd know what about a usual bar?"

"I heard it's more of a sex club."

In truth, I'd heard that once or twice about Club X too, but it didn't matter. I wasn't applying for a job that would have anything to do with sex. All I'd have to do was serve alcohol. "Well, I have enough sex with you, so they'll just have to take me as a bartender."

"That better be all they want."

Elliot's expression told me what all this stalling was about. He was jealous. "I see what you're up to. You're worried."

He shrugged and made a face that looked like he'd just sucked on a lemon. "No, I'm not."

Leaning across the bed, I pushed my face in front of his. "Yes, you are. You're jealous. I thought we weren't about that. This was just supposed to be a good time, remember? Nothing more."

I saw in his eyes this wasn't just a good time for him.

"Whatever. Do what you want. Just know that I don't share well with others, Shay."

Oh the petulance of youth! I knew I better soothe his hurt feelings now or he'd sulk all day. "Elliot, I have no plans to share myself with anyone but you, okay? But I can't do the committed thing. You know that. You don't want that anyway. Twenty-year-old guys like to have a good time, so let's have a good time."

He pulled me down on top of his body, pushed my skirt up around my waist, and thrust his hips off the bed, his sour mood disappearing by the second. Nuzzling my neck, he murmured, "That's all I wanted, baby. Consider it a good luck fuck so you get the job."

I rolled my eyes and tried to wriggle out of his hold. "I can't be late, El. We can pick this up when I get back, okay?"

He ignored my words and pulled my panties off to the side to give his cock clear passage. One quick thrust and he was fully nested inside me, making my legs go weak. Giving in, I sat up and straddled him for some of that morning wood he was sporting. In truth, I had a little time before I had to leave, so why not begin with a breakfast of champions?

X

I didn't make it two steps into the coffee shop before my best friend Carrie looked at me and said, "Shay, you look like you just rolled off that hot man of yours."

Quickly, I looked down my body to check that my clothes weren't wrinkled and screaming "I just had sex!" There was no sign of any untidiness, so I took a seat across from her at our usual corner table and shook my head. "Don't be jealous."

Carrie took a sip of her latte and smiled, pushing her dark blond hair off her forehead. "No jealousy here, girl. That boy isn't even legal. You getting a coffee?"

"No. Not today. I already had a cup at home. I don't need to be jumpy today. And he's perfectly legal. Twenty is legal."

"That boy can't even get into a club, Shay. What do you plan to do with him if you get this job at Club X? It's not like you'll be able to take him there."

Reaching over, I broke off a piece of her coffee cake and popped it into my mouth. "I don't plan to take anyone there, Carrie. It's a job. Do you take people to the boutique?"

"You know what I mean. He's four years younger than you."

"And the problem is?"

Carrie and all her twenty-six years of cynicism stared at me with a look full of judgment in her jaded brown eyes. "He's a child. You're a grad student, and he doesn't even have a job. What exactly are you doing with him?"

"Other than fucking him every chance I can?" I said with a chuckle I couldn't hold back.

"Shay, there are millions of men in the world who aren't boys and have great bodies and penises who are actually gainfully employed. Some might even be good in bed too."

This wasn't the first time Carrie had given me this lecture. Elliot was an acquired taste, and as a woman who'd made a success of her own boutique all on her own, she found his boy-toy act appalling. For her, a man had to wear a suit, and an expensive one at that, and as she always said, "bring something to the table more than a big cock." That Elliot only brought the right size cock wasn't enough, in her mind.

She wasn't necessarily wrong. I knew that. I knew El was a passing fancy. He had no idea what I meant when I talked about my work, and he had nothing to say to my friends, even the ones who didn't think he was one step above gigolo like Carrie thought. I freely admitted that he was merely great sex.

Breaking off another piece of her coffee cake, I leaned forward and nodded. "Gainfully employed penises?"

She shot me a look of disgust. "I know. I know. I don't plan on this being a forever thing. Elliot is just something for now. I'll be leaving in a few months anyway, so we'll be over then, if it doesn't happen before."

"He must be incredible in bed, Shay. You know I wouldn't give you a hard time if I didn't love you like a sister, but he's way too young for you. You need a man who can handle his business. That boy has no business at all."

"I get it. I don't want you thinking he's a freeloader. I never pay for him."

Jesus, I sounded like one of those abused women making excuses for their man.

"He has no job, honey. Where does he get money from?"

I shrugged. "I don't know."

"You've never asked?"

Avoiding her intense stare, I looked away and mumbled, "No."

"Shay, look at me. I've known you long enough to know this isn't healthy for you. Maybe Elliot's a great guy. Maybe he isn't. That isn't the point. You bring a ton of great stuff to the table, and he shouldn't even be let in the house to find the table. There are levels, honey, and he's not at yours."

I looked at her and knew she was right. The problem was I didn't want to let Elliot go. Not yet anyway. "I know all of this, Carrie. And I know you love me, but give the poor guy a break. It must be terrible to be used just for sex."

Her face twisted into a look of disgust. "Uh-huh. A hardship like no man has ever endured before."

"Let's change the subject. I need to go into this interview feeling good."

Carrie pulled her cake away from me and shook her

head. "Speaking of that, why are you bothering with this job at Club X anyway? You're leaving, so why get a new job? What's wrong with the one you have already?"

"I'm not making enough at The Brew House. I need to save up some money for when I go to Copenhagen. I just figured if I could get a job at Club X, I'd be able to have a stockpile when I leave."

"You think you're up for that? I hear that place is wild. Members only and freaky."

I rolled my eyes at her use of freaky. Like I hadn't seen my fair share of that in and out of the clubs I'd bartended in. "I'm not worried. I heard from one of the girls who used to work with me that there's money to be made there, so why not? She worked there for a while and it was fine."

Carrie leaned forward and whispered, "You have to tell me if the rumors of the fantasy rooms are true. I've heard things."

"I don't plan on doing anything that involves fantasy rooms, Carrie. I'm going there to bartend. That's it. My friend from The Brew House got me an interview, so I'm going in with the attitude that they need a bartender and I'm their woman."

"I've heard things about the one brother, Stefan, who runs the nightclub part. Major league player, Shay."

"So?" What the hell did I care about some guy she thought was a player?

"So nothing. I've just heard things."

Leaning back in my chair, I rolled my eyes. "I don't care what this Stefan does when he isn't running Club X. As long as he pays me the money I need, we'll get along fine."

"I hear he's loaded. He and his two brothers run the place and make millions every year off the wild shit our fellow citizens like to act out in those fantasy rooms."

I looked across the table and saw Carrie's eyes light up. "Why do I have the feeling you think this guy would be more appropriate for me than Elliot?"

"Because he's got millions and owns a club. Your guy has some secret stash of cash and goofs around your place all day while you work your tail off."

"Money's not everything, Carrie. I would think everything you went through with Rick would show you that."

Now it was time for her to roll her eyes. Every time I mentioned her most recent ex-husband I got the eye roll of disgust. "He Whose Name We Are Never To Say Again has nothing to do with this. And he isn't even loaded. All I'm saying about your situation is that you might like it if a man with some success behind him began to take care of your business."

"So better to be with a guy who's some kind of world-class player than an unemployed twenty-year-old who's crazy about me?"

Taking a sip of her coffee, her red stained lips spread into a wide smile. "Better to be with a man who's your equal, Shay. And by the way, you have some nerve pooh-poohing players. Isn't that what you're doing with your boy-toy there? Playing?"

I hated when she hit too close to home. Fidgeting in my chair, I looked away again. "It's not the same thing, Carrie. We're having a good time and nobody's going to get hurt. Players like you're talking about leave a lot of emotional carnage in their wake. I'm not up for that, thank you."

Sliding over the rest of her cake, she rested her hand on top of mine. "I'm not saying you are, honey. I'm just saying you're too good for what you're doing now."

Looking down at my watch, I saw I had just enough time to get to Club X for my interview. "I have to head out. I'll let you know how it goes."

"I want all the in depth details, so take lots of mental notes. And don't worry. You got this."

I stood from the table and grabbed the last bite of coffee cake. "Yeah, it's nothing. They want a bartender, and I want a job. I'll make sure to check out this world-class player you've heard about, though. You know, just for shits and giggles."

Carrie nodded. "Exactly. Call me when you get out."

As I headed out the door toward my car, I tried to ignore the little voice in my head telling me Carrie was right about Elliot. I didn't know how she'd gotten my conscience on her side, but I didn't plan to listen to either of them yet. For the next few months, all I planned to do was make as much money as possible at Club X and have the time of my life with the hot young guy sharing my bed.

Nothing more. Nothing less.

TWO

Ç STEFAN

Cash's office door opened and a knockout brunette walked out right past me on her way toward the front door and out of my life if I didn't stop her. Quickly following behind, I caught up to her and tapped her on the shoulder. "Hey, where you going? If you're here for a job, you'll probably be dealing with me."

She turned around and looked me up and down, her gaze settling on mine after she'd thoroughly checked me out. "Yeah? Well, if I get the job, we can talk then."

"I'm part owner here, so you'll definitely get the job. What's your name?" I asked, dying to find out who this woman with as much nerve as I had was.

"Shaylene Callahan, but everyone calls me Shay."

"Well, Shay, whatever job you want, it's yours."

Despite the fact that I'd just assured her she could have a job at the hottest club in town, her expression screamed she was unimpressed. What was with this girl?

"Well, that's good. Guess I'll be starting when your boss calls me."

"Brother, and he's not my boss. He and I own this place, along with our other brother. My name is Stefan March. I manage Club X. What job were you interviewing for?"

I silently prayed to God it wasn't one of Kane's dancers because while I would fight him for her, dealing with that miserable fuck was difficult on any day but especially recently. I didn't know what his problem was, but he'd been downright surly for the last week.

Shay pushed her right hip out and smiled. "Bartender. I need some good money and I've heard this place is where to get it."

"Then you'll be working under me," I said as I licked my lips in anticipation of her being under me in more ways than just at work.

Her green eyes flashed anger. "Under you? Well, bossman, this is the twenty-first century and this act of yours is straight out of chapter one in the how to sexually harass your employees handbook. Perhaps we should say I'll be reporting to you during my working hours. And that's it."

Her words were like a hard slap to my face. I couldn't decide if she was the world's biggest bitch or what could be my greatest conquest yet. Either way, she had sharp tongue in that beautiful mouth of hers. This kitten had claws.

"You don't sound like any bartender I've ever had... working for me."

"That's probably because you don't often get microbiology grad students serving liquor to your guests."

God, every word out of her mouth was a jab, but I liked a challenge. "Do you have any experience bartending, Shay? I mean, you're nice and all, but I don't have the time to train a newbie."

Her eyebrows shot up, and her eyes flashed her anger once again. "I think you'll see by my application that I have more than enough experience for you. I've been bartending since my second year in undergraduate school. That's the first four years of college, by the way."

Ah, now I understood. She was a smart girl. Normally, I stayed as far away as possible from that kind of female. They always had all the answers and never understood how to truly have fun. And worst of all, they always wanted a relationship. Of all the things I wanted in my next woman, intelligence was at the bottom of my list.

"College? Well, I guess that's a nice way to spend four years. I preferred earning money, but to each his own. Microbiologist, huh? Probably will never make enough to afford a membership here anyway. Good thing you're going to be an employee working for us. Employees get free memberships."

In truth, as a bartender, Shay wouldn't be given a membership since she wouldn't be an upper level employee. Only Cash, Kane, and I got them, along with his assistant, Olivia. But as part owner, I could give Shay a membership if I chose to.

At that moment, I couldn't think of anything I'd like to do less.

"I'm not interested in a membership, Stefan. I'm interested in making money at a job. Hopefully, you and your brothers will recognize my talents and hire me. Either way, I have to go."

Before I could say another word, she turned on her heels and marched out the door. Fuck, she was a feisty one. I stood there watching the door close while my brain played tug of war with itself. On the one hand, Shay was smoking hot and I had no doubt having her would be a good time. Long brown hair, a mouth that would have made me hard if it wasn't spewing such sharpness, and a body....fuck, her body was hot! My mind was already filled with thoughts of how incredible it would be to fuck her. What an ass she had! On the other hand, she was smart and possessed a level of bitchiness that even I had to admit I might not be able to overcome.

Might. But if I'd ever met a challenge, it was her.

"She wants a job as a bartender," Cash announced behind me.

Turning to face him, I pretended not to care. "Yeah?" I said with a shrug. "I don't know if I need a new bartender, and we have a list a mile long of people who want to be one."

"Okay. I just wanted to mention it. She seemed nice in the interview. Kane liked her well enough, which says something, I guess. You would have gotten to talk to her if you bothered to join us."

Why I hadn't gotten to the interview on time had to do more with nursing a hangover from the night before than with not caring about Cash's precious hiring process. Not that I really cared to sit through hour after hour of interviews with him and Kane. "We have private investigators for a reason. I don't need to see every goddamn person who walks through the door for a job, Cash."

He put his hands up in surrender. "Okay, okay. Take it easy. You don't want her to work for us, she won't work for us. Case closed."

Cash walked away as I stood still stinging from Shay's barbed jabs. I didn't know if I wanted to bother trying to get with her. With all the women in the world, why take the time to overcome whatever defensive bullshit she had going on?

Kane came around me and stood with his arms folded across his chest. "She's a wild one, isn't she?"

"Wild? I missed the interview, so I wouldn't know."

"I heard how she took you down a few pegs before she left. Looks like there's at least one woman you won't be having."

I didn't enjoy Kane's smugness. Whether it was because he'd been pissed off about something recently or because he never had any women, he seemed to truly enjoy Shay's attitude with me.

"It doesn't matter how fucking wild she is. She's not going to be working here, so what do I care?"

"Seems to have struck a nerve there, Stef. I guess she's just out of your league."

He wasn't even trying to hide his joy over this. "Has nothing to do with leagues, Kane. If it did, we might be talking about how someone like that wouldn't even bother talking to the likes of you if you weren't part owner of this club."

"I'm not the one who thinks he can have any woman on Earth. I'm a little choosier and I prefer to keep my relationships a little more private. You prefer to have them displayed on the bar each night and then in lawyers' offices during depositions. But you're not going to get the chance with this one."

"That sounds like a challenge, Kane. I don't think you're up to it, though."

He chuckled and shook his head. "She's not my type, Stefan. I don't want her, and I won't fight for her."

"Not fight for her. It just sounds like you don't think I could get her."

His chuckle morphed into a full-blown laugh. "I know you can't. That woman is too smart for you. She saw your game coming a mile away. Accept it. Shay isn't a woman you can have. Move on and be happy with those cheap little playthings you prefer to spend your time with."

"You honestly don't think I can get her to go out with me, do you?"

"I honestly can't believe you'd want her. She's too much work for you, Stefan. You'd have to be more than the man whore you've always been. I just don't think you're up to it."

Was Kane serious? "You're saying you think there's a woman I can't seduce? Am I hearing you right?"

"I'm saying seducing her isn't something you know how to do. It's going to take a whole lot more than a few drinks, your charming smile, and whatever smooth lines you use to get with your usual type."

I couldn't believe what I was hearing. Kane, who I didn't think I'd ever seen with a woman, was doubting my ability to charm someone. Kane, who most females backed away from in fear, was saying I wasn't smart enough to get Shay Callahan, science nerd, into bed. He had to be kidding!

"Kane, you're coming dangerously close to insulting me. For a man who has so little success with women, you seem to not know how successful I've been."

"I've seen your conquests. Not impressed. It doesn't take much to get cheap sluts to fuck you. They're going to do it anyway, so if you're the nearest guy around, you luck out."

"Fuck you, Kane!" I spat out, sick of this conversation. It wasn't bad enough I was hung over, but now I'd had to deal with two people giving me shit.

"You know what they say. It's all about location, location, location. I'd bet if you didn't have a constant stream of young ones wanting to work as bartenders here that you'd get far less ass."

The guy was taunting me. I knew it, but something in me snapped and made me want to force him to put up or shut up. Kane was much bigger than I was, though, and I wasn't stupid. I may have wanted to knock him flat on his ass, but the reality was that I'd likely get one or two shots in before he kicked me around my bar.

No, I couldn't beat him physically. But there were other ways to bring him down to size.

"Kane, I could stand here all day trading jabs with you, but I've got a better idea. Let's make a bet. That's if you're up to it, of course."

He stepped back and stared me down. "You want to bet what with me? That you can get with that girl?"

"Yeah. Take the bet or show you're all talk."

"I'm not interested in chasing after that girl. She's not my type. I don't even pretend she is. I'm not interested in her or your bet."

He turned to walk away, but I caught him by the shoulder and stopped him. "Hear me out. I'm not talking about a bet to see if you can get her before I do. I'm saying I'll bet you I can get her to fall for me."

"What's in it for me, other than seeing you make an ass out of yourself?" he asked with the sinister grin he wore so often around me.

"Name it. You set the terms."

He took a few moments to think about my offer and finally said, "Let me see if I got this straight. You're bothered that I don't think you have it in you to get this girl, so you want to make a bet that you can?"

I forced a nonchalant shrug. "If you don't think you're up to it…"

"Is this part of that Stefan charm that gets all the women to fuck you? I don't see it, but if you insist, I'll take your bet."

"Good. Name your terms."

"You have to get this girl to fall for you, and I don't mean just sleep with you. She has to be in love with you or you don't win."

The reality that making a woman fall in love was much harder than making one fall into bed with you could be a real problem. Women like Shay didn't do either easily, I guessed, but sex was a whole lot easier than love.

"Fine."

"And you have only one semester to do this in. She made it clear in the interview that next semester she's not going to be able to work since she'll be studying abroad. That gives you maybe four months."

"Four months? What the fuck, Kane? How long does it take for you to get into a woman's pants? Jesus, I bet I can do it in a tenth of that time."

"You do realize she's not like the other women who work for you, right? She's smart, successful, and from what I already heard from her when she stood right there and dressed you down, she doesn't even like you."

"No matter. I'll take the four months, but I don't plan to need it. What else?" I bragged, secretly admitting to myself that it very well could take half that time just to get her to warm up to me. After that, though, it would be smooth sailing.

"You have to show proof."

I'd always suspected Kane was a kinky one. What did he want? Video? "Proof like what? You planning to watch me sleep with her?" I joked.

"Cash and Olivia are planning their engagement party for just around the time you'd have to get Shay to fall for you. You're going to have to show up to the party with her, and you're going to have to get her to say she loves you."

"As long as I don't have to be in love with her, we have a deal."

"The man whore in love? I'm not ready for hell to freeze over just yet. No, all you need is her in love with you."

I chucked him on the shoulder. "I don't think I've ever seen you this cruel, Kane. It seems heartless to have the girl fall in love with me when I won't be in love with her."

Shaking his head, he smiled. "Not cruel at all. If I thought for a second that this one would even give you the time of day, I wouldn't agree to this bet at all. I don't think you have a chance, little brother. You've met your match this time."

"Yeah, yeah. Whatever. So what do I get if I win?"

Kane grinned. "A gorgeous woman you'd never deserve in love with you."

"Not good enough. I want something from you when I win. Put up or shut up."

"You can't want money. What else do I have that you want?" he asked, genuinely confused about what I could be angling for.

"Your Mustang."

A look of terror crossed his face and he shook his head quickly. "No."

"What's wrong, big brother? Chicken shit?"

"I'm not risking my car. There's no way in hell I'm letting you touch that baby."

I'd wanted to get my hands on Kane's 69 Mustang Boss 429 since the first time I laid eyes on it. Black, sexier than any other vehicle I'd ever seen, it was the one car I hadn't been able to find for my own. I'd get that car and Shay too.

"Seems like you think I might win, Kane. All that talk and when push comes to shove, you're nowhere to be found."

Leaning down, he pushed his face close to mine. "I'm not betting my car, Stefan. I don't care if you fuck this girl or not. No deal."

"Then let me have it for a weekend. I win and you give me your car for a whole weekend."

He seemed to think about my concession and nodded. "And what do I get if you lose? I'm not risking the one thing I care about more than life itself if I don't get something pretty fucking incredible in return."

"My humiliation won't be enough?"

"I don't think you'll be humiliated. You won't really care for her, so your feelings won't be involved. This has to be something worthwhile if my car is on the line, even if it is only for a weekend."

"How about my apartment? You seemed to like it when you came over that one time."

Kane raised his eyebrows in disbelief. "You're going to give me your apartment on the bay?"

"Sure." I was pretty sure he'd never get to step foot into my place.

"So let me get this straight. If you don't get this woman to fall in love with you within four months, you'll give me your apartment. For how long?"

"For an entire year."

"And if you do get her to fall in love with you, you get my car for a weekend?"

"Sounds good. Is it a deal?" I asked, holding my hand out to shake on it.

Kane took my hand and shook it hard. "I'm going to enjoy that place of yours, and seeing you get shot down by a real woman will just be icing on the cake."

"Just get that Mustang ready for me. I plan to enjoy my weekend with it picking up women. If you had any skills, you'd use it to get chicks too."

Shaking his head, he mumbled something as he walked away, no doubt sure he would win our bet. I had no intention of losing this one. That car and my reputation meant too much to me.

I headed into Cash's office to find him staring at his laptop. "Hey, about that girl who came in to be a bartender. Shay was her name, I think. I changed my mind. She'll do fine, so give her a call and see when she can start."

He didn't try to mask his suspicions. "I thought you weren't in need of another bartender. Or was it that we had enough applications? I can't remember. Now you want me to call her and get her in here?"

"Yeah. It's no big deal. If you don't want to, it's fine. I just think the club can use someone like her behind the bar."

Cash shrugged. "Okay. I'll give her a call. I'll let you know when she can start."

"Great! Let me know."

Cash looked confused as I left, but he didn't need to know anything more. This was between me and Kane.

And may the best man win.

THREE

🌼 **SHAY**

By the time I made it home, my blood was still boiling. Who the fuck did Stefan March think he was? And what century did he live in? Slamming the door behind me, I stomped into my apartment, sure I'd barely escaped before that troglodyte moved to pat me on the ass, like I was some 1950s fucking secretary!

"Hey! What's with all the noise?" Elliot yelled from the kitchen.

"I swear to God if I didn't need the money..." I grumbled as I headed toward him standing in only a pair of boxer shorts in front of the stove.

Elliot turned toward me and smiled. "How did the interview go? Did you ace it?"

Leaning against the doorframe, I shrugged, still frustrated by my first meeting with my potential future boss. "I don't know. I guess I'll find out in a few days."

"I'm making breakfast. Want some?" he said with a smile as bacon sizzled in the frying pan, filling the room with its pungent odor.

"Aren't you afraid of getting burned by the grease?"

He turned back toward the stove and moved the

bacon around with the spatula. "Nah. Anyway, it doesn't hurt that much."

"Have you ever been splashed with hot grease? It hurts like hell."

"I have. Did a stint as a cook for a while before I met you. Grease is nothing compared to oil. Now that's painful."

"I don't see the difference. A cook? So you had a job then? When was that?"

I knew I sounded like his mother right there. I didn't want to be that way. It was just that Carrie's words from earlier about Elliot and his lack of gainful employment still rang in my ears.

He turned around and shot me a glance that told me my questions surprised him. "Is something wrong, Shay?"

I shook my head and walked up behind him to wrap my arms around his naked waist. Pressing my cheek to his back, I said, "No. There's nothing wrong. Just idle curiosity."

Elliot turned in my hold and kissed the top of my head. "Ask me anything. I'm an open book. You know that, baby."

Looking up into his hazel eyes, I saw the same gentle gaze as always. Nothing bothered him, not even my residual bitchiness from meeting Stefan March. "It's okay. I know we aren't all about answers."

He moved the pan off the burner and turned the heat off. I stepped away to let him lift the bacon out of the grease, but he pulled me back against him, ignoring his breakfast. "Shay, you're the one who doesn't want that. I've been about all you since the moment I saw you on the beach that day. This thing between us is like it is because you want it this way. I'd be more than happy to answer anything you want to ask."

"No, it's okay. I like you being a mystery, El."

The truth was I didn't want to know all about him. If I did, I might want to send him packing right then and there. Or worse, I might want to stay with him forever, and that couldn't happen. I had plans for my future, and unfortunately, they didn't include him or any man, for that matter.

"Ah, mystery. That's what we're calling what I am?"

He bent down and kissed me gently, like he adored me. Tapping him on the nose, I smiled and backed away. "I have to head down to talk to Dr. Taduch. I'll be back later, though, so we can grab a bite to eat before I head off to work."

"Sounds great. As for me, I'm going to devour this pound of bacon."

I left him standing there with his greasy breakfast, and although I knew it was wrong, a tiny part of me couldn't help but judge him. While I spent my days buzzing around town trying to make money, he spent his time overdosing on the flesh of farm animals.

My phone rang as I slid behind the wheel of my barely running 2005 Taurus. Swiping the screen, I expected to hear Carrie's voice but heard a man's instead.

"Hello, Shay Callahan?"

"Yes?" The man's voice flowed over me like silk and sounded vaguely familiar.

"It's Cassian March. I spoke to my brother and he believes you'd be a valuable addition to the club."

Unable to contain my happiness at the news that I'd gotten the bartender job at Club X, I squealed, "That's great! When do you want me to start?"

"As soon as you fill out the required paperwork, you can start whenever Stefan needs you. Feel free to stop in anytime today. If I'm not around, you can speak to my assistant, Olivia, and she can help you."

"Thanks so much, Cassian. I appreciate this."

"I think you'll like working with us, Shay. We look forward to seeing you."

I thanked him again and ended the call, thrilled at the chance to begin making some real money for Copenhagen. As I drove toward school, I couldn't help but wish Stefan March was as professional as Cassian March. How interesting that one brother could possess such wonderful manners while the other one acted like some frat boy on a quest to fuck as many co-eds as possible. I had no idea how old Stefan was, but even Elliot and his twenty years acted more maturely.

Dr. Taduch had been called away to a department meeting, but he'd left the information I needed to finalize my trip to Copenhagen. Since I had some extra time on my hands, I stopped by Carrie's boutique to share my good news.

I found her standing behind the counter, her eyebrows knitted as she hunched over a spreadsheet. She looked like she desperately needed a break.

"Hey you! Guess who's the newest bartender at Club X!"

She lifted her head to look at me and smiled broadly. "I knew you'd get it!"

"What's with the sour puss face you were wearing when I walked in?"

She pushed aside the stack of papers and shook her head. "Same old accounting and inventory shit. I think one of my girls is stealing from me. God, I wish you were still working for me, Shay. Those were the good old days."

"Good old days indeed. When I wasn't in class or in lab, I was here or behind the bar at Danton's. I don't think I got more than four hours of sleep that entire year."

"Well, it was good for me. Now all I have are wannabes and what I think might be a thief. Tell me something to make my day better. Anything to get my mind off my troubles. Tell me all about the new job."

"There's not much to tell, to be honest. The one owner called me a little while ago to let me know the job is mine. That's the owner I like. The other one isn't too bad either. He doesn't say much, but he's okay. The one I have to work with, Stefan March, is a complete and utter jackass, though. Just my luck."

"Why? What happened?" Carrie asked as she began to fold a pile of pashminas.

"The man is perfectly Cro-Magnon. I swear he borderline sexually harassed me within the first five minutes of meeting me."

Carrie rolled her eyes. "So the player sexually harassed you? Big surprise. Is he hot?"

"Your way of excusing the bad habits of bad men really isn't one of your best qualities, you know that?"

"I have no problem with bad men, Shay. They're fun. And players are the best. You know how I love the game."

"Well, I don't. Players can go play with other women. I don't have time for games."

"So is he good looking?"

I couldn't deny Stefan March was hot. Tall, with light brown hair and brown eyes, he had a body that would make most women bow down and worship him. And between the tats and tongue piercing, he definitely had a bad boy vibe to him. In fact, the only real problem with him became clear when he opened his mouth to speak, and then the man became a total zero.

"He's not as great as I thought he'd be. Lots of muscles and tats, but he's a Grade A jackass. I didn't get a player vibe. Just an asshole vibe."

"So you're not seeing why women love him?"

I shook my head and scrunched my nose up. "No. I won't have any problem not loving Stefan March. Trust me."

"Well, then working at Club X should be a walk in the park for you. No temptation. Nothing to take your eye off the prize."

I picked up a pink pashmina and held it up to my neck to check how it looked in the mirror. "I'm there for the cash, Carrie. Period. End of sentence. If that ass Stefan March has any other ideas, he better go find someone who gives a damn. This girl is disinterested."

"That's good for Elliot," she said in a singsong voice.

Throwing the scarf on the counter, I held up my hand. "Stop it with the Elliot bashing, for God's sake. What did he ever do to you?"

Her mouth turned down into a frown. "Nothing. I'm sorry. I'm out of line. Forget I said anything."

"I know you mean well, Carrie. I do."

"It's not even that I have anything against Elliot, Shay. I really don't. I guess I'm just worried you're going to miss out on something great because you're settling for something meaningless. And before you say I'm bashing him again, meaningless is how you described what you two are, not me."

That had been how I described my relationship with him. I couldn't deny it. No matter how much he wanted us to be more, I'd made sure no meaning had snuck into what we were. Nothing serious. Just great sex and a good time.

"I can't do any more than meaningless right now, Carrie. If there's anyone to feel bad for, it's Elliot, though. He'd like us to be more than just sex and hanging out. It's me who doesn't."

Carrie held up her hands as if in surrender. "Okay, I

get it. You're content to play. Play on playette."

Her words hit me like a slap to my face. "I'm not a player. Elliot knows exactly how I feel. He went into this thing with his eyes wide open, and even though he'd like us to be more, he's okay with how things are."

"Spoken like a true player. Maybe that's why you don't like your new boss. Perhaps you see something in him that you see in yourself."

I scoffed at the idea that there was anything similar between Stefan March and me. The man was a base animal without even the finesse of a twenty-year-old. Guys like him used women for sex, and they deserved whatever misery they got in return.

But Carrie's comment sparked something inside me, and as I moved to walk out of her shop, I stopped. "Player, huh? Well, if anyone can outplay Mr. Stefan March, it's another player, right?"

She narrowed her eyes to suspicious slits. "Where are you going with this, Shay?"

"That man needs to be taught a lesson. He seems to think he's God's gift to women. I think it's time he learns just how common he really is."

"So you plan on doing what exactly?"

"I'm going to outplay the player. He thinks we're just toys for his amusement? Well, I bet I can get him to fall for me. Then he'll see how it feels when the shoe is on the other foot."

"What about poor, dear Elliot?"

I folded my arms across my chest. "Now you care about him?"

"No, not really. I'm just trying to cover all the bases. Isn't your seducing Stefan March going to get in the way of whatever you and Elliot have?" she asked with a sly grin.

"Elliot knows what we are. This isn't going to

change how I feel about him, and anyway, whatever we're doing has to end when I leave for Copenhagen in a few months."

"I think you're playing with fire, girlfriend. Stefan March isn't a twenty-year-old boy. He might just be out of your league."

My mouth hung open in shock. "I can't believe you don't think I can outplay that frat boy wannabe. You watch. Stefan March has met his match."

"Okay, but I hope you know what you're doing."

I turned on my heels and headed out the door. "I'm off to my new job to fill out some papers before I go to my old job. I'll talk to you later!"

"Call me and try to stay out of trouble!" she yelled as I left.

As if some guy could ever be trouble for me.

X

For the second time that day, I entered Club X with butterflies in my stomach. Even though I'd gotten the job, I really wasn't sure what I was getting into. My friend from The Brew House had clued me in on the sexy antics of the place, making sure to let me know how hot some of the patrons were. I cared more about how great they tipped, and she'd bragged about Club X being the best place she'd ever worked for just that reason. But something in the way she kept stressing the part sex played in the job made me nervous.

I should have asked Cassian about it in my interview, but it sounded foolish. What was I supposed to say? "By the way, Cassian, is it true that bartenders routinely were offered money for more than just drinks?"

Now that I'd taken the job, I had to admit I should

have asked something about it. The problem was I needed money. I didn't get the sense that Cassian or the quiet brother would let a female be attacked or anything like that, but Stefan seemed to be something else entirely. I could see him being the one who made sex part of the job.

As all these thoughts paraded through my mind, the quiet owner approached me. Bigger than either of his brothers, the man had a real badass vibe to him. His black hair and blue eyes made him striking, and the fact that he said next to nothing in my interview unnerved me.

"It's Shay, isn't it?" he asked in a deep voice that resonated in the air around us.

"Yeah. Cassian called me and said I got the bartender job. He said I needed to come down and sign some papers. Is he in?"

Kane nodded. "I'll take you back to him. I'm glad you decided to take the job. You'll like it here."

He began moving toward Cassian's office, staying next to me as we walked. "That's what Cassian said."

"A word of advice, though. Keep your eyes open with my younger brother. Stefan doesn't mean any harm, but he likes to think his antics are cute."

I read what Kane was trying to say loud and clear. Chuckling, I nodded. "I understand. It takes all kinds, right? No need to worry about me. I've been bartending for years. I know how to handle myself."

We stopped in front of Cassian's office, and Kane touched me gently on the shoulder. "That's good to hear. You're a smart woman, so I knew you'd be cool about it. Just ignore him and he'll go away sooner or later."

I looked up into Kane's blue eyes and saw sincerity. I couldn't complain about two brothers being all right.

That Stefan acted like a horny frat boy wasn't their fault. No job was perfect, so I could handle it. I'd dealt with drunken patrons at every bar I'd worked at. This would be no different. And while I was at it, I'd teach that boy a lesson.

"Thanks, Kane. I'll keep all that in mind."

"Good. And if you need anything, my office is on the top floor. Stop in any time."

He smiled and walked away, leaving me feeling good about Club X. So far, Kane had been a pleasant surprise. I hoped there would be more like that.

I knocked on Cassian's door and heard him call me in. Offering me a seat, he smiled warmly. "I'm glad you decided to take the job, Shay. There are just a few things we need to go over before you can start. As I mentioned before, there's a non-disclosure agreement we'll need you to sign, and I want to make sure if you have any questions about the contract that you feel comfortable to ask."

"Sounds great! I understand about the NDA, and I'm fine with it. Mum's the word. Although I've never had to sign a contract to work as a bartender, I understand your club is a little different than others, so it's fine. If I have any questions, I'll definitely ask."

He smiled again and pushed papers toward me. "Here's the contract. I'll give you some time to read it over and please ask if you have any questions."

As he walked out of the office, I scanned the document, sure there was nothing in it that would make me not want to sign. The fact was I needed money, and Club X was the place to get it. I'd worked in bars that required me to wear shorts so tiny my entire ass hung out. I'd worked in some where the uniform barely covered my chest, and at all of them I'd made less money in a week than I likely would make in a night or two at

Club X. Whatever Cassian needed me to sign, I'd do it because this bar would get me what I needed.

Signing my John Hancock on the bottom line, I looked around for Cassian to let him know. His gaze met mine from outside the office, and he returned to sit behind his desk.

"That was quick. Do you have any questions?"

"None that I'm sure can't be answered by your brother since he runs the bar, right? I'm sure he'll give me my hours."

Taking a deep breath in, Cassian let the air out of his lungs slowly, as if he was preparing himself to say something he dreaded. "Speaking of my brother, I hope you noticed the non-fraternization clause."

"I did." That I fully intended to disregard it as I played his brother for all he was worth crossed my mind, but that would be between Stefan and me.

"Good. I'm sure you won't have any problems then. If there aren't any questions, let me take you out to Stefan so you and he can get started."

"Great! Lead the way."

I followed him out to where Stefan stood checking over a liquor order. After telling me to find him if I had any problems, Cassian left me standing at the corner of the long glass bar waiting to find out when I'd start. Tugging my T-shirt down to show a little more skin than usual, I stuck my breasts out and put a smile on my face for when Stefan would finally bother to pay me some attention.

I saw him glance over at me out of the corner of his eye, but he said nothing, intentionally ignoring me for nearly five minutes. By the time the jackass turned to look at me, my back was killing me from doing my Barbie doll pose. How bimbos stayed like that all the time I couldn't imagine.

"Oh, you're still here? I figured Cash told you everything you needed to know and sent you on your way since I can't use you tonight."

Not exactly the reception I'd expected, especially since just hours earlier he would have taken me in the back and fucked my brains out if I'd given him even the slightest chance. What was with this guy? No doubt this was some kind of game, but I wouldn't be baited by the likes of him.

"No, he said to speak to you. I can't work tonight, but I can start next week. I figured we could talk so I'd have some idea of my schedule."

Stefan's gaze hardened. "I don't need someone next week. If you can't start tomorrow night, then you're of no use to me."

Ouch.

I stepped toward him and softened my approach. "I wanted to apologize for before. I didn't mean to go all feminazi on you. As for my schedule, I just don't want to leave my old job hanging. It seems wrong to do that to anyone. I'm sure you can understand."

My words seemed to make him happy, and he flashed me a gorgeous smile I couldn't help admitting made him quite appealing. All it took with most people was a pleasant tone and heartfelt words to get them to do what you wanted.

"Shay...that was your name, right?"

I nodded and he continued.

"Shay, I can't even remember what you said to me earlier. I've spoken to at least a dozen women since then, all of them as good looking or more than you and with as much experience and all of them wanting to work for me. So don't bother apologizing for whatever slight you think you caused me. But here's how things are going to go. Either you show up tomorrow night at seven in something showing a lot of skin or you don't. Either way, I'm fine with it."

And then he turned and walked away, leaving me with my mouth hanging open at how fucking rude he'd been. This guy was a total dick! How was I going to ever work for such a person?

I gathered up my copy of the contract I'd signed and made my way toward the door. My mind filled with ideas of how I wanted to tell the bastard off, but by the time I made it to my car, I'd succeeded in calming down enough to think clearly.

Taking a deep breath, I looked at my reflection in the rearview mirror and gave myself a much needed pep talk. *Don't let him get to you, Shay. You need this job and the money it will bring. Billy will understand if you can't work the whole two weeks. And as for Stefan March, when you play him, which sure as God made little green apples you will, you'll get even for what he just did.*

FOUR

🍾 STEFAN

I watched Shay leave after serving up my little spiel about not giving a fuck. When I finally got her under me, I'd enjoy the feeling of conquering such a woman. She had fire, no doubt. And now I knew what I'd suspected since seeing her storm out hours earlier — she could dish it out, but she couldn't take it.

Smiling to myself from this first victory, I heard footsteps behind me and turned to see Kane coming down the stairs with his same surly look from earlier. Whatever. At least one of us was having a great day.

"Kane, big brother? How are you?"

He stopped in front of me and folded his arms across his chest. Looking down at me, he frowned. "I have to say I'm intrigued by your seduction efforts, Stefan. Do most women you have like being treated like shit?"

"All women like being treated like shit, Kane. If they didn't, they wouldn't want players and bad boys. Were you spying on me?"

He chuckled and shook his head. "No. I just happened to hear your conversation with your new bartender. A dozen women? Where have you been hiding them? I've only seen her and Olivia here today."

"All part of the plan. You watch the master in action. She'll be on her knees in no time."

"You'll be lucky if she doesn't cut off your dick while she's down there. You're playing this all wrong, Stefan. Trust me on this."

I threw my head back and let out a full laugh. "Trust you? When was the last time you even had a woman? Take notes, Kane. Maybe your sex life will improve. This one's already on the hook. All I have to do is reel 'er in."

"Whatever you say. I'm going to enjoy your place. It'll be a nice change from my rooms here."

"Don't start moving in quite yet, but make sure that car of yours is all ready to go. I don't need it sputtering on me when I open that baby up. She's going to feel so fucking good when she finally gets the right person driving her."

"You talking about my car or your new bartender?"

Rolling my eyes, I turned back to my paperwork. "The car, of course. Shay doesn't concern me at all. This is a game, Kane. Don't go getting all emotional about it. After today, it's going to feel so fucking good playing her."

"You sound pretty emotional about this, Stef. I think she got under your skin earlier. I stand by my prediction. That woman won't touch you with a ten foot pole. She can get better, and she knows it, especially after what you just pulled."

"Yeah, yeah. You'll see. She's halfway there already. If you want to sweeten the pot on our deal, though…"

I smiled as I waited to see if Kane took the bait. He wanted to see me get my ego handed to me with this girl so much, I was pretty sure he'd want to up the ante.

From behind me, I heard him make a low groan.

"I'll take that. What do you want, and don't say my car permanently because that's not going to happen."

Turning around, I saw his expression telling me I couldn't push the car thing more. No matter. I had bigger plans. "I want your area."

The look of shock that crossed his face made just saying those words worth it, but he took the bait, with reservations. "What about Cash? I don't think he's going to appreciate us using anything in the club as part of a bet."

"If you think I'm going to win our little wager, just admit I'm that good and we can drop it. Just say the words, Kane. You're that good, Stefan. That's all I need to hear."

"No fucking way, Stef. You're not a good enough player to get that woman. No way. No how. I'll bet my part of the club on it. But now I want something."

"What? You already get my condo for a year if you win, which you won't. What do you want, two years?"

"No. I'll take the Ducati. Permanently."

Now Kane wasn't fucking around anymore. Putting my bike on the line made me squeamish. I didn't doubt my ability to get Shay, but if by some act of God or something I lost the bet, I'd lose my bike and not even have Kane's car to ride around in. I'd have a lot riding on this woman.

Putting on my best game face, I nodded my agreement to his newest terms. "Agreed. Do you know how great it's going to be having your car, running the fantasies of this place, and getting that woman to bow down to me?"

Kane stuck his hand out and grabbed mine to shake on our deal. "I've been thinking of buying a bike, but I like taking yours better. I might even sell it and buy another one since it likely won't fit me. All that, your apartment, and seeing Shay rub your face in it when she turns you down flat. This day is getting better by the minute."

I yanked my hand back, already uneasy about what I'd have to give up for Shay Callahan if I lost. I couldn't let my half-brother see I was worried, though. As far as he'd be concerned, I had it all under control.

Now I just had to believe she'd react like I thought she would.

X

I glanced at my watch and saw it was nearly seven. Looking around at the two dozen or so bartenders and servers I had for the night, I didn't see Shay. Well, at least if she didn't come back I wouldn't have to give up my bike to Kane if I lost the bet. Too bad, though. It would have been fun breaking her.

"Okay, everybody gather round!" I barked out to the group spread far and wide across the main floor of the club.

Lola moved to stand next to me and flashed me a sexy smile. "Hi, baby. What's new?" A gorgeous blond with big blue eyes and a rack to die for, she was one of the bartenders I routinely slept with who didn't end up suing us when I blew her off for a few weeks or so. She could always be trusted to give me a good time, so I always gave her the best spot in the bar.

"Not much, Lo. You're going to be at the front bar near the door tonight, as usual."

Sliding her hand over my back, she squeezed my ass. "You're the best boss, Stefan. How anyone can dislike you is beyond me."

I looked down at her and winked, our sign for meeting up later in my office. Smiling, she winked back and walked over to a small group of female bartenders, most of whom I hadn't slept with yet. Quickly sizing them up, I filed their names and what I liked about them away in my mind and returned to the meeting at hand.

"Okay, listen up. Lola is leading off tonight, so she'll be in charge of the front. Tammy, you'll be handling the back near the dance floor. Mika, you—"

Before I could finish my sentence, Shay appeared at my side and interrupted me. "So sorry. I couldn't find a place to park."

Glaring down at her, I continued with my assignments for the night. When I was done, I pulled her aside and tried to hide how much I liked seeing her in her tight black buttoned down shirt and very short black miniskirt. "Next time, get here on time or don't come at all."

Looking up at me through her bangs, she smiled. "Sorry, bossman. I promise to be good from now on. Tell me what you want me to do and I'm on it."

Caught off guard by her almost syrupy sweetness, I nevertheless liked this Shay better than the snapping bitch I'd met the day before. I especially liked how her C-cup tits nearly spilled out of her shirt. Something told me she wouldn't be able to keep up the cute act for long, though. Beneath this accommodating little thing she wanted to playact lay a much wilder creature I knew liked to scratch.

"Go with Lola tonight. You can shadow her to get your bearings. She's my best."

"For now," Shay said with a sly smile.

I knew when a woman wanted me, and all the signs were there with this one already. That weekend with Kane's Mustang and my moving up to the top floors were just a few short days away.

Shay handled herself like an expert behind the bar. I watched her and Lola for about a half hour before I had to admit she knew how to do the job. By midnight, she could man the end of the bar by herself, so I motioned to Lola to follow me to my office.

Closing the door behind her, Lola began to undress quickly, used to our time together being short. "It's been a while, Stefan. I missed you."

I licked my lips at the sight of her incredible body buck naked and walking toward me where I sat behind my desk. Opening up my arms, I eased her onto my lap. "You know how it is, Lo."

Slowly grinding against me, she nodded as she watched her pussy rub her juices into the front of my pants. Her pretty lips pouted, and she said in a tiny whine, "I know. I just wish we did this more often."

"Well, we're here now," I groaned as I slid my hands around to grab her gorgeous ass. If I didn't need to get back out on the floor, I'd have taken her over the desk. Since I was pressed for time, this would have to do. I'd get off either way, so it was all good.

"I guess. I just miss how often we used to get together," she said as she nuzzled my neck.

I tugged her head back by the hair so she faced me. "Take my cock out and let's get going, Lo. We don't have a lot of time."

Lola was nothing if not obedient, and she immediately did as she was told. Already hard, I couldn't wait to get inside her. Even after all these months of fucking one another, she still had some of what I liked in a woman. The rest I could ignore as long as I got off.

Reaching into my desk drawer, I pulled out a condom package and tore it open with my teeth as Lola stroked up and down on my shaft. I pushed her hands out of the way and unrolled the condom over my skin, hating the feel of it but knowing it was just one of the necessities of life.

"Go to town, baby."

Lola lowered herself onto my cock, moving far too slow for my taste. Grabbing her hips, I pushed her hard onto me and then back up a few times before she got the hint that she needed to ride me, not just play fucking games if I was ever going to get off. She bounced up and down on me like an excited girl on her first pony ride, and if I'd bothered to care, I might have said she looked cute.

I didn't care, though, if she was cute or not. All I needed her to be was enough for me to come.

The sound of our fucking filled my ears, helping me move toward my release. I liked hearing her squeal when I rammed my cock into her or pulled on her hair hard to get her to move faster. Nuzzling my neck, she moaned as I slid my finger into her ass and wiggled it, knowing that drove her nuts. It also worked to make her cunt spasm around me, which made me happy.

And women said I didn't care about their pleasure. What bullshit!

Fifteen minutes later, I had a smile on my face and Lola had even gotten off, a bonus because I knew how to take care of business. Bending down, she kissed me and whispered, "Thanks, Stefan. That was fun."

"It was. Now get back out there and show that new girl how to bartend at Club X while I get myself situated here."

I lifted her off me and watched as she put her tiny skirt and shirt back on. She certainly was cute. Turning to face me, she leaned down to kiss me again. "Until next time."

Smacking her on the ass, I winked. "Definitely. See

you out there, Lo."

After she left, I had to admit Lola did know how to ring a lot of my bells. If I had any interest whatsoever in dating someone, she'd definitely be near the head of the line. Thank God I had no interest in that shit. All I had to do was look at my brothers to see how love ruined everything for a guy. Cash walked around like a sad puppy when Olivia wasn't around. Not that my future sister-in-law wasn't great, but the guy was a lost cause. And Kane? Whoever had fucked him up had done one hell of a number on him. The guy worked around gorgeous dancers day in and day out and never even thought of touching them. If that's what caring for a woman did to you, I wanted no part of it.

As I thought about the sad state of affairs both my brothers had ended up in because of love, my office door opened. Pulling up my pants, I zipped my fly just as Shay walked in and closed the door behind her.

"Hey, I wanted to speak to you, Stefan. Do you have a minute?"

Caught with my pants down, literally, I nodded without thinking and sat back down. "Yeah, sure. What do you need?"

"I just wanted to apologize again for us getting off on the wrong foot. And thanks for putting me with Lola tonight. She's been so great in helping me get my bearings."

As Shay spoke, I remembered who I was dealing with. I couldn't put my finger on why, but something in the way she sounded put my suspicions on red alert. "That's good, and don't worry about how we started off. It looks like you're getting settled in fine. Just stay close to Lola for a while."

"Sounds great. Is there anything else you'd like me to do?"

There was no way to mistake the sexy tone in her voice. I'd had enough women hit on me to know Shay was offering more than just learning how to make a new drink. Standing from behind my desk, I walked toward her until we stood no more than a foot away from each other. Looking down, I saw a distinct sparkle in her green eyes.

"Like what? Do you have something in mind?"

Her tongue slid across the seam of her lips before she smiled, and her eyes met mine with a look I recognized from every woman I'd ever slept with. "Lola said you like it when your girls are go-getters. I just wanted to show you I was."

Leave it to Lola to break the new girl in just as I liked. This was why she was my best worker. My eyes scanned Shay's incredibly hot body for a long moment before I returned my gaze to meet hers. "Well, Lola's right. I do like go-getters. I think you'll work out here, Shay. Just follow Lola's example and we'll get along just fine."

"That's great. Thanks! And if you want me to do anything..." Her voice trailed off and she tilted her head to the side. "Just let me know. I'm a quick learner on top of being a go-getter, Stefan."

Her thinly veiled proposition threw me for a second, and by the time my brain reset with an answer, she'd turned on her heels and headed out the door back into the club. My bet with Kane was going to be over before he could warn, "Don't touch any of the dancers," which I had every intention of ignoring.

This girl was all but mine. It was almost too easy.

But I'd been a good boy for a few weeks, so I deserved easy.

FIVE

🍾 STEFAN

Cash and Kane sat in their usual spots on opposite sides of Cash's desk as I strolled in to our one o'clock Monday afternoon meeting at twenty minutes before two. These weekly get-togethers did nothing to help me run the club, so as far as I was concerned, they were optional. That I showed up at all should have meant something.

Unfortunately, neither of my brothers saw things that way. As I took my seat next to Kane, two pairs of blue eyes shot me death stares, intended to make me understand how fed up they were with me and my disrespect for the weekly meeting.

One problem—I didn't care.

"Hey, guys! What's up?"

"Stefan, we have this meeting every Monday at one o'clock. You're nearly an hour late," Cash said through gritted teeth.

"You know how I feel about this whole meeting thing, big brother. You could always just give me the notes and we'd all be happy."

I felt Kane lean closer to me and turned my head to see him glaring at me. "Stefan, we're tired of carrying your immature ass around here. Cash may be willing to take your bullshit, but I'm not."

My half-brother's tolerance for my carefree outlook on life had become extremely limited these days. He used to be more like me. There was a time when he and I would get piss drunk every night and even though he never hooked up with any of the girls we had working for us, he still knew how to have a good time. God, I missed those days.

I looked across the desk at Cash and saw his patience had just about run out too. I needed to diffuse the situation or I risked Kane beating the hell out of me, which he could in a heartbeat, unfortunately. While Cash and I might be an equal fight, a fight with Kane would likely be me getting my ass handed to me or at least knocked around a bit.

Certainly not the way I wanted to begin my week.

"I get it. I'm sorry. I promise to take these meetings more seriously." Seeing the look of disbelief on their faces, I raised my right hand and added, "Scout's honor."

Cash rolled his eyes. "Stefan, we're done already. I have a meeting at three, so I don't have the time to rehash everything Kane and I talked about. Maybe not knowing what the hell is scheduled for the next week will make you realize showing up at the owners' meeting each week is important."

He stood from behind the desk and buttoned his black suit coat, a clear sign he was leaving. I wanted to ask what meeting he had since I imagined it had something to do with Olivia and their engagement. Just the mention of her could put a smile on his face. I didn't like when Cash was pissed at me, even if I didn't show how much it bothered me. Ever since he and Olivia got serious, he'd been in a pretty forgiving mood with me and to see him so angry now because of something I did made me feel like shit. It was stupid, but it did.

Before I could even ask how she was, he marched past me and out into the club, leaving me with an angry Kane who now sat with his arms crossed and glaring at me. Well, if you couldn't piss off both your brothers by midday on a Monday, you weren't much of a younger sibling, right?

I turned toward my half-brother and shook my head. "What? You going to lecture me now?"

"On what? How immature you are? How there's no way in fucking hell I'm ever going to let you take over the top floors, even if you do get in that girl's pants?"

"Speaking of that, you're going to be running the bar soon, so get ready."

Now he rolled his eyes just like Cash had and stood to leave. "Whatever, Stef."

Jesus. Why couldn't I have been an only child?

I followed Kane out to the bar. "Hey, are you planning to just not talk to one of the owners of this place? I think you're going to have to speak to me at some point. I mean, we are equal partners here."

"What do you want?"

Rounding the corner of the bar, I pointed to the upper floors. "I want to know you're going to hold up your end of the bet since she's just days away from giving in."

Kane grimaced and shook his head. "Assuming I believed that, there's no way Cash is going to let you take over anything after you've shown your inability to manage much else than liquor orders and girls who pour drinks."

"Is that all you two think I do here?" I asked in shock at how easily he diminished my part in the running of our club.

His brows knitted and he snorted in derision. "Yeah, you do something else, but fucking women isn't exactly what I'd call managing anything."

"Well, be that as it may, I'm going to win our bet, so be ready."

Kane's expression twisted into one of pure disgust. "You don't get it, Stefan. Both of us are sick of your shit. It's all well and good for us to make a fun bet, but you're making our jobs harder. That bullshit's not going to fly anymore, little brother."

He stormed away, leaving me standing there before I could even defend myself. Making their jobs harder? What the fuck? Did my part of the club ever suffer? Fuck no! While he stood around upstairs with the dancers, who basically managed themselves, I worked my tail off down here to make sure the bar was the best in town. Who the fuck did he and Cash think they were? My part of this club made us money every night we were open, and unlike both of them, a big reason for that was how my staff was with the members. *My* staff, not theirs.

Behind me I heard footsteps and I turned to see John Sheridan standing there. God, he was disgusting. Dressed in a dingy white dress shirt and tan dress pants that looked like they'd never seen an iron, he reminded me of a used car salesman. Greasy chunks of brown hair hung in his eyes, and I could have sworn I smelled the old cigar smoke that clung to those gross clumps. Thankfully, he wasn't there to see me.

"Hey, Sha…uh, I mean John. What's up?" I asked as I tried to avoid focusing on his head.

"I'm here to talk to Cassian. Is he back there?"

I shook my head. "No, he just left for a meeting. Did he know you were coming?"

Shank screwed his expression into a comical grimace

at my news. "Damn. No, I just hoped to catch him."

"Kane's upstairs, if you want him," I offered, happy for the opportunity to make my half-brother's day more miserable by a visit from Shank.

He seemed to consider the idea of making the trip up to the fifth floor but then shook his head. "Nah, that's okay. I'll just come back when Cassian's here. When's he coming back?"

What the fuck? Was I my brother's goddamned keeper or his secretary?

"I don't know. He said he had a three o'clock meeting. I'd guess he'll be back tonight before we open. You can stop back then."

And go the fuck away from me right now.

"Okay." Shank turned to leave and then stopped, turning back to face me again. "Oh, by the way, I want to thank you for taking such good care of my little girl. She can't say enough about how much she loves working here for you."

"Your little girl?"

Holy fucking hell! Shank had reproduced? The horrifying image of what his daughter might look like raced through my mind, sending a shiver down my spine. Which of my bartenders could possibly be his kid? None of my workers looked like that. And then a terrifying thought tore through me. Had I slept with her?

"Yeah. Lorraine. I mean Lola. She loves working here. She can't say enough about how good you are to her." Clapping me on the shoulder, he smiled. "So thanks, Stefan. Anyone my daughter likes is all good in my book."

I nodded and forced a smile as my brain tried to process the fact that the woman I'd been sleeping with came from this disgusting human. Was her mother some supermodel Shank kept hostage as a sex slave?

"Oh, Lola. Yeah, she's great. She knows her way around the bar all right. The members love her."

And until that moment, I'd been enjoying having sex with her.

He grinned and nodded at me. "I wasn't sure about you, but Cassian's always been a good guy so I knew my little girl would be in good hands here. Thanks for taking such good care of her."

"Yeah, my pleasure," I mumbled as he walked away, my brain still having a hard time wrapping itself around the idea of whose loins Lola had come from.

Shank headed out the door and I tore up the stairs to talk to Kane, who I suspected knew all along that Lola was Shank's kid. I found him sitting in that shithole of an office looking like some black and white movie private eye. Jesus, how the hell was I related to this guy?

"When the fuck did you plan to tell me about Lola being Shank's daughter?"

Kane looked up from his laptop and I saw that vicious smile of his and the twinkle he got in his eye when he'd done something to fuck me over. "Is she?"

"Don't act like you didn't know. I told Cash about Lola right after I hired her, and I know he told you to check her out. What the fuck, Kane? You know I've been doing her. You didn't think I should know she's related to the guy we pay each month to keep us safe?"

"Would it have stopped you from sleeping with her?" he asked, cocking one eyebrow like he was judging me.

In truth, it wouldn't have. Lola and I had gotten together the first week she worked behind the bar, and I liked fucking her. She was the perfect woman—hot, a great lay, and eager to please so she didn't make any demands on me or my time. But it would have been nice to know she was Shank's daughter all the same.

"No, but that's not the point. And don't sit there with that judgment face on. It's none of your business who I sleep with, big brother."

Kane huffed his disgust. "I don't give a damn who you fuck until it becomes something we have to deal with because you're too goddamn horny to choose your partners better. I'm sick of women suing us because you promise them something and then treat them like shit. So if I look like I'm judging you, it's because I am. Grow the fuck up and learn to handle your affairs the right way, like a man, or stick with your hand."

I rolled my eyes. "Fuck you, Kane. Maybe if you weren't always alone, even though you're surrounded by gorgeous women every night, you wouldn't be so jealous."

"It's not jealousy, baby brother. See, this is why Cash and I get along so well and you're the black sheep. We understand there was a time to fuck around and now it's time to be men. You don't seem to have gotten the memo. You're twenty-seven years old, Stef. How long do you plan to do this gigolo thing doing every bartender you can? Doesn't it get old after a while?"

"Does sleeping with hot women get old? Uh, no, Kane. No, it never does. What are you, a eunuch or something?"

Kane took a deep breath, like he always did when he was preparing to serve up some bullshit lecture. This time, though, he just shook his head and said, "No. I'm a man, not a boy, Stef. I know what I do here affects all of us. It isn't just about what my cock wants anymore."

"Well, good for you. I hope you're happy with yourself," I said in response, unable to think of anything better. I hated when he did the whole responsible brother thing. That was Cash's role, or at least it always had been. Kane used to be fun, but ever since Olivia tamed Cash, it seemed like Kane was angling to be the next poor sucker to settle down. Not that there was a woman in his life, as far as I could tell.

"You know what screwing around with Shank's daughter means, don't you?"

Closing my eyes, I silently reminded myself not to make the mistake of coming up to this floor again until I was the ruler of this place. "No, Kane. I don't know what that means, but I'm sure you're about to tell me."

"It means you better not mess up with this one."

My eyes flew open. "What does that mean? I'm not planning on marrying Lo, if that's what you mean. This guy isn't lining up for a life of misery. No, thanks."

"Stefan, screwing around with Shank's daughter isn't like screwing around with some ordinary bartender. We need Shank to keep this place open. Cash is working on getting more help in that area, but until he does, Shank is someone we have to keep happy."

"So, what? All of this falls on my head?"

"Welcome to adulthood, Stef. Responsibility sucks, doesn't it?"

"Why is this all on me?"

"Because you're the one who thought it was a good idea to get into Lola's pants. You don't see me or Cash screwing around with her, do you? This is on you."

"Well, maybe someone should have told me who she was when he found out."

"It wouldn't have mattered. I didn't find out until after you started sleeping with her."

"Yeah, I bet. How would you know when we first got together?"

Kane stared at me for a long moment and then rolled his eyes. "Do you think you're fooling anyone down there? All I had to do was walk through one night and notice you not around and I knew what you were up to. A few minutes later, I saw her leave your office and knew."

"Whatever. So what are you saying? I don't have a choice as to what I want to do with her anymore? Now I have to sleep with her or what? Shank will ruin us?"

"You have to make sure she's happy because if she's not, her father might not be so willing to help us."

The realization of what Kane was saying hit me like a fist to the face. Now I had to sleep with Lola. I had no choice. Suddenly, what had always been a good time felt like an obligation, a responsibility.

"Well, how the hell am I supposed to do that and still live like a single man should?"

My half-brother laughed right in my face, as if that question hadn't been one hundred percent serious. "You're not very slick, are you? Have you been exclusively sleeping with Lola all this time?"

"No, but now with all this riding on it, it sounds like I'll have to. I can't do that. It would be like living like a monk!"

"Stefan, monks don't fuck women in their offices when they're supposed to be working."

"You know what I meant. And how the hell am I supposed to live up to my part of our bet if I can't sleep with anyone but Lo?"

"You've got some strange priorities there, baby brother. I just told you that a lot of our safety here is riding on your keeping Shank's daughter happy, and you're worried about how you're going to get into another woman's pants."

"The fact that who I sleep with means so much to this place is fucked up, Kane. Even you can agree with that. But our bet isn't something I'm planning on just letting slide because you and Cash can't find friends in high places."

Kane stood from behind his desk and walked to right in front of me. "You got yourself into this. You get yourself out of it. Don't forget that whatever happens with Shank's daughter will affect all of us, though."

"What about if you hung out with her? She'd probably like you well enough. I mean, you're not me, but you could cozy up to Lola and then I could do my thing like always, including Shay."

The look in Kane's eyes told me he wasn't on board with my plan. "Go back downstairs and do some work, Stef."

"C'mon, it could work. Lo's okay, and she'd probably go for it if I told her you were into her. You look like you could use a good time, and she's definitely that. Even better, you could probably handle Shank, if push came to shove. You know, put that body of yours to good use on all counts. What do you say?"

"I say don't screw this up or we'll all suffer."

And with that, Kane closed his office door in my face, leaving me to deal with this huge burden all by myself. As I walked down to the bar area, I couldn't believe that once again everything in this damn place was put on my shoulders. While Cash spent his time at museum parties drinking champagne and schmoozing with the city's upper crust and Kane trolled the upper floors surrounded by gorgeous women who basically did his job for him, except for the occasional asshole he and his henchmen had to deal with, I had to make this club the best in town. And now I had to act like some lovey dovey boyfriend to Lola to make sure the guy we paid protection to remained happy.

This was definitely going to put a crimp in my lifestyle.

SIX

❧ SHAY

By seven o'clock I was back at Club X and ready to make some good money and some good headway on playing Stefan March. The nightly bartender meeting hadn't begun yet, so I found Lola standing near the back bar. A pretty girl with bleached blond hair, big blue Barbie doll eyes, and boobs I was sure had to be at least a big C cup, she knew her stuff behind the bar, and I could appreciate that. The club's members appreciated the other things about her, I'd noticed.

She seemed to have a tremendous crush on Stefan, so I thought I should feel her out as to just how close they were. It was one thing to play a player, but I didn't want anyone to get hurt, and if she and he had something together, all plans to make Stefan finally see how much of a jackass he was would be off.

"Hi, Lola! You ready for another night at Club X?" I asked as I grabbed myself a glass of water.

"Hey, Shay! Another day, another dollar, right?"

I took a sip from my water and smiled. "I hope so. That's what I'm all about here."

"Oh, that's right. You're saving money to go where?" she asked, her head tilted like she was truly interested in that part of my life.

"Copenhagen. I leave in late December, so I need to get as much money under my belt as I can."

"Where is Copenhagen?"

This wasn't the first time I'd been asked that. It seemed that no one in Tampa knew where Copenhagen was. Smiling, I answered, "Denmark. You know, where Hamlet lived?"

"Hamlet? Who's that?" she asked with those big doe eyes staring at me in confusion.

"You know, Shakespeare? To be or not to be?" I saw in her blank expression she had no idea what I was talking about, so I just shook my head. "Just someone I knew. Denmark is in northern Europe."

"Will it be cold there when you go?"

"Yeah, I think it will be. I guess some of that money I'm planning to make better go to winter coats and hats," I joked.

Lola seemed distracted, and I followed her gaze to Stefan on the other side of the room talking to Mika, another of the bartenders. All I'd learned about her came from her snapping at me every night I'd worked. Cutthroat and worried I'd take her place behind the bar, if not under our boss, Mika had shown herself to be a first class bitch. But she had a knockout look with short black hair and model cheekbones, not to mention an ass that looked like you could bounce a quarter off it, so it wasn't surprising that Stefan couldn't take his eyes off her.

"Do you think she's pretty, Shay?" Lola mumbled as she continued to stare at him with the bitch.

"In a she-probably-eats-her-men-after-sleeping-with-them way, I guess."

Lola turned toward me and giggled. "She probably does, doesn't she? She doesn't like me because Stefan likes me more than her. I heard her complain about him giving me the front bar the other night."

"Mika doesn't like me either, so don't feel bad. And don't feel bad about knowing your stuff behind the bar. You deserve to be at the front of the club."

"You're pretty good too, Shay, and you don't hate me."

I looked past her to see Stefan patting Mika on the ass. What a pig! Looking back at Lola, I smiled, hoping to make her feel better. "I don't hate people who are better than I am. I learn from them. Mika hates people who are better than she is because she's immature, like a teenage girl."

Lola lowered her head just in time to miss Stefan's sexual harassment of Mika. "She likes Stefan."

Why, I couldn't imagine, other than the fact that she was a bitch who deserved someone like him.

"Do you like Stefan, Lola?"

Turning around, she nodded slowly. "He's the best boss I've ever had. Stefan's much nicer than most people think he is. He gets a bad rap, but he just likes to play around is all."

"I think you're being too generous, Lola. What you call playing around most lawyers would call sexual harassment."

She shook her head and frowned. "See, that's what's wrong with this world. Men like Stefan love women. He wouldn't do anything to hurt anyone."

Lola's gentle tone unnerved me and for a moment, I wanted to believe what she saw in our boss was true. Then I saw him practically feel up Kerry and then Kat just after he'd been touching Mika and knew my gut was right about him.

Stefan March was a sexually harassing, male chauvinist pig, pure and simple. That someone sweet like Lola saw anything in him was likely because she was too nice and had nothing to do with him deserving her kindness. But the question was, did she defend him because they were together or just because she was a sweet, if naïve, girl?

"Lola, are you and Stefan...you know...?"

For a moment, I thought I saw guilt in her eyes, but she shrugged and shook her head. "No. I just think that he gets attacked for being who he is. There's nothing wrong with a man who appreciates women."

"Oh, okay."

"Stefan's not the type of man to go with just one woman, you know? I mean, why should he? He's young, hot, and wealthy. Why would he want to tie himself down to just one person?" she said wistfully, making me think she'd just lied to me.

"Gather up!" the man himself barked and I followed Lola to the center of the room to where the bartenders' meeting was to begin.

Stefan seemed to be in rare form this night. Unlike on most nights, he didn't wear a Club X t-shirt but instead wore a long sleeve Henley more like Kane would wear, but as always had a pair of jeans on that accentuated his muscular body. The guy knew how to show off his assets. There was something about him tonight, though—something that seemed even cockier than usual, if that was possible.

"Ladies, my brothers didn't bother to tell me there was a private party for tonight, so you're hearing about it for the first time like I am. We'll do fine, like we always do, so let's show Cash and Kane that this is the part of Club X that makes this place what it is. Showtime is in one hour!"

Everyone around me cheered and hollered, and I turned to see Lola clapping. God, she really did like being his cheerleader!

"So since we need to show our best stuff, tonight Shay will be heading up the front bar, along with Mika. I want to see you two up on the lifts too. The members love that. Lola will be heading up the back bar, along with Kerry. The rest of you know what to do, so it's the status quo for you. And my bottle service girls, I want to see you sell the goods. Now let's show my brothers how this place really runs!"

More cheers and hoots filled my ears, but out of the corner of my eye, I saw Lola's expression filled with disappointment. Why the fuck was Stefan putting Mika up front, where she didn't belong, and shoving Lola, his best bartender, to the back bar?

Everyone moved to their positions, and Lola turned toward me. "I guess I'll see you later, Shay. Watch yourself with her."

She walked off in her usual perky fashion, but I knew she felt like Stefan's assignments meant a demotion for her. He stood at the front bar talking up Mika, which I imagined would be what my entire night would be like, and I made my way over to him.

"Hey, what's with putting Lola in the back? She and I work well together. It's not like she's a bar-back. She's your best bartender here."

"Not that I have to get your permission for anything I do, but I wanted her back there with Kerry because she needs to get up to speed. Why do you care anyway? Mika's just as good."

Now I definitely knew he was up to something with that bitch. Turning my back to her so she couldn't hear me, I leaned in toward him and said, "No, she isn't. She also doesn't get along with anyone, especially Lola and me. You just made my night ten times harder, Stefan."

"Well, then I guess you better get figuring out how to make Mika like you," he said in that snide voice that made me want to push his face in.

With a sneer, I turned away and mumbled, "Maybe if I fucked her and played favorites with her she'd like me better."

Rounding the corner of the front bar, I felt Stefan behind me. I spun around and backed up, unnerved by his angry look. Leaning down, he said in my ear, "Shay, you'd do much better here if you were more like Mika."

"And I let you sexually harass me so I could steal a position that should be someone else's because she's better? No, thanks. But at least I know you aren't all about your libido. You put me as first bartender up here, and I haven't slept with you yet."

That last word slipped out and I watched Stefan's eyes lit up. Fuck! I tried to brush it off, but it was too late. He'd heard it, and I knew all he saw now were green lights where I was concerned. Not that this was necessarily a bad thing. My plan to outplay him didn't revolve around playing hard to get. No, it revolved around what would happen after I got him just where I wanted him.

"Yet? Shay Callahan, I think you're warming up to me. Not that I ever doubted you would."

I couldn't help my natural reaction to his exhibition of swagger. My eyebrows shot up and I snapped back, "Only in your fantasies, Stefan. I'll be the one who forever got away."

He flashed me that sexy grin I had to admit made him look incredibly hot and leaned down close to my face. "Just so you know, I'm even better than I am when you fantasize about me."

My mind went blank as the sight of him so close to

me made my head get fuzzy. Maybe it was his gorgeous brown eyes staring directly into mine, or maybe it was that delicious smelling cologne lightly winding around me as I stood there in front of him, but at that moment I had no witty comeback, no snappy barb to counter his cockiness.

He didn't miss a beat, though. "And I've succeeded in making you speechless, Shay. I even impress myself."

With that, he backed away, still grinning the smile of a victor, and headed into his office. I wanted to march right in there after him and read him the riot act of every feminist writing I'd ever read, but my feet remained planted in their spot and my head felt like some kind of haze had washed over my brain.

Mika's ordering the front bar's wait staff around behind me like some Gestapo brought me back to reality, and I busied myself with getting our area ready for when the party began in less than an hour. Unfortunately, Stefan's belief in Mika's abilities didn't mean she could actually do the job as well as Lola, and it didn't take long for things to fall apart at the front bar. Spilled drinks, mixed up orders, and rudeness to the members seemed to be all she was capable of. For hours, I struggled to clean up her messes only to have more piled on.

As Stefan had ordered, I made sure to climb on the lifts behind the bar to show off my assets to the members a few times. The same bottles that sat perched at the top of the wall actually could be found under the bar, but as he knew, the members loved to see us ride up and down in our sexy little skirts and shorts. Nothing like having men and women clap because you can stand in three inch heels on a tiny platform moving toward the ceiling.

As if that was some skill I should be proud of.

Mika seemed to enjoy balancing precariously on the

lifts and used them whenever possible, but each time she jumped on them, she was as clumsy as she was nasty and when she wasn't dripping liquor onto me, she was dropping entire bottles on the floor. It didn't take long before the area behind the bar felt like a war zone.

Looking up after she let a hundred dollar bottle of scotch sail past me and shatter into a million pieces at my feet, I barked, "Watch yourself, Mika! We sell alcohol here, not wear it."

She whipped me the finger and snapped, "Fuck you!"

She was all class. As I dried the scotch from my legs, a member leaned over the bar and said, "She's all thumbs back there, Shay. Be careful. I think she's trying to kill you."

Finally, just before midnight, I couldn't take any more of Mika or her shit. Pushing her out of the way as she screwed up yet another mixed drink order, I snapped, "Why don't you find some ice or something and I'll take care of these people."

"Fuck you, Shay! I don't have to take your shit any more than I have to take Lola's. Stefan will hear about this."

I stared her down for a moment as I threw out the mess she'd made of a Malibu Bay Breeze. "Well, when you're mouth isn't full, be sure to tell him I said you suck at this job. I hope you're better at what you do for him."

She stormed away as the members huddled around the bar clapped and laughed, and for the first time that night, I felt like I didn't hate working at Club X. Handing the man his drink who'd ordered the Breeze for his girlfriend, I smiled. "It's an incredibly complicated drink, you know."

As he leaned toward me, he laughed and stuffed

money in my tip jar. "You're the best, Shay. Love your style!"

He may have loved my style, but by night's end I knew Stefan didn't. Mika never returned to the front bar, leaving me alone to handle things, which I did, but as the crowds began to thin, Stefan stormed up to me with a look in his eyes that told me the time for playful banter was long gone.

"My office. Now!" he ordered as Mika stood a few feet behind him smiling like she'd won some contest of wills.

"Stefan, I have no one to man the bar," I answered as I poured a glass of scotch on the rocks for the man who stood right in front of me.

"Lola's coming up to take your place. My office. Now!" he barked.

I saw her as she walked behind the bar, her face ashen. "I'm here, Shay. Don't worry."

Turning away from Stefan, I quietly said to her, "Are you okay? You look white as a ghost. Did he yell at you too?"

She took my hands in hers and squeezed them. "No, no. I'm just worried about you. Kerry told me that Mika has been filling Stefan's head with lies all night. I don't want to see you get fired."

I couldn't help but smile. "Don't worry, Lola. I can handle myself. And by the way, whatever Mika told him I said is probably true. She sucks at this and I let her know."

Lola giggled, but her smile quickly faded as the sight of Stefan standing in front of us frightened her.

"Shay, now!"

I gave Lola a quick wink to let her know everything would be fine and followed Stefan and Mika into his office. It became obvious immediately that Mika had the upper hand. Standing next to his desk as he sat behind it, she looked like some goddamned first lady of Club X perched there wearing that smug face of hers.

"Shay, I can't have bartenders doing what you did tonight."

Was he serious? Did he really intend on sitting there and backing Mika? I said nothing, sure if I opened my mouth that whatever I said would make matters worse. Out of the corner of my eye, I saw Mika smirk, like she knew the outcome of this meeting would be all in her favor.

"Do you have anything to say for yourself?" he asked, his voice full of an edge I didn't know Stefan had.

"I don't have anything to say that you want to hear, boss. You've already made your mind up and have no interest in hearing what I have to say."

"See? She's such a bitch!" Mika whined. Pushing on his arm, she added, "Just fire her. I can take the front bar and do a great job if I don't have to deal with her shit."

Stefan jerked his shoulder to get away from her, but I couldn't hold my tongue any longer. I leapt out of my chair and began saying what had been on my mind all night. "A great job? Are you fucking kidding? You couldn't find your ass with both hands. You're nothing compared to Lola, who should never be anywhere but the front bar. All you're good for is what you two do in here, and I doubt you're even very good at that!"

Stefan's eyes grew wide at my outburst. "Shay!"

Mika came at me, screaming, "Who do you think you are? I'm a better bartender than you any day!"

I didn't move quickly enough, and she caught my cheek with her nails, scratching all the way from the corner of my eye to my jawline. Stunned, I staggered back as she continued coming at me until I ran into the wall behind me. Stefan darted around his desk to grab her, but she was like a wild animal and got me once more before he could take hold of her hands.

"Mika! Stop!" he bellowed, but she kept swinging at me, even as he held her tighter.

"Let me go! I'm going to scratch the bitch's face off!"

Hiding my face to protect myself, I heard him say something to her about waiting outside for him and then they were gone. I lowered my hands and saw blood on my fingertips from where I'd touched my face. In all the years I'd worked in bars, never before had anyone attacked me like that. Drunks were usually too disoriented to do much harm, and even if co-workers didn't like me, they never jumped me like Mika just had.

I sat back down and tried to calm myself. Taking a few deep breaths, I looked down at my hands and saw them shaking uncontrollably. All of a sudden, my emotions became jumbled and before I knew it, the tears were rolling down my face mixing with my blood and creating a pale red liquid that dropped onto my white shirt.

Stefan returned and sat down behind his desk with a stunned look on his face. If I didn't know better, I'd say he was upset I'd gotten hurt. But that wasn't his style.

"She's going to demand that I fire you, and I'm probably not going to have a choice."

My anger burned inside me and made me want to cry again. Before I let him see me shed a tear over him or his bullshit, I stood up and told him what I thought of the whole damn mess. "Maybe if you weren't fucking her you'd be able to stand up for someone who deserves it. I get it. You don't want another sexual harassment suit. I hear you're an expert on them. Fine. I'll save you the trouble. I quit."

I spun on my heels and headed for the door, but Stefan caught up to me before I could leave. "Shay, wait.

You don't have to go."

His brown eyes stared down at me with concern. What was he so worried about? "It's okay, Stefan. You've never done anything with me that should make you worry. Look after your girlfriend. You've got more to lose with her than with me."

The truth of what I'd said registered on his face, and his hand slid from my shoulder. I knew he had no choice. The way he behaved with all his other employees made his decision for him.

"I'm sorry."

I opened the door and shook my head. "Whatever, Stefan. You turned out to be just what I knew you were from the moment I met you. Have a nice life."

SEVEN

STEFAN

Even though I knew what waited for me at the weekly meeting with my brothers, I showed up on time and ready to work. For three days I'd felt like shit about losing Shay behind the bar, and Mika hadn't made my decision to let her go any easier. My bar needed Lola and Shay, but if I pissed off Mika, I knew what would come next was the all-too-familiar lawsuit.

Cash wore a look of amazement when I strolled into his office before one. As I took my seat in front of his desk, his mouth fell open. "I didn't think we'd see you today, at least not this early."

"Yeah. Well, your lectures finally got through this thick skull of mine."

His expression changed to one that showed me he didn't believe a word I said. "Really? Well, five years doesn't seem like too long to learn a lesson."

Kane walked in just as Cash finished his verbal jab and sat down next to me. "Nice of you to join us, Stef. And on a day when you're going to get your ass handed to you too. Channeling your inner masochist today?"

"Don't start, Kane. I'm here. Appreciate it for what it's worth."

My half-brother raised one eyebrow and stared at me. "Touchy. Problems in your area getting you down, Stefan?"

The fucker knew what had happened with Shay and had waited until our weekly meeting to bust my chops about it. Why couldn't I have been an only child?

I shot him a look and turned back to face Cash. "Well, let's get this show on the road. I'm eager to see what I've been missing at all these meetings."

"Wait a second. I missed something. What's Kane talking about with problems in the bar? Is something going on?"

Looking away, I mumbled, "No."

"Since you did that thing you always did when you were little and tried to lie, I know there's something wrong. You might as well tell us, Stefan, so we can discuss it and figure out a solution."

Discussing it was the last thing I wanted to do. Discussing it meant that I'd have to listen to the two of them lecture me once again on how I shouldn't sleep with my bar staff. Thanks, but I already figured that out.

"There's nothing to discuss, Cash. Two of my bartenders had a problem at the private party last week and I had to handle it. That's all."

"That's not what I hear," Kane said in that snide voice that made me want to hit him. "I hear that shitty bartender Mika took a shot at Shay, and you let Shay go."

"Well, you heard wrong."

Cash's eyes darted back and forth between Kane and me like he was watching a tennis match. When neither of us offered any more information, he asked, "Well? What happened if what Kane heard isn't right?"

"There was a problem between Mika and Shay at the front bar. A misunderstanding more than anything else. I spoke to them and settled it, but Mika got a little excited and ended up scratching Shay. Nothing big."

Out of the corner of my eye, I saw Kane lean back and smile. "He's conveniently leaving out the part where Shay was bleeding from this scratch and quit."

"Is this true, Stefan? Did Mika actually attack her? Did Shay quit?" Cash asked, his voice getting more impatient by the second.

"It wasn't an attack so much as she was excited and her hand caught Shay's cheek."

"Jesus Christ, Stefan! And then, after Mika attacked Shay, you let Shay quit? Have you lost your mind?"

"Maybe if he wasn't fucking the attacker Shay would have fared better," Kane said with a chuckle.

I turned toward Kane and let my anger explode. "You're just pissed off because of our bet! You don't give a fuck about my bartenders and their problems, which by the way are nothing compared to what my people and I do to make this bar a success."

"What bet?" I heard Cash ask as I stared Kane down.

"Why don't you tell him, Kane? Tell Cash how you made a bet with me that involved your area of the club."

Kane's face twisted into an expression of disgust. Turning to face Cash, he explained, "Stefan and I made a bet about Shay. He believed he could get her to fall for him and I bet against him. He seems to think that because I agreed to putting my part of the club on the line in this bet that you'll be angrier about that than his sleeping with yet another bartender, a shitty one at that, and losing a good one because he couldn't defend her or risk another lawsuit from the girl he's fucking." When Kane finished, he turned to look at me and sneered. "Sound about right, Stef? I hope I didn't miss anything."

"Fuck you, Kane."

"Enough!" Cash bellowed. "Stefan, as much as I know I should care that you two are making bets about you sleeping with yet another bartender, the immediate problem is that you let one of our employees get attacked by another employee and then let her quit. That's a whole different kind of lawsuit. Why didn't you discipline Mika?"

Kane laughed out loud at Cash's mention of discipline. This was why I didn't bother attending these goddamned meetings.

"I told her she couldn't do that. She knows. She was just excited about something Shay said."

Cash pinched the bridge of his nose and sighed. "I'm not going to bother asking what Shay said to upset Mika so much, but regardless, we can't have bartenders attacking one another. Mika needs to come see me immediately, Stefan. As for Shay, I suggest you find a way to get her back."

"I can handle my staff, Cash. I don't need you to talk to Mika."

More laughing from Kane. Fuck, I was sick of his shit! And I was supposed to be the immature one?

Cash didn't find any of this amusing, though. Grimacing at both of us, he shook his head. "No, Stefan, it's obvious you can't handle this one. I'll speak to her as soon as she comes in tonight."

I stood to leave. "Well, this has been fucking fantastic. I'll make sure to do this again sometime next year."

"We're not done yet, Stefan. In fact, we haven't even begun the meeting."

He couldn't be serious. There was more than that? I stared down at Cash in stunned amazement. "Are you kidding?"

"No. Sit down. We have a private party to discuss,

and you're going to love this one."

Whenever one of my brothers said that, I knew I wasn't going to love anything that came out of his mouth after it. Taking my seat again, I waited to hear about this private party I knew I'd hate.

"Cabot Marshall booked his birthday party for next Thursday last month, but he didn't tell me until today what he wanted the theme to be. You ready for this?"

"Let me guess. A circus theme? Marshall has a freaky vibe going for him," Kane offered.

Cash shook his head and a huge smile spread across his face. "No. Even better. Stefan, you want to take a guess?"

"In so many ways the answer to that is no."

"Fine. Marshall wants the party to have a Seventies theme. You know, disco, bellbottoms, Charlie's Angels?"

"Who the fuck are Charlie's Angels?" I asked, already sick of this meeting and talk of this party.

"Do you know anything other than what immediately involves you?" Kane snapped.

Ignoring his sarcastic insult and my quiet "Fuck you" in return, Cash continued, "Marshall wants the whole nine yards with this one, and since he's a platinum member, we're going to give it to him. Most of the staging will fall on your shoulders, Stefan, so you need to get up to speed on the Seventies."

"Are you talking about the 1970s?" I asked, still confused.

"Yes. The 1970s."

"And I have to do what concerning this?"

Cash looked over at Kane and then back at me. "The biggest thing you'll need to do is have your staff dress in costume. Look it up online before you tell them about it. Other than that, you need to get a disco ball."

"And this is on top of Halloween, which is the next

day?"

"No. Marshall wants the party to be open, so we'll be doing the club's Halloween party that night too. It will just be the Seventies theme for anyone invited and the staff."

"And what about Kane's people? They don't have to dress up? What the fuck, Cash? Like I don't have enough to deal with already."

"My people will be in costume, Stefan," Kane said in his usual annoyed tone. "But the first thing people see when they enter this club is your part, so your bartenders will need to be in the right look."

"Fine. I'll Google the 1970s and see what I can find."

"And after you do that, you need to convince Shay Callahan to come back to work here. I've seen her behind the bar. She's good. A whole hell of a lot better than Mika, Stefan. I'm not saying I'm going to fire her when she comes to see me tonight, but you need to get your priorities in order, little brother. Lawsuits are bad enough, but you've never let the bar suffer before. You need to fix this and fast."

I wanted to sit there and take my brother's scolding like I wanted to tear my arm off and beat myself with it, but he wasn't wrong. I'd messed up with Shay and needed to make that right. Not that I wanted him to know all that, though.

"If we're done, I have a full day's work to do," I said, trying to hide how much this whole Shay thing bothered me.

Looking over at Kane, Cash said, "Unless Kane has anything to add."

"I have nothing. I haven't lived in a self-involved cave all my life, so I don't have to research anything for Marshall's party. As always, my people will be ready."

Standing, I looked down at my half-brother. "Maybe

if I had a costume designer like you, my life would be easy too."

Before he or Cash could give me more shit, I left our weekly Monday afternoon meeting, sure I didn't want to go through anything like that again anytime soon. I was also sure of one other thing. I had to find a way to get Shay to return to Club X.

EIGHT

SHAY

Leaning in toward the bathroom mirror, I examined Mika's handiwork on my cheek. A thin scab covered where she'd scratched me with her fake nails, except for near the corner of my eye where it still remained red. Thankfully, it seemed to be healing well and I wouldn't be scarred for life because of that crazy bitch. Shaking my head, I still couldn't believe all that had happened because of Stefan March.

The worst part of the whole damn thing was I wouldn't be able to make all that money at Club X that I needed for my trip, and now I didn't even have a job at all. How I'd pay rent and all my bills I had no idea. This was what I got for being so stubborn.

Elliot padded up behind me and wrapped his arms around my waist. Looking at me in the mirror, he said, "You look tough, Shay. Chicks with scars are hot."

Rolling my eyes, I shook my head. "Not funny, El. That crazy bitch could have literally scratched my eye out."

He nuzzled my neck and mumbled, "Is that really

possible?"

I couldn't help but smile. "Don't try to make me happy about this. I'm still angry about the whole thing."

Elliot looked up at me in the mirror. "Okay, stay pissed. It's good for the soul."

"You're no help at all, you know that?"

He backed away from me, patting me on the ass. "I do what I can."

I returned to staring at my bruiser look and heard a knock on the front door. I so wasn't in the mood for dealing with anyone. I waited for Elliot to answer it, but the knocking continued, so I trudged out and opened it to find standing there in the hallway none other than the person who'd caused all my problems.

"Hey, Shay. Can we talk?"

Stefan March looked out of place asking to talk to me at my home, and my first inclination was to slam the door in his face. Nothing he had to say could make the situation better.

"I don't think we have anything to talk about, Stefan. You showed me who you were the other night, and I don't want to work for someone like that."

The hurt from my words registered in his eyes, and for the first time, he looked truly bothered by one of my comments, even though I'd said much worse to him nearly every day since we met.

"If you'd just give me a minute, I really think you'll want to hear what I have to say."

"Unless you plan on apologizing and offering me my job back with a raise, I'm not interested."

"Well, that's pretty close. Can I come in so we can talk for a minute?"

An apology and more money? It certainly was tempting. But I knew how this would end up. I'd go back to Club X and the whole Mika problem would still be there. "I don't think so, Stefan. Nothing's changed at the club. I can't work like that."

I began to close the door, but he grabbed the edge and stuck his face in close. "Come on, Shay. Hear me out."

He looked so silly with his face pushed in between the door and the jamb that I couldn't help but chuckle. "You remind me of Jack Nicholson in The Shining."

Smiling, he shot me a wild look. "Here's Johnny!" His expression softened, and he said, "Please let me in."

"That you knew what I meant by my Nicholson reference impresses me, Stefan."

"Enough to let me in?" he asked as he gave me his best puppy dog eyes.

I backed away from the door. "Yeah. Come in."

Flashing me that fabulous Stefan March smile, he pushed the door open and came in, happier than I'd ever seen him. Elliot moved close by my side as the door closed, and we all stood there awkwardly staring at one another.

Stefan leaned forward and extended his hand to shake Elliot's. "Hey, I'm Stefan March. Shay's boss. Nice to meet you."

"Former boss," I corrected him as Elliot grabbed his hand to return the handshake.

"Nice to meet you, Stefan. I'm Elliot."

And then we stood there awkwardly silent again until finally Elliot kissed me on the top of my head and quietly said, "I'll be in the bedroom if you need me."

"Nice to meet you, Stefan."

"Yeah, you too."

I waited until I heard the bedroom door close and said, "Do you want to sit down?"

Stefan looked around at my old living room sofa and hand-me-down chair my aunt had given me when

I moved in and nodded. "Sure. Okay."

It wasn't what he was likely used to, but I wasn't about to be ashamed of what I had. It may not have been the kind of place he had with his millions to spend, but it was my home. I took a seat on the sofa as he sat on the edge of the chair like he planned to bolt out the door at any moment.

"So what did you want to talk about, Stefan?"

He looked toward the bedroom for a moment and then back at me. "So, is that your boyfriend?"

"Elliot? He's a...my..." I wasn't sure how to categorize Elliot. We lived together, had sex like rabbits, and acted like boyfriend and girlfriend, but at that moment, calling him my boyfriend seemed wrong. "I'm sure you didn't come here to talk about my personal life, so what did you have to say?"

The look on Stefan's face was pure confusion at my inability to answer a simple question about the man who obviously lived with me, but he simply nodded and smiled. "Okay, fair enough. I want you to come back to the club. I made a mistake and I need you back behind the bar."

I had nothing to lose, so I came out guns a' blazin. "Not if Mika's still getting preferential treatment."

"She's not."

"Oh? And she didn't scratch your eyes out when you told her?" I knew I was pushing my luck, but I didn't care.

"No. She understands one more problem and she's gone."

"I won't come back unless you promise that Lola never gets stuck at the back bar again, especially during a party."

"I'm not going to discuss Lola's—" he began, but I cut him off.

I stood and shook my head. "Then we have nothing to talk about."

"Wait. Shay, wait. Why do you care about where I schedule Lola? I thought your problem was with Mika."

"Stefan, my problem the other night was that you made my job next to impossible because you showed Mika preferential treatment and stuck Lola at the back bar, where she made next to nothing, I bet."

With a look I assumed wasn't intentionally meant to be drop dead sexy, he smiled up at me and said, "I've shown Lola preferential treatment on many occasions, Shay."

I had a feeling he'd just confessed to sleeping with Lola, but I couldn't be sure. Not that it mattered. Shunting Lola to the back bar not only hurt her but me too. "That has nothing to do with me, Stefan. All I know is that Lola is your best bartender and she belongs up front. You seem to want me to man the front bar, but if you want me back, I want Lola up there with me when we're scheduled together. Yes, she's a great teacher for newbies like Kerry, but at what cost? That party could have gone much better if there were two good bartenders at the front bar."

He sighed and nodded. "Okay. Done."

"And about that raise?"

"Fifty cents more an hour," he said with a smile.

"Done."

"You drive a hard bargain, Shay. I better leave before you convince me to give up my bar to you and Lola."

Stefan stood to leave but stopped just before he made it to the door. "Oh, before I forget. Thursday we have a private party again. You'll have to be in costume. Know anything about the 1970s?"

"The Seventies?"

"Yeah. The member wants the party to have a

Seventies theme. You know, disco ball and all? So you'll have to wear a costume."

Immediately, old Dukes of Hazzard reruns jumped into my mind and I knew exactly what I'd dress up as. "Got it. I'll be ready."

"Good. Any chance you can be back at work tonight? I know it's short notice, but I'd consider it a personal favor if you could."

Stefan turned on that charm that was so him, flashing me a smile and giving me his trademark sexy look I'd seen time and again with other bartenders and members at the club. It seemed odd to have him acting like this toward me, but as I stood there in jeans and a t-shirt with no makeup on, I suddenly realized why women found him so appealing. He had a way of making a woman feel beautiful, even when she felt anything but. Raising my hand to cover the scratch on my cheek, I nodded. "Sure. I'll be there by seven, as always."

"Thanks, Shay. Oh, and I'm glad to see you're healing nicely. See you later."

He left me standing there unsure how I felt about Stefan March. An arrogant asshole since the first moment I met him, he now seemed different in some way, as if some of that arrogance had been wiped away leaving a nicer person in its place.

I liked this Stefan much more than the old version.

The bedroom door opened, and I turned to see Elliot staring at me with an icy look. His lips pursed, he said nothing, but his body language screamed his unhappiness.

"Well, now you've met Stefan March. See what I meant all those times I complained about him?"

"All I saw was you not able to even call me your boyfriend, even though I live here with you. What's that about, Shay?"

I had to turn away to avoid the accusatory look in his eyes. I knew what he was saying. I didn't know how to make things better, though.

"It's nothing, El. Don't make it into something it's not."

"What's going on here, Shay? We've always been up front with each other from day one. I think I deserve to know the truth."

I walked past him toward the kitchen, not wanting to have this conversation even though I'd known for a while that it was inevitable. Elliot and I had been good for a long time, but whatever this was between us had run its course. That I couldn't even call him my boyfriend in front of someone I didn't care about said more than Carrie ever could about the state of us.

He followed me, refusing to let this go. I couldn't blame him. He deserved to know how I felt. The problem was I didn't know how to say it.

"You're into him, Shay. Just tell me."

My eyes grew big as I stood there stunned at his statement. "Into him? No. No way."

"I saw it all over your face. Maybe you don't even know yet, but you want him."

I'd pretty much abandoned my plan to play Stefan March, so whatever Elliot thought he saw on my face in front of Stefan was wrong. "No, you're mistaken. He's my boss, and that's it."

"Whatever. I know what I saw. He's into you too. All I know is that whatever we were isn't there anymore. I don't know what happened, but things are different with you ever since you started working at that club."

I didn't know what to say to that. I hadn't meant for things to end with him like this. Elliot and I had never been something that would last forever, but I'd always thought we'd part ways better than this. It was just that

I didn't feel like I had before.

The hurt in his eyes bit at my heart. "Don't do this, Elliot. We've had a good time, but we both knew this wasn't anything permanent."

He hung his head. "I think it's time for me to go."

As much as I didn't want things to end with him like this, I didn't move to stop him as he turned toward the bedroom to get his things. When he came back out with his black duffel bag in his hand, a lump formed in my throat. All those months together and things were ending just as they began with him and that one duffel bag he brought with him that first night.

He walked up to me and kissed me softly. "Have a good life, Shay. Remember to have some fun on your way to the top."

"El, I'm sorry." I didn't know what I was apologizing for. I just knew I was sorry it was ending like this.

"Don't be sorry. I knew what we were. I always hoped for more, but you never lied and even though I think you and that guy are into each other, I don't think you cheated either. You have nothing to feel sorry for."

Hating how awkward this felt, I fingered his collar, wanting to feel him one last time. "I never cheated, El. When I was with you, it was only you."

He pressed a kiss onto my forehead and gave me a weak smile. "Take care, smart girl."

I watched him leave, unable to move from where I stood staring at my front door for a long time before I looked around my apartment and realized that day I'd always known would come had finally arrived. It had come a little early and not in the way I'd planned, but it had come.

Heading into the bedroom, I saw his side of the closet empty, hangers taking up the space where his clothes had been. As I grabbed one of my work shirts, I slid my hand over those hangers and took a deep breath. "Bye, El."

X

Lola stood against the front bar wearing a huge smile as I walked toward her just as the nightly bartender meeting was about to begin. "Nice to see you again, Shay."

"Yeah, you know how it is. I couldn't stay away."

"Stefan told me I'm back up at the front bar tonight and every night. Isn't that great?" she beamed.

"Right where you belong, if you ask me."

"Maybe he'll put us together again. He should. We work terrific together."

I looked over toward Stefan and smiled. "Well, you know how Stefan is. I can't figure out why he does the things he does."

"Gather up! We've got a big night ahead of us!"

Lola and I made our way to the circle of bartenders and servers who surrounded Stefan, and I saw Mika hang back away from the crowd. He hadn't lied. I hadn't been sure of what I'd find when I came back, but he'd been true to his word, it seemed. Hopefully, there wouldn't be any more problems with Mika from now on.

I listened as Stefan handed out the night's assignments, loving how happy Lola looked as he announced her new position as permanent head bartender and everyone but Mika clapped for her. Once or twice our eyes met and I smiled at him, surprised at how much I was beginning to like this new Stefan. I was sure he'd show me that arrogant asshole part of him again, but for the time being, I enjoyed the bossman.

When he finished, everyone scattered to their places to get ready for a busy Monday night. Assigned to the front bar with Lola, I had to laugh when she asked how I really got the scratch on my face.

"You heard right. Mika tried to scratch my eye out."

"I bet Stefan saved you, right?"

Still his biggest cheerleader. "Not exactly, but now that I think of it, I should have asked for combat pay to come back."

"He really does appreciate you, Shay. I can see it in the way he talks to you."

"I must have missed the appreciation side of our boss, Lola. All I've seen is the sexually harassing side and the one where he was so angry I thought flames might shoot out his eyes the other night."

She giggled and said, "You're funny, you know that?"

"I guess. I just say what I think."

Handing me a bottle from under the bar, she smiled. "I think that's a good thing. There aren't enough people in this world who say what they think."

I couldn't help but wonder how someone who'd obviously spent a lot of time in bars could be so gentle and naïve. Lola seemed to be at least my age, if not older, but she had the soul of someone who'd never seen ugliness in the world.

"You're too nice, Lola."

"Not always," she said as she twisted her face into a fake grimace.

"You always make excuses for Stefan, and you seem to like the one part of me that pisses people off the most."

"Well, I told you, men like Stefan are just being true to themselves, like you are. I think that's why I like both of you. There's nothing phony about either of you. That's how people should be."

Kerry interrupted us with a laundry list of questions, so Lola headed off to the back bar to help her. As I crouched down to get the area under the bar ready for the night, I looked up to see Stefan leaning over staring down at me. "You need something, bossman?"

"Just wanted to see if everything's okay with my new bartender."

I stood up and shook my head. "I'm not new, Stefan."

"Well, I was hoping that maybe we could say that this is your first night so we could get off on the right foot this time around."

He had that same look on his face that he'd worn earlier as he left my apartment. His brown eyes sparkled, like he was enjoying himself. Maybe he was right. Maybe we should try to get along instead of always being at each other's throats.

I reached my hand out in front of me to shake his. "It's nice to meet you. I'm Shay Callahan."

He shook my hand and smiled. "And I'm Stefan March. Nice to meet you, Shay. I think you're going to love working at Club X."

His grip was light, even though his hand dwarfed mine. For the first time, I noticed how truly built he was and how attractive he could be. As I took my hand back, I smiled to him. "I'm sure I'm going to love it here."

"Hey, Shay, glad to see you back."

I turned to see Stefan's brother Kane come from behind him. Always a nice surprise, he was all smiles for me tonight. "Well, I couldn't stay away for long. Stefan convinced me everybody wins if I came back."

"I'm sure they do. Mind if I steal my brother away for a moment?"

"No problem. I'll leave you guys to it."

Stefan's expression had morphed into a sneer, and I walked down to the end of the bar to cut up some fruit.

The two of them were still within earshot, though, and I heard Kane say, "You look like you're making progress, but you're still going to lose, Stef. And I'm going to enjoy it."

"Lose my ass. Get ready to learn how to run a bar, Kane. And make sure the Mustang is ready because I am."

I looked up to see them both staring down at me, Stefan with his new kinder look and Kane with a look that made me think Elliot might have had the right idea but the wrong brother.

NINE

My return to Club X turned out to be even better than I imagined. Whatever Stefan said to Mika worked because she practically avoided me like I had the plague and when she was forced to be around me, she made every effort to be civil. It looked at times like she wanted to bite through steel, but she remained polite, if cool. Cool was fine with me, though.

Lola's new position as head bartender suited her, and I liked to think that I might have had something to do with her getting the recognition she deserved. As for me, I liked working with her and most of the other staff, and even Stefan had begun to grow on me. Not like he did for Lola, but at least I didn't despise him anymore.

The night for the private party with the Seventies theme rolled around, and I showed up at work in my Daisy Duke costume, impressed I still fit into cutoff shorts I'd worn in my freshman year in college six long years before. A bunch of the girls had said they were coming dressed as Charlie's Angels, so at least I wouldn't look like one in a line of Farrah Fawcett clones. Nearly everyone had arrived already, so I took my place behind the front bar with Lola and hoped Stefan would assign me there for the party.

Lola looked me up and down and giggled. "I'd know those shorts anywhere! You're Daisy Duke from that Dukes of Hazzard show, aren't you? I love it!"

"Yeah, I figured since so many people would naturally go to the Charlie's Angels look that I'd do something different." Twirling around, I looked down at my shorts and said, "You don't think they're too short, do you? I mean, it is Club X but I'm not dancing."

"They're perfect. You have a good body, so you can carry them off. What do you think of my costume?"

Lola wore a dark wig tied into ponytails right below her ears with red ribbons, and her costume included a red tank top and blue shorts that resembled hot pants. I knew exactly who she was, but I couldn't remember what TV show she was from. "Her name is Maryann, but what show was she on?"

"Gilligan's Island! The guy at the costume place told me it would be perfect."

"Definitely. We look perfect together up here. Let's hope Stefan thinks so too."

"I think he will. I asked him to put you up here whenever you're on."

She was too sweet. "You know as head bartender I think you could just tell him you want that, Lola."

Shrugging, she smiled. "I know, but he's so used to telling us what to do. I don't want to give him a hassle."

Behind her, Stefan walked up to the bar looking at a stack of papers and chimed in, "A hassle about what? Don't tell me it has anything to do with this party because I'm already fed up with this Seventies shit. Between the disco ball and the DJ with his music, I can't wait to get back to the present once tonight is over."

"Do you like our costumes?" Lola asked quietly,

obviously hoping for some validation from him.

Looking up, he studied her and then me and smiled. "I have no idea what you two are supposed to be, but I like what I see. As long as it works with the theme and Marshall that freak is happy, I'm happy."

Lola beamed her pleasure at hearing Stefan was happy, but he just walked away, preoccupied with his paperwork. She so wanted him to like her, but from everything I'd seen, if he had been with her already, it was just to play.

The party began around nine, and I could tell immediately that the birthday boy liked to party hard. He and his friends downed glass after glass of top shelf scotch and cognac, tipping Lola and me like they had the ability to print money themselves. After just a few hours, my rent and all my utilities were covered.

The party raged on for hours, with some of my favorite oldies songs blasting through the room, and when regular members joined in to celebrate Halloween, Club X came alive like I'd never seen it before. The bar and dance floor were packed with people all in costumes, most of them far more revealing than mine or Lola's, and the place had a sexual vibe to it usually reserved for the upper floors.

Even the ruler of the fantasy area came down to party, and while Lola handled a group of members dressed in togas who only wanted to talk about the orgy they'd love us to join, Kane hung out on my end of the bar waiting to talk to me. When I finally got to him nearly a half hour later, he offered me a tour of the upper floors.

"I thought maybe you'd like to come upstairs and see how crazy Club X gets on this, the wildest night of the year."

Kane's suggestion surprised me, but my curiosity

got the best of me and I agreed. "I can't do it until the crowd dies down, though. Will the offer be open later?"

"Any time. Just come up to the fifth floor. I'll be there."

I smiled at the chance to finally get a look at the fantasy area of the club, but Stefan had seen Kane's visit too and quickly pushed his way through the crowd to find out why he'd been there. Yelling over the crowds, he leaned over the bar and said in my ear, "What did Kane want?"

I stopped pouring a glass of cognac and looked at him in confusion. "Just to offer to let me see the top floors. That's all. I think I might go up if the crowd thins out down here later."

"I need you down here, Shay. Lola can't handle the entire front bar by herself."

Was he losing his mind? "I wouldn't leave her alone to handle everything, Stefan. If it doesn't slow down, I'll just go up another night. It's okay. It's a standing offer."

My willingness to be a good employee didn't make him any happier, and he stormed off toward his office without saying another word. The crowd didn't slow down until nearly two in the morning, but when I had the chance, I told Lola I'd only be gone for a few minutes and hurried upstairs, too curious not to take the opportunity to check out the fantasy area of the club.

Kane stood at a counter at the top of the stairs watching the costumed crowds as they filed past him down the hallway. Far more serious looking than he ever was with me, he seemed as hard as a statue so no one stepped out of line in front of him. I stopped at his perch and with a smile said, "I only have a few minutes, but maybe a mini-tour can happen?"

"Did it finally slow down in the bar? That explains why my floors are mobbed. My guys keep telling them if they don't have a room reserved it won't happen, but it doesn't keep them from hoping something will open up. This is typical Halloween behavior at Club X, though."

"Maybe it would be better another time when it's not so crowded?"

Kane's blue eyes lit up and he gave me a smile. "Come around here. I've got an idea."

I walked around behind the counter almost chest high on me and saw a bank of nearly twenty monitors he used to watch all the rooms. The scenes they showed were in black and white, but even in those bland colors I instantly saw what Carrie had meant by the freaky side of Club X.

He pointed at the screens and said, "Each one belongs to a room and I can use the bigger ones to take a closer look. Which one would you like to see better?"

A feeling of exhilaration raced through me. "I don't know. This feels like spying on people's private moments together."

"If they wanted privacy, Shay, they'd stay home." Looking down at me, he smiled. "Take your pick."

My eyes traveled from one screen to the next, each one showing me sex and lust at its finest. A dark haired beautiful woman dressed in a nearly see-through black dress that fell to the middle of her thighs danced behind a window for a man who kneeled just inches from it staring at her like a starving man seeing food for the first time in months. I pointed at the screen and looked up at Kane. "He looks like he's having a good time."

"That's exactly the fantasy he requested. He wants her close, but not too close as to tempt him. He won't risk losing his wife and kids for his fetish, but he can't stop himself either. So he has us stop him."

"What's his fetish?" I asked, studying the scene

playing out in front of me.

"See-through clothing," he said with a deep chuckle. "Gets him off every time."

I turned toward Kane and shook my head in confusion. "Why doesn't he just have his wife wear something see-through and save himself some money?"

"It's not the same for him. Nothing to fight against."

Rolling my eyes, I couldn't help but think men were silly creatures. "Leave it to a man to want that."

"Oh, you think this is just men? Look over here." Kane pointed at the monitor farthest from me and I moved to stand in front of him to see better. "Sex is an equal opportunity game, Shay."

I looked down and saw a woman sitting on a couch watching a man slowly undress another woman. As Kane and I stared at the monitor, the man removed a long white glove one finger at a time and then held it up for the woman next to him to examine. The entire scene had a surreal feel about it.

"What are they doing? Will he and the woman he's undressing have sex right there in the room?"

Kane looked down at a sheet of paper and nodded. "After he removes every single piece of clothing she's wearing, he'll have sex with the woman on the couch. Simone had to find two of everything to wear tonight. The member has a thing for watching her husband undress another woman before she sleeps with him. See? Freak isn't just a male thing."

"Do you watch these every night, all night?"

"No," he said with a grin as he sat back on a barstool. "I've seen everything here, so my eyes are trained to merely scan the monitors for any signs of problems. Other than that, I don't watch because I don't care."

"Doesn't anyone just have hot sex in these rooms?" I asked and felt my cheeks grow hot as I realized the words that had just come out of my mouth.

He nodded. "Sure, but most of what happens at clubs like this has little to do with just sex and almost nothing to do with love, so what you might think of as hot probably wouldn't be what you'd see in any of my rooms."

"This is an interesting place you have here. Thanks for the closer look."

I felt someone's hand touch mine and turned to see Stefan standing in front of me. His knitted brows and frown told me my boss was none too happy with me.

"What are you doing up here, Shay?" he asked sharply.

"Just getting the tour of Kane's area."

"You need to get back downstairs. I'm sure Kane can handle things on his own."

I turned around toward Kane and bit my lip. "I think I'm in trouble with the boss. Thanks for the closer look," I whispered.

"My pleasure. Come back anytime."

As I walked toward the stairs, I tried to avoid Stefan's angry stare and hoped I hadn't ruined the good relationship we'd developed since I'd come back. I heard him snap at Kane, but didn't quite understand what he said as I hurried downstairs back to see how Lola was holding up.

After the club closed, Lola and I stood in stunned amazement at how much the two of us had earned for just one night of bartending. This was what I'd come to Club X for.

"Can you believe this, Shay? I've never made this much in my life!" Lola squealed as we counted out our tips.

"I guess dressing up like this was a good idea, after

all. A little T and A gets some great T-I-P-S," I joked.

Stuffing her earnings into her purse, she finished the last of her clean up and motioned toward the door. "Want to get some breakfast? I'm starving."

As much as I liked the idea of hanging out with Lola, after a long night all I could think of was hitting the bed, even though it would be another night alone. "Another time, okay? I'm feeling pretty beat."

"No problem," she said with a big smile. "I'm off tomorrow night, so I'll see you Saturday?"

"I'll be here. Be careful walking out."

"I always ask Stefan to walk me out when I leave this late, so no worries. See you later!"

Lola headed toward Stefan's office, and I finished the rest of my work. The idea of going home to bed had seemed like a great idea, but the fact that Elliot was gone and I was headed to an empty apartment made it more sad than anything else.

Lost in thought, I didn't see Stefan approach the bar until he was right in front of me. "Hey, Shay. Good job tonight. You and Lola handled this front bar like the experts you are."

Forcing a smile, I said, "Thanks, Stefan. I hope you weren't too angry about me checking out the fantasy rooms upstairs."

He narrowed his eyes to slits and stared at me. "You okay? You look like something's wrong?"

"Yeah, I'm fine."

"Mika didn't give you any more problems tonight, did she? I thought she understood once more and she's gone."

"No, nothing like that."

He came around the end of the bar and grabbed a bottle of whiskey off the top shelf. Putting it on the bar in front of him, he grabbed two glasses and turned toward me. "Neat or on the rocks?"

"I don't know, Stefan. I probably should get going."

"You don't look like you're in any hurry, Shay. Something happen between you and your boyfriend?"

Ignoring his question, I simply said, "Neat, please."

He poured me a glass and I downed a few gulps hoping to push the whole Elliot thing out of my mind as quickly as possible. I'd finished the entire glass without saying another word, only realizing afterward that I'd gone into my own head right there and ignored Stefan.

I pushed the glass back toward him. "Another one, thanks."

He did as I asked without a word, and I closed my eyes as the alcohol hit my tongue this time. I'd believed that ending things with Elliot would be easy since I'd always kept him at arm's length, but now that the reality of his leaving settled into my brain, I couldn't be so cavalier about it.

"You want to talk about it?"

I turned to look at Stefan and shook my head. "No. Talking isn't going to make it better."

He threw back the last of his first glass and nodded. "Okay. I'm sure you two will work things out sooner or later. I wouldn't worry."

I took another swig and looked away. "Elliot moved out right after you left. We're over."

"Oh. I'm sorry, Shay."

"Yeah. Thanks." I turned back to face him. "Pour me another."

"You sure? I wouldn't think a little thing like you could handle much more."

I leveled my gaze on him and snorted my disgust. "Little thing? You must have me confused with someone else. I'm no little girl. Hit me with more of that whiskey."

A sexy grin spread across his lips. "Okay. Your wish

is my command."

"Good. I'm in no mood to be told no tonight, Stefan."

"I would never tell you no, Shay."

I took a drink and felt it burn as it went down my throat. Rolling my eyes, I chuckled. "You never tell anyone no, Stefan. You're the definition of a man whore."

He didn't say anything, and I thought I saw him cringe ever so slightly at my mention of him being a man whore. I couldn't imagine why. He'd meticulously built that reputation with many women, and never before had I seen any evidence that he didn't enjoy every minute of his conquests. In some way, there was something to respect about that.

"I guess you have me all figured out, don't you?"

I raised my glass to him. "Hey, there's nothing wrong with knowing what you want and going after it. That you don't want one woman is perfectly fine, in my mind. You've got looks, money, and freedom. Who would want to give any of that up? You can have any woman you want. It's hard to believe you wouldn't take advantage of any opportunity that presents itself."

"What about you? You have all that going for you."

"What about me? I don't have the money you do, Stefan. If I did, maybe I'd be like you. Who knows? But you're not going to get a lecture from me about your being a man whore. Play on, player."

I swallowed the last of my drink and pounded the glass onto the bar a little harder than I'd intended. A giggle escaped from my lips. "I didn't mean to let that slam like that. I think I might have had my fill."

"Maybe I should give you a ride home. You might not be okay to drive."

Taking a step forward, I walked straight into the edge of the bar. I looked down and then over toward

Stefan. "I was going to say no, but since I just walked into the bar and there isn't a priest or rabbi around to make it a joke, I guess I better take you up on your offer."

He stepped behind me and wrapped his arm around my waist. "Always a smart ass, huh? Come on. I'll take you home."

I wasn't too drunk to walk, but by the time I hit the warm night air outside, I definitely knew I shouldn't be driving. I walked beside Stefan and wondered what kind of car he drove. I guessed it would be something expensive and definitely fast. Maybe a Porsche. Or maybe a Jag. Yeah, he had a Jag vibe to him. Looking around, though, I didn't see any car that fit.

"Where's your car? I'm in heels here, Stefan," I said as I clutched his arm tighter.

"I don't have a car. My bike is behind the club."

A bike? I should have known.

We turned the corner of the building and there it was. Stefan's motorcycle. I'd never seen a bike like it, and it definitely was expensive and fast. Big, black, and with him sitting on it.

With a way too sexy look, he said, "Climb on."

I slid my leg over the seat and wrapped my arms around him. "Shouldn't I wear a helmet?"

"Not tonight. Hang on!"

He revved the engine, and the bike vibrated beneath me, powerful and loud. I tightened my hold on him and pressed my cheek to his back as he took off flying through the streets of Tampa. His body felt powerful like the bike, and I moved my hands down over his stomach, feeling his washboard abs beneath his t-shirt. When my palms touched the top of his jeans, I stopped their movement, sure I felt his hard cock just beneath my hands.

"You okay back there?" he yelled back as we turned

the corner onto my street.

"Yeah, I'm good," I answered, unsure of what I was now that my buzz had vanished on the ride there.

He stopped in front of my apartment and shut the bike off. I swung my leg around to stand and tried to fix my hair, sure the wind had blown it into a look that resembled a brown Darth Vader helmet. "Thanks for the ride home. See you at work!"

Turning toward the front of my building, I heard Stefan get off the bike and say, "I'll walk you to your door."

He followed me all the way down my hallway, and I knew where this was going. The desire to go through with my plan to play the infamous Stefan March mixed with the emotions I was feeling over Elliot's leaving. I knew I should have just closed the door on him, but at that moment, I didn't want to be alone.

"Well, I got you home safe and sound, so I guess I'll get going, unless you need me for something…"

He let his sentence drift off as he slid his gaze over my body. I knew what he wanted, and I wanted it too. Stepping toward him, I looked up into his eyes, and then as I backed through my front door, smiled. "I'm in no hurry to sleep."

"Good. Me either."

TEN

🌼 SHAY

Following me inside, he slid his hand through my hair and cupped the back of my neck, pulling me into his body. His mouth slanted over mine, and he kissed me with a passion I never expected from someone like him. My head felt like it was swimming, and every inch of my body felt like it was alive.

Stefan moved fast and quickly unbuttoned my blue and white plaid shirt I'd loosely knotted at the bottom. Running his hands across my ribs, he slid them up over my bra, cupping my still covered breasts and murmuring, "This needs to come off too."

I smiled up at him, strangely amused by what he'd said. "Well, I'm sure you know how to work one of these."

His tongue slid over his lips and the corners of his mouth hitched up in one of those sexy grins only he could give. "I do. Turn around, princess."

Struck by his nickname for me, I did as he ordered. His hands made quick work of my bra, and it slid down my body as he took my breasts in his hands. Moaning in my ear, he pushed his hips forward and I felt his hard cock behind me. "Mmmm…as gorgeous as I thought they'd be."

I arched my back and leaned my head against his muscular chest. Closing my eyes, I moaned as he began rolling my nipples between his finger and thumb with exactly the right pressure to make me wet. Elliot had never cared much to pay much attention to anything above my waist, preferring to spend his time in foreplay almost exclusively on my pussy, so I'd missed what Stefan was giving me.

"Ohhh…that feels so good," I groaned as his mouth nuzzled my neck.

He nipped my earlobe with his teeth and squeezed one nipple harder. "I want to see what's beneath these shorts, baby."

His hands slid down from my breasts to unbutton the top of my Daisy Dukes. Hooking his fingers in the belt loops, he tugged my shorts off my body, taking my thong along with them. Naked, I moved to turn around to undress him, but he stopped me. I turned my head to look at him. "Am I the only one getting naked here?"

Behind me, he slipped his shirt over his head to reveal the gorgeous body I'd always known was under those Club X shirts. The man obviously spent serious time at the gym. Spinning around as he inched his jeans down over his legs, I saw for the first time how stunning Stefan March truly was. Every inch of him seemed to be covered in muscle, from his enormous shoulders to abs that couldn't have been more defined to incredibly toned legs.

I stared at the tattoo I'd never seen on him at the club. I was used to seeing his sleeves full of women and what looked like mythological creatures on his arms, but now as he stood shirtless in front of me, I saw a tattoo that was only writing across his ribcage. In black and red, the words ALL GOOD THINGS ARE WILD AND FREE spanned his torso.

"Interesting tattoo," I said, curious about this one.

He stood there naked in front of me and nodded. "Yeah. Wild and free. Come here."

Pulling me to him, he kissed me and I felt my body come alive again. I slid my hands over his body, amazed at how soft his skin was over all that hard muscle.

Stefan crouched down, and I looked down as he leaned in toward my body. His fingers spread me wide open, sending strings of desire racing through me. Then the tip of his tongue lightly touched my pussy, and my legs went weak. As if he knew what effect he had on me, he slid his palms up the back of my thighs just as he pressed his tongue flat to my clit, his piercing creating sensations in me I'd never felt before.

"Oh…my…God…"

Before I could finish my sentence, he hooked my leg over his shoulder to gain even better access to the most sensitive parts of me and went down on me better than any man had in my life. Maybe it was the way that metal stud in his tongue slid over my clit, each time sending a jolt of pleasure straight to my core. Maybe it was how he seemed entirely focused on me, his tongue devoted to getting me off.

Whatever it was that he did, I came harder than I'd ever come before, barely able to stand from the quaking in my thighs. He sat back, his mouth still wet with my juices, and looked up at me with an expression of pure satisfaction, as if I'd just given him the best oral sex of his life.

Licking his lips, he smiled. "Mmmm. Nice."

I wanted to speak—to say something sexy or snappy—but I couldn't. My brain seemed to have gone blank the moment he buried his face in my pussy, and it hadn't come back online yet.

He stood up and in a commanding voice ordered, "Face that way, Shay."

Turning me around so my back faced him, he pulled my hair off to one side and whispered in my ear, "I want you on your hands and knees, princess."

His voice was raw, like every syllable came straight from somewhere dark and deep inside him. This Stefan made me want him more than I thought I ever could, and my body reacted to his every word and touch as if he'd already mastered me.

"In the bedroom," I squeaked out as I began walking toward my room, needing to buy time before he overwhelmed me and I lost control.

He caught me just as I crawled onto the bed, pressing his hands onto my hips and pulling me back toward him until his cock nudged my ass. His lips dragged along my neck to my collarbone, and he whispered against my skin, "I've fucking wanted you since the first time I saw you."

I closed my eyes, loving the feel of his mouth on me as he spoke those words. It meant nothing that I'd always believed he'd wanted me, but to hear him say that now excited me more than I wanted to admit.

Thrusting his hips forward, he skimmed the head of his cock through my pussy to my clit, sending a rush of pleasure racing through my body. "Oh, God…" I dropped down onto my forearms and pushed back against him, wanting him inside me so bad.

"That's it, baby. Let me into that pretty cunt."

He backed away from me, and then I felt the head of his cock at my entrance for the merest moment before he thrust his hips forward and buried himself inside me. His fingers dug into my hips as he retreated from my body only to thrust forward again. My body felt filled like never before, as if every time I'd ever been with a man had been a dress rehearsal for this.

I gripped the sheets in my hands, and he began fucking me better than I'd ever been fucked in my life. Every stroke into me, every deep moan that escaped from him inched me closer to that moment when I'd come. I wanted to feel that release he gave me more than anything else in the world at that moment.

"God, you feel so fucking good—" His sentence trailed off on a groan, and he slid his hand up my back to fist my hair. "Up on your hands, baby."

I obeyed his command, never even thinking of not doing what he wanted. He felt so good inside me, his thick cock sliding over raw nerve endings and making each come alive with every push into me. No man had ever made me want to submit like he did.

Stefan leaned forward and buried himself to the hilt inside me. Next to my ear, he whispered, "Show me that fire I saw that first day, Shay."

He wanted fire, but I wanted to let him control this tonight. To make me forget Elliot and the mess I'd made of that relationship. To not be the one with all the power for once. But I could do fire too.

I moved forward and felt him leave my body. Climbing onto his lap, I slid my wet pussy over his cock and grinned. "You want fire, Stefan?"

"I want whatever you're bringing, baby."

His hands gripped my hips as I raised up over his cock, and slowly I lowered myself onto him, loving the feeling of him filling me.

"Why did we turn around? I liked it the other way."

I raised up on my knees again, leaving just the head of his cock just inside me to tease him. "I like to see the man I'm having sex with."

Stefan pushed me hard down onto him, and his cock

hit a spot deep inside me that made my eyes roll back into my head. God, he felt so good!

"You want to see me? Then look at me while I fuck you, princess."

I opened my eyes as he slid his fingers over my cheeks and into my hair, gripping it tightly in his hands. His dark gaze fixed on me, he looked like hunger personified. He was need, desire, and appetite all right there in front of me.

"Ride my cock. I want to watch you ride me until there's nothing left inside either of us."

I did as he commanded, riding him with an abandon that I didn't even know existed inside me. My body bucked against his, and his invaded mine over and over as we searched for that one moment where we weren't boss and bartender, player and challenger, and even man and woman.

Staring into one another's eyes, we searched for that one sweet place and time where we were nothing more than just Stefan and Shay.

I wanted to kiss him, to plunder that mouth that had infuriated me so many times. He may have wanted me from the moment we met, but my want had been something entirely different. More often than not, the man had enraged me to my very being, yet there I was on his lap, his cock deep inside me as he edged me inch by inch to my release, and I couldn't imagine any other place on Earth that I'd want to be right then.

He held tight to my hair to keep me looking at him, and for a fleeting moment, I thought I saw something even more in them than the Stefan I'd come to like. In those dark brown eyes focused entirely on me, I saw a look that made me think he was so much more than what I'd believed.

I cradled his face and kissed him, wanting to feel

him against every part of me. His lips fed on mine as mine did on his, as eager to taste me as I was to taste him. His tongue with its metal piercing slid over mine, exciting me as the memory of what it felt like gliding over my needy clit danced through my mind.

My body ached—for good and for bad—with every time I slid him inside me. Legs spread as wide as I could to take all of him, my hips hurt but the tender ache inside me overruled any idea of stopping. Each stroke of his cock into me brought me closer to release, but if I was to be truthful, I didn't want this to end.

Of all the incarnations of Stefan I'd seen, I preferred this one best. For all his cockiness and swagger, he knew how to handle a woman and give her pleasure. I'd doubted that before this, but no more.

Now I just wanted more—more of him, more of the feelings his body created in mine.

More.

He slid his hands down my back and cupped my ass, kneading the skin slowly with his fingers. In my ear, he whispered, "Let me feel you come apart, Shay."

I was so close. Just once more to feel him fill me, the head of his cock touching that one spot as our bodies pressed together.

Then I felt it begin. A tiny spark of release that grew from somewhere deep inside that uncoiled slowly until every inch of my body felt like my nerve endings were wide open and more alive than they'd ever been before. I clung to him as my orgasm finally tore through me, and I rode him until the final quiver inside me had subsided.

Stefan came just as I finished, his cock pulsing against my tender walls as he groaned my name low and deep into my mouth and tugged roughly on my hair. He was power and passion, and as I watched him come, I couldn't help understand why women found him so sexy. Everything about him signaled his pleasure at satisfying me, a very attractive trait I hadn't seen before now.

We sat there quietly, our bodies still entangled as the haze of sex gradually faded away. Part of me wanted to say something, almost as if I should be sexier after all that we'd done, but another part enjoyed the silence of being in someone's arms and sharing nothing more than my body with him.

Stefan sat with his eyes closed and his mouth slightly open, as if caught between the same two choices. Like most men, he said nothing for a long time, preferring silence over most anything else. I could appreciate that more often than other women could. There was something about not having to speak that gave off a sense of power.

Finally, he whispered, "If I don't get a drink, I'm going to turn to dust right here in your bed."

I couldn't help but chuckle. Leave it to him to break the moment with something cute. After giving him a tiny kiss on his parched lips, I smiled. "You're going to make me get off you for a drink?"

"I'd say I could walk to the faucet still inside you, but I'm not sure my legs could handle it. That was some marathon session."

He kissed me and pressed his forehead against mine. "No kidding. I think I'm already beginning to turn here."

Rolling my eyes, I lifted myself off him and walked toward the kitchen, asking, "Water or something a bit stronger?"

"Water's usually what I drink after workouts."

I grabbed him a glass of iced water and returned to the bedroom to find him still buck naked and sitting on the bed, the only change the lack of condom on his still hard cock. Why I had thought he'd quickly dress and down his drink before bolting out the door I didn't know, but he appeared perfectly at home sitting there waiting for me.

"A workout, huh? I didn't think I was that hard on you," I teased as I handed him the glass.

He gulped down the water like a man who been stranded in the desert and placed the glass on the nightstand. Turning back toward me, he leaned back on his elbows and grinned. "I knew you'd be like that. It's good. Nothing worse than a woman who just lays there and doesn't participate."

And there right in front of me he morphed into the Stefan who'd gotten under my skin from the first moment I met him.

"Participate? Maybe that's a reflection of the partner, not the woman."

He reached out and snaked his arm around my waist to pull me toward him. "Maybe, but I don't think so. Whatever. You don't have to worry about that. You're definitely a partner worthy of a workout."

"You're pretty cocky, aren't you?" I teased, secretly loving the feel of his body against mine and wishing he wouldn't leave as soon as I feared he would.

He looked down toward where our bodies touched and back up at me. "Shouldn't I be? I thought you liked the way I am."

Arching one eyebrow, I pretended to be skeptical. "I didn't say I didn't."

"Good. We need to do this again."

"Really? Need to?" I mocked.

"Yeah. Good sex is a need thing."

Smiling, I said, "Well, when you put it that way…"

Stefan nuzzled my neck and kissed me on the sensitive area just under my ear. "Good. Then we'll definitely do this again."

He leaned back with a satisfied look in his eye. Tapping him on the nose, I continued my teasing. "For a player, you're not very non-committal. I thought players hit it and left. You're all about making plans for next time."

"Who told you I was a player?" he asked with a genuine look of confusion in his eyes, as if he thought he wasn't one.

"Everyone. I mean, it's no secret, Stefan."

He shook his head. "Like I told you at the club, you think you know all about me, but you don't. I might just surprise you, Shay Callahan."

I climbed off him and slipped a t-shirt over my head. "I look forward to it, Stefan March. Few people in this world surprise me, so it would be a nice change."

Leaning back on his elbows, he nodded. "That sounds like a challenge I'll accept. I like surprising people who don't believe I have it in me."

Was he trying to charm me? Whatever he was doing, it was working, and I couldn't have that. Regardless of who he was there lying naked on my bed looking more incredible than a man should joking around with me, Stefan was a player, pure and simple. Forgetting that would only lead to me getting hurt, and I couldn't let that happen.

"Well, Mr. Surprise, I need to get some sleep or I'll never get back to that place I work with the boss who cracks the whip, so you better get going."

Stefan sat up and stood in front of me wearing a playful expression. "Crack the whip? That sounds kinky."

"Yeah, yeah. Let's find your clothes so you don't have to ride that bike of yours buck naked all the way to your place."

I turned to head out to the living room and he followed me. Scooping up his clothes, I had to smile. The man had already surprised me more than I thought possible. Not that I wanted him to know, though.

"Shay, are you trying to get rid of me?"

I shook my head. "No. I just figured since this is just a hook up, you wouldn't be staying the night. Player, remember?"

He took the clothes from me and began to dress. "Yeah, but I'm getting a bum's rush vibe here. Did you and your boyfriend really break up?"

His feelings were hurt. Damn, I couldn't figure this guy out. He definitely was a player, yet he seemed bothered by me not wanting to have him spend the night. It was odd player behavior, but what did I know? No matter what Carrie believed, I wasn't a player and my experiences with them had been limited, at best, but none had ever wanted to do the cuddling after sex thing.

"Yes, we did, Stefan. I wouldn't do that to someone. If I'm with a man, then I'm only with him. I don't cheat. It's something I can't abide."

"Okay. Good. I mean, I don't want to have to fend off an attack from that skinny guy. It wouldn't be hard, but putting the beatdown on your poor boyfriend would really kill the good time we had, don't you think?"

Chuckling, I brushed a piece of lint off his shirt. "There's no boyfriend, so no need to kill our good time. But it's time for me to get to sleep. I had a good time."

In another classically un-playerlike move, he leaned down and kissed me long and deep, like we were separating for ages and he needed to remember the feel of my lips on his. "See you at work, princess."

And then he was gone and I was left trying to figure out what the hell had just happened.

ELEVEN

🍾 STEFAN

Stretching my arms above my head, I closed my eyes and thought about how good the night before had felt, loving the memory of Shay completely giving herself to me. Rarely had I enjoyed fucking a woman as much as I did her. I had a feeling she'd be wild, but I never imagined she'd be so…so able to make me want her.

Not that I'd gone over to the dark side like Cash had with Olivia, all lovey dovey and ready to race down the aisle. Fuck that! I was a confirmed bachelor committed only to the single life, and that wouldn't be changing any time soon. I had the world by the tail. Why would I give that up?

I did enjoy myself, though, and I planned to get back inside Shay's tight body as soon as possible. Now that she'd warmed up to me, it would be nothing but smooth sailing from here on out.

A knock at my office door tore me from my daydreaming, and before I could even yell to tell the person to come in, Kane appeared in my doorway with a look on his face that told me he knew. I didn't know how, but he knew.

"What can I do for you today, Kane?" I asked wearing a grin I couldn't wipe from my face.

He studied me for a long moment and closed the door behind him. Arching an eyebrow, he stared and said, "Just wondering how that bet of ours is going."

I laughed. "You know what, big brother? Today's your unlucky day, or my lucky day, depending on how you look at it. I was with her last night."

His steely blue eyes narrowed. "No way. I can't believe that woman would ever go with the likes of you. She's too good for you."

"Believe whatever you want. Even after you pulled that shit by inviting her upstairs to check out your area, I had her and it was fucking fantastic!" I bragged. "And now, it's just a matter of time, Kane. I got the girl, and I'm getting your car and your place in this club. I'd say that's a complete win."

My half-brother stood stunned, his shoulders hunching slightly under the weight of my gloating. But he wasn't giving up yet. "You know, Stefan, it's way easier to get a woman to sleep with you than it is to get her to fall in love with you. Revel in whatever last night was all you want. You're still miles away from winning."

"What last night was, Kane, was just some of the best sex I've ever had with a woman. Face it. It's just a matter of time. The woman is primed. I win."

"Not so fast, Stefan. The hard part is only beginning, and you only have a couple months."

I couldn't believe this guy. What the hell? I'd bedded Shay and all he wanted to talk about were hurdles, as if I hadn't overcome the most important one. "Maybe you didn't hear me correctly. I slept with her last night. As in we had great sex and she's going to want more and I'm going to want to give it to her."

"Sex and love aren't the same thing, baby brother. Our father was the poster child for that truth. No, getting a woman to sleep with you is easy. You're going to have to work to get Shay to fall for you, and I still am willing to bet you don't have what it takes."

Suddenly, my day wasn't looking as rosy as before he'd showed up. He was definitely harshing my post sexually triumphant buzz. I didn't need to be reminded of the fact that a woman like Shay would be hard to break. I'd recognized that fact within thirty seconds of meeting her. But fuck, he at least could give me some credit for getting her into bed.

My head began to throb, which I suspected was all part of Kane's intention in coming into my office in the first place. Taking a deep breath, I worked to keep myself calm. I didn't need to let myself get goaded into some asinine argument with him today.

"Whatever, Kane. Just remember today as the day I told you this is all but won. She'll fall into line like all other women do and that's that. So go back upstairs to your miserable, lonely existence and know that soon I'm going to be in that shithole you call an office surrounded by gorgeous dancers and you'll be down here dealing with bartenders, liquor orders, and all that comes with running the bar."

My insults didn't faze him in the least. Grinning like some cat who'd just eaten a canary, he leveled his gaze on me and said, "It's not over till the fat lady sings."

Turning on his heels, he headed out of my office, leaving me with the hard truth I hadn't wanted to admit to him. Shay likely wasn't going to fall into line like every other woman I'd ever been with. Those women would have lined up to fall in love with me. Some even had. Shay Callahan wasn't those women, though.

Kane wasn't entirely wrong. She was going to take some work. But I hadn't met a woman I couldn't get before in my life, and I didn't plan to make her the first one. I might need to bring in reinforcements, though. This had "needs a woman's touch" written all over it.

Olivia. Who better than my soon-to-be sister-in-law to help me get the girl and win my bet with Kane?

I beat a path over to her office and found her sitting behind her desk with her nose to the grindstone. Typical Olivia. Thankfully, Cash's fiancée had liked me from the moment she met me, unlike Shay, so I figured she'd have some good ideas how to seduce her since my tried-and-true method likely wouldn't work this time.

"Hey, Olivia! What's up?" I asked as I sat down in a seat in front of her desk.

She looked up and gave me one of her terrific warm Olivia smiles that lit up her dark brown eyes. "Not much. What's going on, Stefan?"

"I'm not bothering you, am I? If I am, I can come back later."

My polite offer was met with a suspicious look. "No, we're good. What's up?"

"I want your advice on something."

I figured it was best to try to ease into this conversation. Olivia and I were more than friendly, but it wasn't every day your future brother-in-law with a man whore reputation came into your office to ask how to get a girl.

She closed her laptop and sat back in her chair. "My advice? Okay. What's up?"

Taking a deep breath, I let it out slowly and began. "Well...how should I put this?" Suddenly, easing into things seemed all wrong. Best to just jump into the deep end. "I need your advice on how to get a woman to fall for me."

Olivia's eyes grew as wide as saucers. Looking around like she was being punked, she shook her head. "What?"

"You heard right. I want to get a girl, but I'm pretty sure none of my tricks are going to work on this one. So I thought I'd ask you since she's sort of like you and you know what you'd like a guy to do. Well, if you weren't with Cash. You know."

Nice. Two minutes in and I'd already devolved into some rambling teenage boy. All I needed was a big zit on the end of my nose to make this whole thing complete.

"You want me to tell you how to seduce a woman? Stefan, is this some kind of joke? I doubt anything I could tell you would be more effective than what you already do. Cash tells me everything, and I know how successful you are with women."

"Yeah, yeah. I know. I am. But this one's not like those women. That's why I want your help."

Still confused, she seemed to consider what I'd just said and then she got a faraway look in her eyes. "Hmmm…so are you asking me what I'd like a man to do to seduce me?"

I nodded. "Yeah. What would a guy have to do to get you to want to be with him?"

"Well, when Cash and I began to get together, he—"

"No, no," I said quickly, cutting her off before she gave me any details of how my brother had gotten her to fall for him. "I don't think I'd ever be able to look at you the same way again if I knew what moves Cash put on you. Let's just stay away from that, okay?"

Olivia giggled at my discomfort. "Okay. So you want to know what someone like me would like in general from a man to make me fall for him. Well, he'd have to be a good man first and foremost."

A good man was not who I was.

"A good man, huh? I think I'm already out of the running."

She reached across her desk to give me a sympathetic squeeze on my wrist. "That's not true, Stefan. You're not a bad man. You just do things good men don't usually do. There's a difference."

"Oh yeah? So if I didn't do those things I might have a chance?"

"Um…maybe. I can tell you that a good man would treat a woman with respect. I'm not saying you don't do that with the women you date, but maybe you could be less about sex and more about what interests her."

All I knew about what interested Shay was that none of it interested me. She was a science geek. I didn't give a damn about science.

"I don't think we like anything the same."

"Stefan, is she a bartender?"

"Yeah. Don't tell Cash. He'll have a stroke or something and ruin your whole wedding."

Olivia rolled her eyes and smiled. "I won't. He'll be up all night pacing about future lawsuits, and I don't want to see him upset like that. But you have that in common with her. You both work here. Maybe you can start there."

"Maybe. It's not much to go on. Any other advice?"

"Stefan, how well do you know this woman?"

"Pretty well. Well, not really." I hesitated a moment and then confessed, "We've already slept together."

For the second time in our talk, Olivia's eyes flew open. "Oh. Okay. Uhh…do you think you might have gotten to know her before you slept with her? Not to sound all old fashioned or anything, but it would have made getting her to fall for you a little easier."

"I guess, but that's all water under the bridge now.

So you think I should just talk to her about the club?"

My question made a grimace come over her face for a moment, but then her expression softened. "I don't think that's the way to go, Stefan. Think of it this way. If you really want her to like you, she has to see the person I see. What she sees now is the player. You have to make her see the fun guy who made me smile when your brothers intimidated me, the guy who jokes around and drives Cash and Kane crazy. Then she'll see the real you."

"Okay. This is good. I can use that. A few jokes, some sweet talk, and I should be in like Flynn. Thanks, Olivia!"

I rose to leave, but she stopped me. "Wait a second! That's not exactly what I meant. You need to be genuine."

"Yeah, I'll be genuine. You know me," I said with a smile as I headed out into the club.

So I needed to be funny and genuine. No problem. I had this under control. Kane's Mustang and his part of the club were all but mine.

X

My plan couldn't have been simpler. I'd see Shay at work that night, turn on the genuine and funny charm, and let nature take its course. I ran home for a quick shower right after six to make sure I looked as good as I could. I guessed Shay was more of a button down shirt kind of girl, so I broke out my favorite black dress shirt and checked out my look in the mirror. A little too close to Cash's style for my taste, but I wasn't trying to seduce me.

I got back to the club in time to see Shay walk in with Lola, ruining any chance I had for flirting with her. Why was Lo here? Tonight was her night off.

"Hey, Lo! Come here!" I yelled as they headed toward the bar. She came running, as she always did when I called, a look of worry on her face.

"What's up, Stefan?"

"What are you doing here? You're not scheduled."

Lola looked up at me with fear in her eyes. "Is it okay? Kerry called and said she had an emergency and asked if I'd take her shift tonight."

"Yeah. I guess. I just didn't have you scheduled. Now I'm going to have to rearrange everything."

She smiled and gave the answer I knew she would. "Oh, that's okay, Stefan. Just put me anywhere. I know it's not my night, so wherever you were going to put Kerry is good. I'm just here to help out."

"Thanks, Lo. That helps."

Flinging her arms around me, she hugged me tight and whispered against me, "You're the best, Stefan."

The familiar scent of her flowery perfume drifted up from where her head pressed against my chest, and I remembered what Kane had said about keeping her happy. The thing with Lola was going to be a problem. Nothing I couldn't overcome, but a problem nonetheless. As for tonight, I could separate her and Shay, but I'd promised Shay I wouldn't put Lola at the back bar anymore and I didn't want to put her there. But she was filling in for Kerry, so I had a little more wiggle room.

I gently pushed Lo away and forced myself to smile at her. "Time for work."

With just a nod, she walked away toward Shay to await the nightly meeting. As I stood there quickly growing frustrated by the whole situation, I saw Kane stroll down from his perch on the top floor and walk right up to Shay. What the fuck was he doing?

I watched as he stood way too close and laughed just a little too much at whatever the hell she was saying. When he touched her shoulder, a clear sign he was up to no good, I walked over to break up their little whatever it was. Deep in conversation, they didn't even notice me standing there for nearly a minute.

"Hey, Kane. I need to talk to you," I finally said, interrupting them.

He turned to look at me, still wearing a silly grin that seemed to have been charming Shay just a moment earlier. "Look who it is! Stefan, what's up, baby brother?"

"I love that you call him baby brother," Shay cooed in a voice that I never heard when she spoke to me. "That's too cute."

Kane made some joke about me as a baby, ridiculous since he didn't meet me until I was nearly twenty, before he flashed Shay another smile and finally tore himself away to follow me. We got to my office, and I barely closed the door before I barked, "What the fuck was that all about?"

"What?"

"Don't give me what. What are you doing with Shay?"

"Nothing, Stefan. I just saw her standing there and stopped to talk."

"Why didn't you talk to Lola then?"

He chuckled. "I did. It's just that Shay seemed more interested in talking back to me."

My blood pressure steadily rose until my temples throbbed. "I know what you're doing. You think I'm going to win our bet, so you're throwing up roadblocks to make sure I don't. This is bullshit, Kane. Step back out of my way."

"Or what? Planning on taking a shot at me, Stef?" he asked, intentionally egging me on.

I stepped closer to him. "You may be bigger than me, but you've been asking for a beatdown for a while, big brother."

He looked down at me with amusement in his eyes that only pissed me off more. "So you're going to fight me over her now? What happened to this just being about winning?"

"It is about winning, Kane, and you're fucking with me because you don't want to give up what you bet. This is bullshit!"

"Don't get excited, Stefan. I don't plan on doing anything with Shay. Now if she likes me, there's nothing I can do about that."

Before I could answer, he walked out leaving me standing there feeling like a jackass. Fucking Kane! If he wanted to play hardball, I could do the same. And I had an ace up my sleeve he didn't—I'd already slept with her. That was important. He could smile and flirt all he wanted. I'd gotten there first and that counted for something.

I headed back out to the floor for the bartenders' meeting with what to do about Lola and Kane roiling around in my mind. There was only one other place in the club that she could make anywhere close to the money she made at the front bar. The fourth floor station stayed pretty low key, but the tips the bartender got up there sometimes bested what the front bartenders earned. I never sent her there because I'd always considered her too good for that, but if it made getting closer to Shay possible, it had to be done.

What I'd do with Kane was a different story. As I caught a glimpse of him walking back up toward his floor, I wished my father hadn't liked women as much as he did. At least with Cash I knew I could trust him.

"Okay, listen up!" I called out to my bartenders for

the night. "I know last night was incredible, but we're done with that Seventies shit and back to modern day. Shay is at the front bar tonight with Kat, and Gabe and Mika are at the back bar. Everyone else is where they usually are, either waiting tables down here or on the upper floors. Lola, I want you to take the fourth floor bar."

Out of the corner of my eye, I saw Shay give me a look of disapproval. Everyone broke up and went to their assigned places for the night, including her, and I headed to the front bar to make sure she knew I didn't break my word.

Shay crouched down behind the bar, so I leaned over and quietly said, "I saw that look you gave me. It's not even Lo's scheduled night."

She looked up and gave me a little smile. "It's not a problem for me. As long as Lola is happy, Stefan, I'm happy."

"Well, you seemed pretty hot about it when I was at your house that day."

"I didn't think it was right to choose Mika over her. You didn't do that tonight. She says the fourth floor is a pretty plum assignment."

Shay stood up and began to rummage around with the glasses beneath the bar. She smelled like she had the night before, minus the alcohol, and I inhaled deeply as my mind replayed how she'd tasted when I'd kissed her. "I had a good time last night."

Her green eyes flashed a scolding look as her face remained placid. "Shhh. I don't need everyone in the club knowing we were together, Stefan."

"I'm the boss, Shay. I can be with whoever I want."

"Whomever, and that's fine but I can't. I don't need everyone talking about me and making my life miserable."

She may have been saying that, but I saw in her eyes she wanted me as much as I wanted her. Quietly, I said, "First slow part of the night, come see me in my office. Kat can handle the bar for a little while."

"Your office?" she asked with her eyebrows raised, like she was surprised.

I winked and leaned back away from her. "Yeah. First slow time you get."

As if the gods were smiling down on me, the crowds at Club X were thin so by one I shot Shay a knowing look to let her know she could follow me. Kat could handle the few members still left milling around the front bar, so I headed to my office.

By ten after one, I was still sitting alone wondering if there'd be some massive influx of members suddenly, but when I opened my office door, there were still just those few men standing at the bar with Kat but Shay was nowhere to be found. I scanned the room for her and then I saw her coming down the stairs.

Why the fuck did she go up there?

TWELVE

✿ SHAY

I saw Stefan glaring at me as I stepped off the last stair onto the club floor and knew he'd grown inpatient. Not that I wanted to hang out in his office and play doctor with him. The night before had been off the charts phenomenal. All those months with Elliot and I'd thought he was great in bed, but one night with Stefan March and every inch of my body craved him already.

My head needed to be my ruler, not the area between my legs. That would only get me into places I couldn't afford to be in. Stefan was like a rich, decadent dessert — incredibly desirable yet very bad for you. Once, maybe twice, you could indulge, but any more than that and nothing good could come from it.

But I couldn't avoid him. He was my boss, first and foremost, and if I was honest, I'd grown to like him, despite myself. From the look on his face, though, he likely believed I was playing games with him by going up to see Lola instead of running to his office the first chance I got.

He turned away and closed the door even as I walked toward him. Not good.

I grabbed for the doorknob but stopped myself from walking in uninvited, knocking instead since it felt like that eagerness he'd shown me earlier had changed to something else. He barked for me to come in, and I opened the door to see Stefan sitting behind his desk wearing a tight-lipped smile.

"Hey, what's up?" I asked tentatively as I leaned back against the door to close it, sensing an iciness in his dark eyes.

"Not much. What did you go upstairs for?"

Definitely chilly, but why did my going upstairs to see Lola bother him?

"I wanted to see how Lola was doing. The fourth floor isn't too bad. She's making a killing up there tonight since we've got next to no one down here."

"Yeah, not too bad," he repeated quietly, his mood improving as he said the words.

"Lola's got a fan up there too. Some guy who's got deep pockets, if her tips are any indication," I added, hoping as I talked that he'd go back to his old, playful self.

"Yeah? Good. That would be good for her," he said with a smile.

Slowly, I moved toward his desk, glad to see his mood change for the better. "So what did you want to see me about, bossman?"

That old sparkle reappeared in his eyes, and a very Stefan grin lit up his face. "Bossman? Are we back to where we were that first day we met?"

I stopped a few feet away from him and shrugged. "I don't know. You tell me."

He opened his legs slightly and crooked his finger to beckon me. "Come here."

Stepping in between his thighs, I looked down at him and felt my body come alive, betraying all my intentions to keep aloof. The man had that effect on me.

Stefan leaned forward and slid his hands down the backs of my legs, making them go weak from his touch. Against my ever-lessening will, they buckled slightly and I pitched forward toward him, crashing into his muscular chest.

"Oh, sorry," I said as I half-heartedly tried to push myself off him. The truth was I liked how he felt against me and didn't want to have to pretend to be disinterested, but I knew who he was and who I was. Stefan was a player, and I was a woman who was chasing a dream that didn't include any man right now.

His arms snaked around my waist and held me to him. "No need to be sorry. I like a woman who goes after what she wants."

I rolled my eyes at his ego. "I wasn't trying to jump your bones, Stefan. I fell into you."

Winking, he smiled. "Sure. I'd think after last night we'd be past this kind of thing."

"What are you talking about? What kind of thing?"

He licked his lips so seductively I almost forgot what I'd just asked him. But then he opened his mouth and that cocky Stefan I'd met that first day I'd come to Club X came out. "This shy girl thing you're doing. No need for that, Shay. Not after what we did last night."

Something inside my brain exploded and I pushed against him with all my might to get back on my feet. His expression registered his surprise, and I said, "So you think that because I had one night with the spectacular Stefan March that I'm ready to be the flavor of the week?"

Even though I'd shocked him by not falling at his feet and worshipping him, he reached out to pull me back to him. "Still got that fire, huh? Good. I like that."

I couldn't help but laugh. He thought he had me all

figured out. One night with him and I'd be putty in his hands. Typical man. I'd all but reconsidered my plan to play this player, but now as I watched him stare up at me with a look full of expectation, I decided it was game on.

Leaning down, I brushed my lips against his and whispered, "Oh, you like my fire, baby?" My hand slid down the front of his jeans that covered his quickly hardening cock. "How hot would it be if I dropped to my knees and sucked your cock right here, Stefan? Would you like that?"

He moaned something about wanting that more than I could imagine and a surge of power raced through me. There he sat, his head back and his fingers fumbling with his fly, thinking that I'd be like every other female who'd passed through this office. It was time for this man whore to learn a lesson.

I lowered myself to the floor and kneeled in front of him. Slowly, I ran my palms up his thighs until my thumbs could stroke the base of his cock through his jeans. I applied pressure to where I knew would excite him most and moaned, "Close your eyes and imagine my lips wrapped around your thick cock, taking all that I can handle. You want that, don't you?"

"Fuck, yes…enough talk, Shay," he said in a low voice full of need.

I ran my hand up the front of his pants and stood. Looking down at him, I couldn't help like how this made me feel. For a moment, I wondered how many woman had actually said no to him, and I doubted the number would take more than one hand.

But he'd met his match this time.

"Time for me to get back to work. See you when you get out there, bossman," I chirped playfully as I spun on my heels and headed toward the door.

From behind me, I heard Stefan say, "What? Where are you going?"

I stopped as I reached the door and turned around to see him, his face the picture of confusion and his deep brown eyes wide in frustration. A twinge of regret pinched at me when I looked into those eyes, but I couldn't forget who he was simply in a moment of weakness.

"I need to get back to work. Kat can't be expected to man the front bar all by herself."

"Don't worry about Kat. You have time. Come here."

"Not tonight, Stefan. Another night, maybe."

And with that, I turned around and walked out of his office, leaving him hard as a rock. As I walked back to the front bar, the thought crossed my mind that he'd just find someone else to relieve the frustration I'd caused in him. That the idea of him with someone else made my stomach knot up irritated me. Why should I care who he slept with?

X

A knock at my front door jarred me out of an incredibly sexy dream about Stefan, and I shuffled my still sleepy self to answer it. I opened the door and saw Carrie looking at me the way she always did when she disapproved of my look.

"Going with the homeless look these days? Sweatpants, Shay? Who the hell wears sweatpants to bed?"

"People who want to be comfortable. What are you doing here at the crack of dawn waking me up?" I asked as she pushed past me and sat down on the couch.

"The crack of dawn isn't eleven o'clock in the

morning, Shay. Even people who work in bars are up before eleven. And we had a breakfast date this morning, remember?"

"Oh yeah," I lied. "Give me a few minutes. I'll get ready."

I slouched away to my room to try to bring myself back to life, but Carrie followed me and threw herself onto my bed. Folding her arms behind her head, she studied me as I peeled off my sweatpants and shirt. "So how's the Club X gig going?"

"Good. Making lots of money, which is good."

"Well, at least it's all good. Now tell me all the details, Miss I-Seem-To-Have-Forgotten-Who-My-Best-Friend-Is. I know you have something to tell me. It's written all over your face."

I snuck a look at my expression in the mirror and instantly saw what she saw. I was wearing the self-satisfied look of the victorious. Turning toward her, I grabbed a towel and wrapped it around me as I moved toward the bathroom. "Let's just say you're looking at the first woman to ever serve up the just desserts to Stefan March."

"Shay! You get back here right now! I want details!" she yelled after me as I stepped into the shower.

She could wait. It would make the telling of the story all the better. I turned on the water and closed my eyes, not even trying to stop the smile that spread across my face. As I lathered up the shampoo in my hair, I heard on the other side of the shower curtain, "Spill your guts, girl. What happened with your boss?"

With suds rolling down the sides of my head, I peeked out and saw her standing there in my steamy bathroom. "Privacy mean anything to you?"

"Not when it comes to hot talk. Now spill it," she ordered.

"Let me rinse, for God's sake!" I said as I dipped my head under the water.

"Fine, but I'm not leaving this bathroom, so you might as well just get on with it."

I rinsed the shampoo and conditioner out of my hair and gave myself a quick soapdown before I turned off the water and prepared to tell Carrie all the sexy details of my time with Stefan. Pulling back the shower curtain, I stuck my hand out for a towel. "I don't kiss and tell without drying off first."

She threw a bath towel at my head and sat down on the lid of the toilet. "Let's go. I'm dying here. Did you sleep with him or what?"

"You know, when you diminish all my hard work down to just sex, you really hurt me, Carrie."

Raising her eyebrows in faux disbelief, she grinned. "Just sex? I'm sorry. I didn't realize this was an achievement like climbing Everest."

I finished drying myself off and headed back into the bedroom. "You have no appreciation for my hard work. None at all."

Carrie followed me and sat back down on the bed. "You know, Shay, as much as I love acting like some puppy dog and following you around, could you please begin this story before you start blow drying your hair or giving yourself a full facial?"

I stopped and took a deep breath, trying to stifle a laugh at Carrie's impatience. Finally, when I knew I'd pushed her far enough, I slipped into a pair of shorts and a tank top, sat down with her on the bed, and began to towel dry my hair. "Okay, I think I'm ready now."

"Finally!"

"So, let me start at the beginning. Do you remember that first day when I told you that Stefan March was a player and nothing else?"

Carrie rolled her eyes. "I think we can skip the details from way back when and get to the meat of this story. Did you sleep with him or not?"

"Yes."

"And?" I didn't answer immediately as I considered how I'd want to report Stefan's sexual prowess, and Carrie continued, "Players are always good, so I don't know why I even asked for more details. Let's cut to the chase. What happened after you slept together?"

"He wants to sleep with me again."

"Of course. But other than that, what's going on between you and the master player?"

"He's getting played."

Carrie's jaw dropped. When she finally could speak again, she asked, "You really went through with that?"

Her surprise bothered me. "You didn't think I would?"

"Well, to be honest, no. You may be a player in your own right, but you're no match for a man whose whole existence is based on playing women."

"I can't believe your lack of faith in my abilities. Some friend you are."

Her dark eyes stared into mine, telling me she was serious. "Shay, this has disaster written all over it. I'm warning you now, girlfriend. Stop this or you're going to get hurt. Stefan March isn't Elliot, and this isn't going to end up with you barely missing him like you did with that boy-toy."

The mention of Elliot made me feel like a real shit. I hadn't even missed him that much, and I hadn't really mourned the loss of the relationship before sleeping with Stefan.

"Still being a harpy about poor Elliot, huh?" I asked, intentionally deflecting, but Carrie saw right through my attempt.

"Don't try to change the subject. I'm worried about you. One of the women who comes into the boutique knew an awful lot about Stefan March, and she told me he's a player like no other she's ever seen."

I couldn't help but laugh. Something about a woman telling Carrie all about Stefan as she shopped for high-end accessories was funny. "That you asked about him is touching, honey, but your concern is unnecessary. It's all good fun for both of us — well, more for me since he's not getting what he wants right now."

"From you or anyone?" Carrie asked.

I felt my expression stiffen as the thought of Stefan with someone else sent a twinge of jealousy through my chest. "Me."

"I saw that, Shay. You flinched when I mentioned him with someone else. This is exactly what I'm talking about. You're going to get hurt with this one."

Waving away her concerns, I tossed the damp towel onto the bed and moved over toward my dresser to finish getting ready. "Nonsense. All this is between him and me is sex. Period. Trust me. No one can keep her heart closed off like I can. Just ask poor Elliot."

In the mirror, I saw Carrie furrow her brow. "Indeed, but poor Elliot wasn't a major league player. He was simply a horny kid you took a shining to. This one knows his way around women."

I finished coating my eyelashes with mascara and swiped cranberry gloss over my lips, smacking them together to spread it around. "I know you're trying to help, but there's no need. It's all good."

She said nothing for a long while as I put on the rest of my makeup. When she finally spoke, her words were far more serious than I was prepared to hear.

"I'm curious, Shay. Why the need to play this guy? I mean, so he came off like a 1950s Cro-Magnon the first day you met. So what? Why are you hell bent on this? You're not a vicious person, and if you do play him and he falls for you, you're going to hurt yet another guy."

Ouch.

I turned around to face her judgment, far too defensive about what I was doing with Stefan. "Another guy? You make me sound like a black widow. And why do you care what some player ends up feeling anyway? Stefan March sees women as playthings, at best, and at worst, sperm receptacles. I would think you and all of womankind would be cheering me on."

"I'm all for showing men we deserve better, Shay. Sign me up for that crusade. I'll wear the uniform. But leading someone on, even a player, seems to make us even worse than men."

Leave it to Carrie to drive the point home. I hated when she hit the nail on the head like that. I wasn't worse than Stefan March. He went through women like water. I'd never been that way with men. That I'd never found the right guy and settled down wasn't because I was some vicious creature out to break the hearts of all men who came into contact with me. It had never happened because I had goals and becoming someone's girlfriend and someday his wife would derail those goals. Wanting to succeed in life shouldn't make me the bad guy, but at that moment, I was feeling that way as Carrie looked at me as if I was no better than some callous player.

"So what are you saying?"

"I'm saying don't do this. Someone's going to get hurt. You had your fun, but if you don't want to be with him again, tell him and be done with it. You already can say you got the best of him. The player wanted a second round with you. I doubt many females who've been with him can say that."

I saw in her eyes there would be no changing her mind on this, so I did my best nonchalant shrug and smiled. "Okay, I hear you. I guess I thought I was striking a blow for all women, but I see I'm acting no better than all those players we've hated all these years. I won't go through with it."

Carrie studied me for a long moment to judge my sincerity and then nodded her approval. "It's the right thing to do. Somebody was going to get hurt, and that's never good."

"You're right. I know. Let's get a bite to eat and forget all about this. My treat."

"Your treat? You must be making a killing at that club, Shay. I thought you were saving up for your trip."

"I am, but money's been good at this job. I can afford the nicer things in life now, like taking my best friend out for brunch," I said with a chuckle.

"The nicer things, huh? Well, this girl's never been one to look a gift horse in the mouth, so let's get this show on the road."

"Sounds good!"

As I followed her out my front door, I pushed down the tiny pang of guilt inside me from lying to my best friend. No matter how right she may be, I'd gone too far into this thing with Stefan to turn back now.

THIRTEEN

🍾 STEFAN

Standing hunched over the back bar, I hoped to avoid Kane and his entirely unamusing way of making my day even shittier than it already was. My older half-brother had a knack for ruining even my best moods, and in my present state, all it would take was one of those goddamned smirks he liked to give and I'd want to smack the hell out of him. That I wouldn't simply because I knew it would result in even more pain than I already felt from the worst hangover ever experienced by mankind didn't change the fact that I'd want to.

I'd hoped a night of heavy drinking and fucking would take the edge off Shay's rejection, but even though the sex with Kat and Jana had been more than good, as it always was when the three of us got together, and the tequila had numbed me enough to forget how it felt being left sitting there with my fucking rock hard dick hanging out, when I woke up this morning all I knew was I wanted Shay and for some reason, she didn't want me.

Or she was playing some game.

That idea made me feel a little better since games I could win. Whether it was high school football where I excelled as the star quarterback or poker where I could beat the best players Tampa could throw at me, I could play games. Nobody played games like I could, so if she wanted to play, I was up to it.

"Examining the top of the bar for any particular reason, Stefan?"

And there went my fucking day. Kane, who I swore had been put on this earth for the single reason of bringing me misery, stood behind me ready with his snarky bullshit even though he likely knew I was hung way over.

"Go away. It's too early for your crap," I said as I attempted to lift my head without feeling like it was going to explode all over the back bar.

"Just wondering how you're handling all those balls you have in the air," he said in that tone that told me he thought I wasn't handling anything at all.

I groaned and slowly turned around to see him smiling down at me. "Don't worry about my balls, Kane. Concentrate on your own balls, which I suspect are a nasty shade of blue by now."

Kane threw his head back and laughed way too loudly for me in my state. "You never fail to go for the sex joke. Trust me. My balls are fine. Thanks for caring. It's your balls and the people you share them with that's the concern of all of us here, Stef. Are you still managing Lola while you try to get back into Shay's pants? Any luck with that, by the way?"

He knew I'd struck out with Shay the night before, even though I doubted she'd said anything to him about it. Probably watched my office door from the second floor like some kind of fucking stalker.

"I told you I'd handle Lola. As for Shay, it's in the bag, big brother. Just sit back and watch how a master works."

He pursed his lips and smacked them loudly. "In the bag, huh? I didn't get that last night."

I walked around him toward the front bar, wishing he'd just leave me alone with my booming headache. He followed and after I downed my fifth glass of water since I woke up, I felt slightly better.

Good enough to spar with him, at least.

"You said yourself that she would take something more. Isn't that how you put it? Well, that means she's going to take a little more time than my usuals. Don't worry, Kane. I'll win our bet and then you'll finally see how to handle a woman so if you ever get another one to spend any time with you, you'll know what to do."

"Stefan, I'm more concerned that you know how to juggle all these women. If it was just Shay, I'd be far less interested in your nightly activities. It's not, though. Lola needs to be taken care of."

"I told you I'd handle it, so I'll handle it! Get off my back about it, for fuck's sake!"

Kane narrowed his eyes to slits and stared at me. "Don't mess this up, Stefan. We can't carry your ass forever. It's time you carried your weight around here. I will say this, though. At least we haven't been sued in the last couple months."

Before I could tell him to fuck off, he headed off in the direction of Cash's office, likely to discuss at length how little they thought of my abilities in running this place and how big a pain in the ass I was to both of them.

Whatever. They could both fuck off.

I knew how to handle my business. When the time came, I'd manage Lola like I managed everything else in this fucking place. Until then, my focus would continue to be on Shay and whatever game she was playing.

What was she up to? Our time together had been hot, so it couldn't be she didn't want a repeat. She may be that science nerd everywhere else, but around me she couldn't hide the sexy, even if she wanted to. There was no way she didn't have a good time at her apartment. So why did she give me the rebuff last night in my office?

Pouring myself another glass of water, I trudged back to the scene of her rejection and sat down behind my desk to try to get some work done. Cash's repeated demands for my monthlies played in my head, but as much as I wanted to get them done just to get him off my back, I couldn't concentrate. In part, it was the hangover, but even more it was Shay.

Someone knocked on my office door, and I silently promised God I'd give up anything he demanded if only he could make it not be Kane. Quietly, I called out, "Come!" and waited to see if my prayer had been answered.

The door opened slowly and through the crack Olivia's red hair peeked through. *Thank you, God.* Olivia I could handle. In fact, she might be just the person I needed at that moment. I hadn't made any headway on my Shay problem, so maybe she could point me in the right direction.

"Stefan, do you have a minute? Cash wanted me to bring you up to speed on next week's party. Angie has made at least a half dozen changes since I sent you the details, so I thought I'd come over and go over them with you."

"Sure. Just speak quietly because you're competing with the effects of last night's tequila binge, okay?"

Olivia gave me that knowing look she often had when I said things like that to her. While I didn't think she'd ever been much of a partier—she was far too much like Cash to ever be a wild girl—I did get the sense that she knew all about that life. Maybe she'd had a boyfriend like me at one point?

"Another wild night, Stefan? Your brother told me he thought you were settling down a little. I guess that was just wishful thinking?" she asked as she sat down in front of my desk.

"Settling down? Why would he think that?"

She shrugged and smiled. "I think maybe Kane said something to him about it. And what you said to me the other day led me to believe..."

"Ugh. Kane isn't someone you or Cash should believe about anything concerning me. As far as settling down goes, I'm happy the way things are, so no, I'm not, girl or no girl."

"Okay. I'm sure they didn't mean any harm. It's just that you're so different from them I think sometimes they don't understand you."

"They want me to be just like them. Well, I'm not and I'm never going to be."

She rifled through the papers on her lap. "I think that's part of it. I knew from the first time I met you that you were different from them." Looking up, she said, "You've got what my mother calls Youngest Child Syndrome."

Youngest Child Syndrome sounded like something that came from a nuclear disaster. That couldn't be good. "What's that?"

"The youngest child is always a little wilder, a little more carefree than his or her older siblings. By the time parents get to the last child, they're more relaxed and easygoing about things."

"Are you trying to say my parents had lower expectations for me than they did for Cash? The heir and the spare?" I asked, the defensiveness creeping into my voice even as I tried to hide it.

Olivia quickly shook her head. "No, no. Nothing like that. It's just that younger siblings are more carefree. Your brother is by his nature serious, Stefan. You know that. Do you know that the first time I met your mother that day we were all out at her house for Labor Day I instantly understood why you are like you are? You're just like her. I imagine Cash is just like your father."

I thought back to the last few years of my father's life and had to agree. "He is. They named him right. Cassian March IV. He's just like my father. A hardass until his last breath."

"See? You can't blame him for being so serious. He comes by it naturally."

"And Kane? What's the explanation for him? He's not the youngest or the oldest."

A sly grin brightened up her face. "Kane's the outsider here, so it's not surprising he's like he is. He didn't grow up a March."

"More like a pain in my ass. Outsider? He owns just as much of this club as Cash and I do."

"I know, but he's had to deal with being your brother without being a member of your family all his life. That was likely very hard for him."

I couldn't bring myself to feel sorry for Kane at that moment. Not after he'd intentionally set out to piss me off as soon as he saw me today.

"I wouldn't worry about Kane. He and Cash are more alike than Cash is with his own brother, so I'm more the outsider than he ever could be."

Olivia's brown eyes filled with a look of sympathy. "Maybe they're jealous of you, Stefan. Serious people like the three of us see people like you as having a much easier time of it. You never seem to worry about anything. We'd like to be like that, but we can't be. It's not in our natures."

I liked the idea of Cash and Kane jealous of me. They rode me so much about everything from how I ran the bar to who I slept with that I'd convinced myself they practically hated me.

"All you have to do is have a good time in life. No regrets. No worries. If what I want doesn't come to me, there's something just as good coming right after it. That's how I live."

A chuckle escaped from her lips, and she shook her head. "If only it was that easy, Stefan. That kind of thing only works for people like you, though."

As we talked over the details for the party, that last thing she said repeated in my head over and over. *That kind of thing only works for people like you, though.* Maybe she was right about that. Maybe that's why my brothers seemed to resent me so often. It didn't make dealing with their shit any easier, but the thought of them seeing me as some golden boy did make me feel better.

Olivia left and slowly my hangover eased up, so by dinnertime I looked forward to the night in front of me. Shay would be working again, and I'd have another chance to work my magic with her.

I heard another knock on my door and prepared myself for Cash or Kane to walk through after my talk with Olivia, but instead Lola appeared in front of me. Lately, she caused me almost as much grief as my half-brother. I knew I had to keep her happy, and I didn't really have a problem with her as one of my workers. She knew how to handle the bar, and the members loved her. The problem occurred when what she wanted from me came into play. Ever since Kane told me I had to sleep with her to make sure we kept on that scumbag Shank's good side, all the things I liked about her seemed to just disappear.

Dressed in her usual—the tiniest skirt that barely covered her ass and a Club X t-shirt a size too small so her fake tits nearly busted through the thin fabric— she looked like she was trying too hard. Why I'd never noticed before I had no idea, but now, I couldn't imagine wanting her ever again. Twirling the ends of her blond hair around her forefinger, she batted her eyes at me and smiled. "Hey, Stefan. I just wanted to stop in and see how you were doing."

I knew what she was wondering about. Why hadn't I called her into my office for our usual fuck sessions? "Hey, Lo. I'm good. Same old, same old. You know how it is."

She bit her lower lip either to signal her nervousness or to look sexy and said quietly, "Are you busy? Do you want me to come back later tonight?"

"No. I'm fine. Do you need anything for the bar or have a problem with the schedule?"

Her expression told me she was confused. I'd never acted so businesslike with her. From the first night, I'd always been all about getting in her pants.

Lola took a few steps toward my desk and stopped. Looking down toward her fingers fidgeting near where her black skirt hit the tops of her thighs, she frowned and asked in a voice barely above a whisper, "Is something wrong, Stefan? Did I do something...?" She let her sentence fade away before she mentioned us together.

"No. You're golden out there. I don't have a better bartender than you, Lo."

She smiled and looked up at me. "Even Shay? She's good, don't you think?"

"Yeah, she's good too, but even she knows you're the best out there."

As I finished saying the last word, Lola's smile fell away, and I watched her shoulders sag slightly. "Oh.

Thanks. I try."

Instantly, I felt like I should change the topic. "You're here early. Want to get a jump on the night?"

"Yeah. I wanted to talk to you about something, but I think you answered my question even before I asked it."

I knew where this was going, but I didn't help her. It was shitty of me, but I let her stand there wearing her heart on her sleeve and did nothing to make her feel better. Kane and Cash may have thought I had to sleep with her to protect us, but at that moment, I didn't want to follow their rules. I'd sleep with who I fucking wanted, not who they deemed necessary.

She turned to leave but stopped just as she reached the door. "Stefan, why don't you want to do anything with me anymore?"

Surprised at her directness, I knew by the hurt in her voice that I'd underestimated Lola's feelings for me. I searched for a way to tell her I didn't want to sleep with her anymore, but I couldn't be that cruel. A lie was the only way out, and I had to play this right.

Standing, I moved from behind my desk and walked over to her. She looked up at me with those big eyes full of fear at what I might say. Kane's words echoed in my mind, so I constructed a lie vague enough to sound truthful but still nice enough not to hurt her. Hopefully, that would be enough to keep her father happy.

"Lo, you know how it is with us. On and off and all that. You know I still like you, don't you?"

She reached out and ran her fingertips down my forearm as she stared up at me. A look of relief came over her, and she said, "I thought maybe you met someone and that's why you never call for me to come in here anymore. But then I saw Kat and Jana last night..."

"You know me, Lo. If anyone knows how I am, it's

you. I'm not the "meet someone" kind of guy."

"Oh. You don't think you'll ever settle down?"

I smiled and winked at her. "No way. I like being me too much."

"Yeah, that's what I was telling Shay the other night. No one could blame you for being like you are, Stefan. You have everything going for you. Settling down would be like denying yourself things you shouldn't have to."

Curious why she'd have to defend me to Shay, I didn't stop myself from asking, "Why? Did she say something?"

Lola moved into defending her new friend. "Oh, no. It wasn't anything bad, Stefan. She's just not used to how you are is all. I told her someone like you who's been blessed with all the good things you have going for you shouldn't be expected to settle down with just one woman."

"Shay thought I should?"

She paused for a moment and said, "She doesn't understand you like I do. She likes her men to be the kind to settle down. She'd never see what I tried to explain to her. To Shay, even a man with looks and money should want only one woman."

"Well, then thank God we don't like each other, huh? Sounds like we'd both be miserable."

"Shay's nice, but she's not like us, Stefan. We live this life because we love it. She's only working here on her way to bigger and better things. She's good at it, but she doesn't love it like we do."

Lola left my office placated by my vague lie, but I couldn't help but be bothered by what she said about Shay. Were Lola and I really that much alike and so different from her? Was that why Shay seemed to be able to brush me off so easily after a night of great sex?

The idea that I'd finally meet a woman I couldn't have had always been impossible to me. Now it seemed entirely likely that Shay Callahan was that woman.

FOURTEEN

❋ SHAY

Even though I'd given Carrie my solemn promise that I'd put any thoughts of going further with my plan to play Stefan March completely out of my mind, I couldn't stop myself. Part of me had some strange need to prove to him that he'd finally met a woman in this world who could stop him in his tracks and make him want to give up his player ways. Another part, though, craved being with him again. I had to admit that part confused me. I didn't know how, but Stefan had wormed his way into my thoughts to the point that I liked being around him, and sleeping with him had only intensified those feelings.

That both parts were entirely incompatible wasn't lost on me either. Sometimes when he was nearby, I had to remind myself that all of this was just a game because he'd do something cute or look at me with those deep brown eyes and all I could think of was when we'd be alone again.

Hiding the fact that the man had a serious effect on me became a full time job. I didn't want him to know how I felt, but keeping it from Lola and the rest of the

Club X staff was just as important. I didn't need to create some huge issue at my job and leave hurt feelings all over the place.

My skill at concealing my desire for Stefan wasn't very impressive, if Lola's sideways glances and repeated questions were any indication. At first, I just brushed her off with an eye roll or noncommittal shrug when she noticed me staring across the room at him. When she began asking what I thought of Stefan, I'd initially found it pretty easy to rage on about his male chauvinist pig tendencies. I wasn't lying. Between his borderline sexual harassment of every single female who worked under him and the fact that I knew he'd slept with more than a few of my coworkers, sneering at the thought that he was anything more than just a player was almost second nature to me.

But then he showed up at my apartment to ask me to return to the job after that Mika mess, full of apologies and willing to give Lola her rightful place among the staff, and it began to be harder to see him in such an entirely negative light. He'd turned into someone I could like and respect, at least a little, and once those feelings weaved their way into my brain, lying to Lola grew harder and harder.

Not that she wasn't lying to me too. I had no doubt that she and Stefan had something between them, whether it was in the past or still going on. That was probably why she was so curious about my feelings about him.

I walked into the club with all of this on my mind and wondering what kind of reception I'd get from Stefan after leaving him high and dry the night before. Most men would be complete and utter bastards after being teased and dropped like that, so I prepared myself for an even angrier version of the Stefan I'd met that first day. How I'd explain his sudden change toward me to Lola when she was standing right beside me I had no idea.

I found her behind the front bar getting ready for the club to open and steeled my expression to hide what I expected to come from our boss. She greeted me with her usual sweet smile, and I noticed her outfit looked even tinier than usual.

"Hey, Shay! How's it going?" she chirped.

"Pretty good. What's new with you?"

For a moment, a strange look crossed her face but then it was gone and she was back to her usual happy self. "Not much. Just getting ready for the night. I'm thinking Stefan will have the two of us up here again, like usual. It should be a good crowd tonight, so we'll make a killing."

"That's what I'm here for. Bring on the money!" I said with a chuckle.

Lola nodded. "How long do you plan on staying, Shay? I know you said you were going somewhere, but when?"

Only once before had she expressed any interest in anything about me other than my work with her, so instantly my suspicions were raised. Something in her eyes told me this newfound curiosity about my life outside of Club X had more to do with Stefan than truly wanting to know more about me.

"I'll be here until the end of the semester, so once the new year rolls around, I'll be gone."

"That's only a few months," she said in a faraway voice like she was thinking about something other than how long we had to work together.

"Yep. You only get a couple months more of me and then I'm Copenhagen bound."

Lola was quiet for a few minutes while we busied

ourselves behind the bar until she asked, "Does Stefan know?"

"That I'm only here until the end of the year?"

"Yeah."

I remembered back to my interview with Cassian and Kane. I'd definitely informed them of my leaving in January, but since Stefan hadn't showed up that day, he'd never heard from me what my plans were. I had to assume, though, that one of his brothers had told him.

"I've never said anything about it to him, but I'm sure he knows. I made sure to mention it when I interviewed for the job."

Lola smiled fakely and nodded again. "Oh. Well, I'm sure he knows, but maybe you should mention it to him, just in case. I'd hate to see the club suffer because he didn't hire someone to replace you."

I couldn't put my finger on it, but something about her tone of voice made me think she was counting down the days until I was no longer around. A stab of hurt hit me at the thought that Lola had turned from someone I'd considered a friend to just another coworker like Mika.

"I guess," I said, feeling slightly shell shocked at her behavior toward me.

We went back to getting the bar ready, and I tried to make myself feel better by remembering that if it weren't for work, someone like Lola and I would never have even spoken to one another. We had nothing but the club in common.

It didn't make her change toward me any easier to take.

Silently, I resigned myself to feeling defensive and let the walls I often kept around me rise until I could think it all didn't hurt. From behind me, I heard Lola finally say, "I think Stefan will miss having you around,

Shay."

I turned to look at her, unsure of where she was going with all of this but pretty fed up with her sneaky attempt to find out if I was competition for him. "I'm sure he will, Lola. We work well together, he likes to put the two of us here on the front bar because he never has to worry, and the few times he and I have spoken alone, he seems to have enjoyed himself."

Her eyes opened wide in surprise at my comment about us being alone. "I didn't realize you two were close like that. You know, to have spoken alone. You don't really have anything in common."

I couldn't help but smile. She was fishing to find out if Stefan and I had slept together. Maybe I should have played her game and led her to believe there was some big thing between us, but at that moment I was too hurt by her treating me like I was Mika to play along.

"We aren't. He's my boss and I'm his employee. That's it."

She looked like she wanted to pump me for more information about how close Stefan and I were, but I was done. Turning on my heels, I walked out from behind the bar and headed for the ladies' room to be alone.

Before I could get there, though, Stefan caught me. Grabbing my arm, he stopped me and flashed me a smile. "Hey, what's up?"

Suddenly, a flash of anger spiked inside me. First Mika and now Lola had given me a hard time because of this guy. And I hadn't even gotten much but a night of great sex for my trouble. "I want to be up on the fourth floor tonight. I need a break from the front bar."

A look of surprise settled into Stefan's features, and then as if what I'd said triggered something in him, his face darkened. "Why? What's up there that you want?"

Was everyone in this place crazy? What the hell did he mean what did I want up there? "Money? You said yourself that the fourth floor bar often does as well as the front bar."

"Is that it?"

I stared at him in confusion and shook my head. "What's with you? I just want to be away from the front bar, okay? You know I can handle it. Lola told me it's definitely a one-person job."

"Is there some problem with Lola? If so, I can send her upstairs again," he offered, as if he was worried about me. Maybe he wanted me to experience job satisfaction. I couldn't tell what the hell was up with him or Lola.

"No. I really want to be upstairs tonight."

"I don't know, Shay. I like having you down here at the front bar. It's good for business."

I didn't want to spend my night fielding sly questions from Lola about him. Now that I didn't see her as a friend, I wanted to be as far away as possible from her. "Stefan, I'm asking you as an employee who's always done what you asked. Please let me man the fourth floor bar tonight. It would mean a lot if you'd be cool about this."

I wasn't sure what part of what I said convinced him, but any qualms he had about me heading up to the fourth floor seemed to vanish. "Okay, Shay. You got the fourth floor. I'll find someone else for the front bar with Lola. Any suggestions?"

Shaking my head, I moved toward the ladies' room. "Nope. Whoever you choose."

I didn't stick around for the bartenders' meeting since I knew where I was stationed for the night, so after I'd hid out in a bathroom stall for a half hour telling myself I was stupid for feeling bad about Lola turning on me, I quietly headed up to the fourth floor bar to get it ready for the night. Since Stefan hadn't assigned anyone before I asked, the area had to be prepped from top to bottom, but at least that would keep my mind occupied instead of having it wander to why suddenly the only real friend I had in the bar had turned me into her competition.

Unlike the bars on the main floor, the fourth floor bar was dark and secluded. Located at the far end of the floor away from the stairs, it was technically above where the front bar was located down on the first floor but it couldn't have been more different. Nestled in a corner just past the fantasy rooms, it was dimly lit and without any reflective surfaces on the wall behind it. No mirror, no glass at all. I imagined that had something to do with the purpose of this floor.

Who wanted to stare at themselves while they grabbed a drink after getting freaky in a fantasy room?

I got to work in my new secluded area and became so involved with making sure it was ready when members arrived that I didn't notice Kane leaning against the bar as I crouched down to clean a sticky spot on the floor.

"Hey, what are you doing up here? Stefan exile you for something?" he asked in that husky voice so unique to him.

Looking up, I smiled and stood to my full height. "No, I asked to be put up here tonight. I needed a break from downstairs and heard this bar was as good as the front bar."

Kane leaned his body forward and rested his forearms on the top of the bar. "That's what I hear too. You should do well tonight. Tuesdays are pretty busy, and every room on this floor is booked all night."

"Sounds good to me. I'm all about the money for the short time I'm here."

His crystal blue eyes flashed a look of recognition. "That's right. We only have you for a few months more before you leave us. I'm sure Stefan will miss you. I know he relies on you and Lola to take care of things downstairs."

"He'll be fine without me, I'm sure. I bet bartenders come and go here, so he'll just replace me with someone else."

Kane's usually serious expression softened, and a slow grin spread across his lips. "He does go through them pretty fast, I admit, but it's rare when he gets one of your caliber."

I couldn't decide if I should interpret his words to refer to me as a bartender or me as a woman. Kane likely didn't know his brother and I had slept together — or maybe he did. The vision of Stefan bragging about his latest conquest the morning after having sex with me marched through my mind, and it didn't take much to convince me that it had happened very much like that.

"Yeah, well, I'm sure I'll be forgotten as soon as I leave, Kane."

He stared directly into my eyes for a long moment and then in low voice said, "Then he's a bigger fool than I thought he was." I stood there surprised by Kane's words, and as if my reaction made him uncomfortable, he leaned back away from me and added, "But that wouldn't surprise me. Stefan's always had a streak of stupid in him."

Now it was my turn to feel uncomfortable. Kane had never unnerved me before, but as we stood there in the dim light and not more than a foot away from one another, I couldn't help but feel a sense of power coming from him that I'd never recognized before. Maybe it was his size or maybe it was his deep voice, but something made me feel small next to him at that moment.

A nervous giggle escaped from my throat as I tried to understand what I was feeling. "Well, you know what they say. There's always one in the family."

"And we have Stefan," he said with a laugh. A few members began filtering in from the stairs and in a second Kane changed back to that friendly guy he always was with me. "I'm just up one floor if you need anything, Shay. Don't hesitate to ask."

"Thanks, Kane. I might since this is my first real experience with your part of the club."

"Don't worry. You'll be fine. There's always security on each floor, but I'll put Jason here tonight. Members don't even think about messing with him."

"That's nice of you. Thanks! I'm sure I'll be fine then."

He backed away down the hall, the whole time wearing a sly smile. "Come up and see me. We can talk more about my stupid younger brother or other more interesting topics."

I didn't know if I'd take him up on his offer, but I had a feeling hanging out with Kane would be nothing like spending time with Stefan. As different as night and day, the two men intrigued me each in their own way. Whereas Stefan was all fun and good times, Kane always seemed to be reserved and mysterious, even when he was smiling and making jokes. The serious side of me found that so appealing. His younger brother might act like the consummate player, but Kane appeared almost disinterested in women. I didn't think he had a girlfriend or liked men, but I'd never seen him spend any time even talking to women other than me. If I was a real player like Carrie claimed, I'd have gone after Kane. For as much as Stefan seemed to be the perpetual bachelor, his older brother might have been one of the most aloof men I'd ever encountered, and I had an inkling he was friendlier with me than most people. A player would set her sights on that prize.

I left my thoughts on the two available Club X brothers behind as a crowd of people began to form in front of my bar. For five hours I waited on members as they prepared to enter their fantasy rooms and after they'd left them, loving how different this area was from downstairs. It had a sexy feel the front bar lacked, and the members were even friendlier here. I couldn't believe Lola hadn't mentioned how much better this was and the money I made even rivaled the night of the private party when she and I had made a killing. She probably didn't like it as much as the front bar because Stefan was nowhere to be found.

I'd never had any real interest in the fantasy part of Club X, but now that I stood right in the middle of it all, I couldn't help but be curious. A few of the girls had talked about wanting to take advantage of this area of the club, but even making the money I did at private parties and here on the fourth floor I couldn't afford a membership to my workplace or what I imagined a fantasy room cost.

During lulls, my mind traveled back to my first conversation with Stefan that day I'd interviewed for the bartender job and his offer of a membership. Maybe I could take advantage of Kane's part of the club, but what fantasy would I want to live out?

By the end of the night, I'd set myself to figuring out what my fantasy was and I'd convinced myself I deserved the title of Most Boring Woman On Earth. Over and over, I'd wracked my brain to think of what I could ask for in a fantasy room, and each time I came up with something, it was either incredibly mundane or ridiculous. I doubted Kane and his people could help me secure a position at a good university. Obviously, whatever I thought I was, first I was an academic—a boring academic. God, I was the queen of dull!

Then my mind would swing to an idea so wild that my cheeks would flush with heat. Kane's offer for me to come see him replayed in my mind, weaving itself into my thoughts on possible fantasies. Did he ever partake of the good times in his part of the club, I wondered. What would he be like alone with me in a room devoted to sexual pleasure? I'd heard rumors from some of the other bartenders that unlike Cassian and Stefan, he had a dark side. I didn't see it, though. I could imagine him being super Alpha and possessive, maybe even domineering, but he worked too hard to be restrained for me to believe when it came down to it he was a sexual freak.

But then again, maybe that's why he was so restrained all the time.

"You look a million miles away. Everything okay up here?"

I turned from the spot on the bar that I'd been cleaning as I considered what to do in a fantasy room and there stood Stefan right in front of me. Flustered that he'd caught me daydreaming, I hurriedly threw the rag aside and pressed a smile onto my lips.

"Just lost in doing my job, I guess. What's up? Why are you up here?"

"I wanted to check on you and make sure you were okay. Members sometimes get a little wild up in this part of the club. Everything good?"

"Oh yeah. Making lots in tips from happy people either dying to get into their rooms or even happier people coming out after their time is up."

"I meant to come up earlier but things got pretty busy downstairs. Lola said she loved the money up here but prefers the front bar down there."

The mention of Lola's name made me bristle with anger, and I shrugged in the hopes that my lack of interest would make him change the subject. "I bet. You're not up here, so of course she wouldn't like this bar more. I like it just as well as the front bar, but then again, I don't need to have the approval of my boss with every damn drink I pour."

Okay, that came out a little bitchier than I'd intended. I saw by the look on Stefan's face that my rudeness had surprised him too. He settled his dark gaze on me and in a nicer tone than I think he'd ever used on me, he asked, "Something wrong? Did Lola do something?"

I shook my head and waved him off. "No, it's nothing. Thanks for asking, but I'm good. I'm just going to get things cleaned up here and head home."

He nodded and then took a deep breath in, releasing it slowly. I thought for a moment he would reprimand me for not getting along with yet another person I worked with, but instead he leaned over the bar until his face was no more than a few inches away from mine and looked up at me with those deep brown eyes that at that moment nearly made me melt.

"I thought maybe we should talk about the other night."

"I think firing me because I wouldn't have sex with you in your office is grounds for a lawsuit, Stefan," I said half-joking. I knew what night he was referring to.

"Not that night, Shay."

I looked away, unable to handle that doe-eyed puppy dog look he was using on me. Jesus, he could be sweet when he wanted to be. "I know. I was kidding. Sort of."

"Give me fifteen minutes and I'll come back up so we can talk."

I didn't want to talk about that night or anything

else with Stefan. Something about Lola turning on me made me feel vulnerable. I nodded to let him know I'd stay, but as soon as he walked away, I hurried to finish up my work and get the hell out of there.

Being alone with him to talk about when we had sex wasn't a good thing when I was so weak.

FIFTEEN

🍾 STEFAN

Only Lola still remained downstairs by the time I got back, and there was no way I wanted to spend any more time talking to her when I had Shay waiting for me on the fourth floor. Before I could slip into my office unseen, though, she followed me in, closing the door behind her.

"What's up, Lo? I'm in a little bit of a hurry, so if it's not serious, can we leave this for tomorrow?"

She stared up at me with big blue eyes full of disappointment. "I wanted to know if...maybe if you weren't busy tonight, we could get together?"

"I can't tonight. Sorry. I've got something to take care of upstairs."

I knew she remembered Shay had worked the fourth floor bar, and her look hardened as the thought that I was going up to see her settled into her mind. "What? The club's closed."

"Kane. He's got a mess up there he needs my help with."

"Oh. Would you like my help?" she asked softly but

there was a hint of suspicion in her voice. She didn't believe me.

I walked toward her to escort her out of my office. Opening the door, I shook my head. "No, it's nothing I'd want you involved in. We got it."

With my hand on her lower back, I guided her out into the club as she asked if I'd walk her out to her car like I always did. Jesus, this woman was a worse cockblock than Kane.

Just as I was about to tell her I couldn't, we ran into my half-brother standing there watching as I gave Lola the bum's rush. Quickly, I devised a plan to push her off on him. "I can't, but Kane can, right?"

Kane looked at me like I'd just committed some heinous crime, and Lola shook her head, confused. "But I thought you had to help him upstairs with some problem?"

"I do, but while I'm upstairs taking care of things, he can walk you out and then come up to help me." Turning to look at Kane, I hoped he'd be cool about things like a brother should be. "Sound good?"

For once, Kane didn't do his best dick impression and said nothing to blow my cover. "No problem, Lola. I can walk you out. Then I'll come back and help Stefan since there's no way he'll be able to handle things upstairs without my help."

"Okay, thank you," Lola said, giving Kane one of her cute smiles that made me think maybe she could fall for him and all my problems would be solved.

"Great! See you later, Lo!"

I watched Kane walk her out of the club and bolted toward the stairs to get up to Shay but remembered I hadn't grabbed a condom from my desk in all the nonsense with Lola. Fuck! Quickly, I ran into my office and found a pack where I kept them in my office drawer, but before I could get upstairs, Kane stopped me by blocking my way out the door.

"What the fuck are you thinking, Stefan?"

I was thinking that Shay was waiting for me and between Lola and Kane, I couldn't decide who the bigger killjoy was. "You're in the way. Can we talk about whatever you want to talk about tomorrow?"

"You know what I want to talk about. Blowing Lola off isn't going to work. We need to be on her and Shank's good side, and treating her like you just did isn't going to make that happen."

All the happiness I'd felt after talking to Shay had all but ebbed away by now, leaving me cranky and horny and stuck talking to Kane, the last person on Earth I wanted to hang out with tonight. If I didn't know better, I would have thought he was keeping me talking to him there on purpose to ruin any chance I had with Shay.

"Kane, I told you the other day. I'm not going to be responsible for Lo's happiness, no matter what you think. If you want her to make sure Shank continues to help us, you cozy up to her. She seems to like you, so it wouldn't be too hard, assuming you still know what to do with your dick."

My ass busting didn't go over well, and he leaned in toward me to crowd my space until his face was just inches away from mine. "You made this fucking mess. Now you're responsible for it. Maybe if you weren't always thinking with your cock you wouldn't have to do things with it you don't like."

The look in his blue eyes made me think he had plans to fight me right there. Jesus! Why the fuck did this guy always seem to be on my ass about something. "Back the fuck up, Kane." He didn't budge, so I leaned in and glared at him. A few seconds of that told me he wasn't going to give in, so I resorted to my foolproof tactic.

I lied.

"Fine. I'll make it up to Lo tomorrow, okay? Now get the hell out of my way!"

He gave me one final nasty glare and backed up to let me past, but not before he threatened me one last time. "Stefan, I'm not fucking around with you. Cash may have a soft spot for you, but I don't have those feelings. We need Shank, and for good or for bad, you're the one who has to make sure his daughter is happy. You fuck this up, and I'll fuck you up, and Cash won't be able to stop me this time."

"Fine."

I left him standing there outside my office and tore up the stairs hoping that he and Lola hadn't totally ruined any chance I had to hang out with Shay again. Hitting the fourth floor, I looked down the hallway and didn't see her near the bar. Disgusted, I caught my breath and leaned against the wall, silently cursing both Lola and Kane. Fucking A!

A noise from one of the fantasy rooms caught my attention, and I walked toward it hoping I didn't find some orgy. Seeing that would be like the universe rubbing my face in shit. I peeked my head in and there stood Shay looking around like she was in awe of the place.

"I thought you left," I said quietly as I closed the door behind me.

"I was just taking a look around. I didn't realize I was in here that long."

"You mean long enough to still be here when I returned?"

She gave me a tiny smile and looked away. "I don't know what to say, Stefan. I did have a good time."

Stepping toward her, I slid my arm around her waist and gently pulled her toward me. "And we can have a good time again. There's nothing standing in our way, unless your boyfriend is back in the picture."

She looked up at me and I saw questioning in her green eyes. "He's not."

"So what's the problem? I can feel you want me like I want you, Shay."

"That's the problem, Stefan. I do. But everyone else in this place does too, and I don't like feeling like I'm one in a cast of thousands."

"You're not." Even though I'd been with Kat and Jana the night she left me hanging, as I stood there with Shay's condemnation of my lifestyle staring up at me, I didn't want anyone else.

"Stefan, we had fun, but I can't be who I'd need to be with someone like you. I just can't."

"What do you mean? You don't have to be anybody but you."

Shaking her head, she frowned. "That's not true. I'm not like Lola or Mika or any of the other women you get together with here. That's not the kind of woman I am. Every one of them seems to be okay with being just another notch in your belt. I'm not."

"You're not like them, Shay. I know that."

"So maybe it's best if we just leave whatever there is between the two of us where it was the other night at my apartment. Maybe we're just too different to be anything but a one-time thing, Stefan."

Shay turned to leave, but I pulled her back into my arms and kissed her. "Maybe I don't want to leave it there. Maybe we're not so different, after all. As Lola reminded me earlier tonight, you're leaving in a few months. Why can't we just enjoy one another until then?"

"Because of what you just said. Lola. And Mika. And Kat. And Jana. I may not be the poster child for monogamy. Trust me, I'm not. But that's just too many people I don't really even like in my personal life."

I didn't know why, but the thought of any of them did nothing for me now that I'd been with Shay. And the idea that my ever being with them could mean she might not want me bothered me more than even I understood. This had all started out as a bet between me and Kane, but it had gone way past that for me now.

"They don't mean anything to me. I already decided not to be with Lola and Mika anymore, and that thing with Kat and Jana the other night..." I stopped talking before I said something that would only prove to Shay I wasn't the type of guy she'd want, but I saw by the look on her face that it didn't matter.

"We come from two different worlds, Stefan. You're a player, and as much as some people think I am, the reality is that as soon as I saw even just a few of the women I was lumped in with, I didn't want to be there. That's never going to change either."

I didn't want to hear that. Never before had I not been able to change a woman's mind, and there was no way in hell Shay Callahan was going to be the first. We may have been as different as night and day, but that was no reason we couldn't get together.

"We both work in this club. That's something we have in common, right?"

Her green eyes stared up at me, unconvinced. "I don't think that's enough to base having sex with a person on."

Maybe it was my ego, or maybe it was the bet with Kane. Or maybe it was the feeling of emptiness when I thought of not ever being with her again, but I had to do something to convince her to at least give us a chance. "What if we start over?"

"Stefan, we already started over, remember? I don't

think pretending not to know one another again is going to work."

She began to back away from me, but I grabbed hold of her wrist. "Wait. What if we started over as friends?"

Shay's eyebrows shot up in surprise. I had to admit even I was stunned I'd said that word. I'd never been friends with a female. To be honest, I couldn't even imagine how to do that, but if being friends with Shay was the way to have a chance to be with her, then friends it was.

"Do you really think we could be friends, Stefan? You're a man whore and I'm a female. That doesn't sound like a recipe for success."

"Sure. Why not?"

She seemed to think about my challenge and smiled. "One of the most important parts of friendship is honesty. Can you handle that?"

"Absolutely."

Looking around, she nodded. "I bet you've been in one of these rooms hundreds of times."

The first test of our friendship. She did like to go big. "You'll probably be surprised to hear I haven't been in one of these more than a handful of times."

"Really?"

"Yeah. It's not really my thing. I have my office downstairs, Shay."

There was a long pause and then she said, "I'm guessing I shouldn't ask how many times you've used your office to be with someone, huh?"

"Probably not."

Even as she continued to smile up at me, I saw the distance in her eyes. She was pulling away emotionally as the idea of me with all those other women registered in her brain. Never before in my life had I regretted what I was, but at that moment, the way she looked at me made me wish I hadn't been that man whore.

"It's late, Stefan. I think I better go."

"Don't. Come with me. I know a beach we can go to and hang out."

Shay's face twisted into a grimace. "You don't seem to understand how to be friends with a female, do you?"

"I didn't say we can go and fuck on the beach. Just hang out. That's it. Get to know each other. Isn't that what friends do?"

"What beach are you talking about?"

"Just say yes."

She took a deep breath in and sighed. "Don't make me regret this, okay?"

Taking a step toward the door, I held out my hand to take hers. "You're going to love this place. We'll be the only two people on the beach."

"How do you know?"

I tugged her toward me as we walked out into the hallway. "It's a private beach—we call it March Beach."

Shay looked surprised. "You have your own beach? Do Cassian and Kane live there too?"

"No, none of us live there now. It's where Cash and I grew up. My mother still lives in the house, but she's in Italy until next week. It'll just be you and me."

We walked down the stairs as I told Shay about how great the house was, and she asked, "You're taking me to your mother's house?"

"Yeah. Come on!"

"She won't mind? Do you often bring people to her house to enjoy the beach?"

I knew what she was asking. She wanted to know if I routinely brought women to my parents' house to fuck them on the beach. Assuming I could leave out the girls from high school I'd done exactly that with, I told her the truth.

"I've never brought anyone to my mother's house since I moved out of there when I was nineteen. And not because that would mean having to meet my mother, not that I've ever introduced anyone to her."

"And it will just be us?" she asked with a hint of curiosity in her voice.

"Well, the caretaker and the other people who work the estate are there, but they won't bother us. It will just be the two of us enjoying the beach and the water, if you want to swim."

As we walked out to my bike, she shook her head. "I don't have a bathing suit with me, Stefan."

The idea of Shay buck naked next to me in the water made my cock swell. I winked and said, "Then you can skinny dip. Nobody will see you."

Climbing onto the back of my bike, she slipped her arms around my waist and leaned in next to my ear. "You're still struggling with this whole friend thing. Women don't skinny dip with their male friends, Stefan."

I started my bike and revved the engine. Fuck, her body felt incredible pressed up against me. Turning my head, I looked back at her. "It was just a suggestion, but I'll make a mental note of that for the future. No swimming naked with friends."

She smiled and rested her chin on my shoulder so our lips were nearly touching. "You'll get it someday. New things take time."

I hoped her words meant more than just figuring out this whole friend thing.

SIXTEEN

SHAY

The house we rolled up to could only be described as breathtaking. An enormous Victorian home right on the waterfront, it made me feel like we'd traveled back in time to the days when all of Tampa looked like this. I'd seen paintings of neighborhoods full of homes just like this in my faculty mentor's office, who in his spare time liked to trace the history of the area's more distinguished families. He'd never talked about the March family, but if this house had been theirs for more than a few years, Dr. Taduch would know about them.

Stefan climbed off the bike first and held out his hand to help me off. "Welcome to the March House."

"You grew up here? Wow!" I wanted to say more, but that's all that came to my mind as I filled my eyes with the view of the gorgeous house in front of me. How wealthy were the Marches?

"Yeah, it was pretty great living here. Cash and I used to love running up and down the hallways when we were little. Then when we got older, we'd dare each other to do dumber and dumber things in the water.

We're lucky we're still here."

"It's stunning, Stefan. Just stunning."

"I'll give you the grand tour later. For right now, let's relax on the beach."

"Lead the way. After tonight, I could use some relaxing. Any chance there's a hammock?"

"Sure! We'll probably fall asleep, though. It's pretty relaxing down there just listening to the waves."

Stefan walked toward the beach, but I stopped, unsure this was a good idea. He wasn't getting the idea of how to be a friend, and I wondered if I'd been duped into coming here just so he could put the moves on me as a captive audience.

He got about twenty yards ahead of me and noticing I wasn't right behind him, turned around. "You coming?"

I could have asked him what the hell we really were doing here, but what was the point? The guy wasn't going to hurt me. He hadn't shown himself to be a rapist or ax murderer. The worst that would happen would be he'd put the moves on me and I'd have to shoot him down again. He stood there staring at me as all this ran through my head, his brown eyes and their sexy look beckoning me.

"Yeah. Let's go."

As long as I didn't fall for those eyes and all the other incredibly hot parts of him, I'd be fine.

My feet slid into the cool, damp sand, the tiny grains getting between my toes, and I leaned back on my elbows to look up at the night sky dotted with stars. A typical early November night, a tiny chill cooled the air as it brushed my skin.

I looked to where he lay on the sand next to me. "It's gorgeous here, Stefan."

"Yeah, it is." His eyes widened a little as he looked at me, and he said, "Is it okay if a male friend takes his shirt off when he's sitting on the beach with a female friend? I don't want to break any of these friend rules, which by the way, there seem to be a lot of."

The man could seduce a woman with just that cuteness of his. Even if I didn't want to smile, I couldn't help it when he said things like that. He waited for me to answer, to give him permission to take his shirt off, so I pretended to think about it for a minute and then answered, "I guess. It's nothing I haven't seen before, so I don't think it would break any friend rules."

I knew what he was doing. Between the cute and charming thing and the sight of his perfectly ripped half-naked body, he thought I'd forget all about this friend nonsense and sleep with him right here on the beach. As he stripped off his shirt to reveal his toned pecs and abs, I couldn't help remember the feel of him against my body as we made love that night in my apartment. As much as my head told me no, the rest of me wanted that again.

No! Do not let yourself get seduced by all these things, Shay! You may want to play him, but Carrie was right. He's out of your league and the only one who's going to get played is you.

With a smirk that made me want to kiss him or punch him—I couldn't decide which—he said, "Either you're staring because you like what you see or…well, I can't think of another reason why you'd be staring."

His comment shook me out of my silent adoration of his body and I rolled my eyes, hoping to convince him that I didn't want him more than anything else in the world at that moment. "You know, if you're going to get all those tattoos, you shouldn't be surprised when people look at them. Isn't that the point?"

Stefan looked down at his arms and torso and shook his head. "No. I don't get them for anyone else but me.

If they were for everyone else, I'd get cartoon characters and Chinese symbols all over my body."

"Instead of mythological beasts and half-naked women."

There was that smirk again. It made me feel like he thought he had my number and all he had to do was give me one of those sexy trademark Stefan looks and I'd be on top of him begging him to fuck me.

"For someone who's only seen me naked once, you seem to know a lot about my tats."

I felt my cheeks grow hot under his direct stare. That's what he wanted, though. He wanted to seduce me with his tattoos, his muscles, and every other delicious part of him.

Quickly, I changed the topic before he was successful. "So if we're going to be friends, Stefan, maybe we should know something about one another."

"More than how incredible we were in bed together?"

I rolled my eyes again. I knew it! This was all a ploy to get in my pants again.

"I'm guessing by that look that you think we should know more about each other. Ask away. I'm an open book."

"What's your favorite thing to eat?" The instant the words came out of my mouth, I regretted them. Stefan was just going to say something sexual and my first attempt at being friends would be ruined.

But then he surprised me.

"Meatloaf."

"Meatloaf?" The man came from a family that lived in a multi-million dollar waterfront house with its own beach and meatloaf was his favorite thing to eat?

"Yeah, meatloaf." He leaned back onto the sand and folded his arms behind his head. Looking up at the stars above, he continued, "Sometimes when my father was gone, which was most of the time, my mother would let the cook go for the night and she'd go into the kitchen and make us the most delicious meatloaf you'll ever taste. I have no idea what she does to make it so good, but I think she puts some kind of tomato sauce and pepper in it. Whatever she does, I love it."

"Wow. I figured you'd say something like caviar or escargot."

Turning to look at me, he made a face like he'd just eaten something rotten. "No thanks. Neither one of them even sound good. What about you? What's your favorite food?"

"Blueberry pie."

"I don't know the rules for this game, but I figured the favorite food had to be something you love more than anything else. How often do you have blueberry pie?"

"Not often enough. And there aren't any rules to this. Just has to be your favorite food. Still want to stick with meatloaf?"

Stefan nodded. "Yep. Still my favorite, hands down."

"Ok. What's your favorite place?"

"Right here on this beach on a warm fall night under a clear sky. And if you're going to ask me when, the answer is right now."

"Don't ruin this with cheesy seduction talk, Stefan."

He rolled over on his side to face me and propped his head up on his hand. "I wasn't. It's the truth. Remember, we're supposed to be honest."

"I don't believe that. You've had twenty — how old are you anyway?"

"Twenty-seven."

"You've had twenty-seven years of experiences, and you want me to believe this is your favorite with me right here on this beach?"

"Why not? You've seen what my life is about. I spend my nights in a bar watching everyone have a good time, and the only enjoyment I've ever found from it was chasing women. Do you know no one has ever asked me what my favorite food was? No one has ever asked me what my favorite anything was."

"I'm sure your family has," I offered, wondering if the person staring up at me was as lonely as he sounded.

"You mean Cash and Kane? I'm just the pain in the ass little brother to them. I create problems they have to clean up. And they never let me forget it."

"Well, what about your mother? Moms are always good for that kind of stuff."

His face lit up at the mention of his mother. "Yeah. She doesn't ask, but if I tell her I'm coming over she'll make me that meatloaf she knows I love. I'm her favorite."

"You're the youngest. Moms always love the baby most."

"I think it was more that Cash was my father's favorite, so she didn't want to see me left out."

And with that, his smile faded away and an uncomfortable silence settled in between us. I didn't know how to deal with this Stefan. The asshole who I thought of as a borderline misogynist I could handle. The decent guy at work I liked. The man who rocked my world in bed I had to resist falling for. This Stefan, though, made me want to take him in my arms and ask what his favorite everything was. He just seemed so alone that I had to fight reaching out to make him feel better.

But I did fight that urge, as overwhelming as it was, because no matter who he was right now, there with me as the water gently lapped against the shore just a few feet away from us, the reality was Stefan March was that player I'd intended on playing. Even if I didn't want him to be.

Even if I really wished at that moment he was the guy next to me who I could fall for.

He looked up at me and quietly asked, "Do you think people can change, Shay?"

"What kind of change are we talking about?"

"The kind that matters."

I looked at him, unsure of what he meant but knowing people don't change. "Leopards can't change their spots, Stefan. They are who they are. Like in the story about the scorpion and the frog."

Chuckling, he shook his head. "Who?"

"Haven't you ever heard of the story about the scorpion and the frog? The scorpion asks the frog for a ride across a stream, and the frog says no because he knows he'll sting him and he'll die. The scorpion promises he won't. Why would he, right? He'd die too. The frog is convinced and lets him get on his back, but halfway across the stream the scorpion stings him. The frog can't believe it and asks him, 'Why would you do that? Now we'll both die.' The scorpion simply says, 'This is my nature.' He couldn't change who he fundamentally was, so they both died."

"So you don't think people can change?" he asked, his brown eyes wide with interest in my opinion on what seemed very important to him at that moment.

I thought about it and shook my head. "No, I don't think they can. You are who you are, no matter how much another person wishes you weren't that person."

"What if the part of you that you wanted to change wasn't who you really were? What if it was just something that wasn't really you?"

"What do you mean?"

He took a deep breath and blew it out slowly,

frowning as he sighed. "You're smart, but what if you weren't and you were just pretending to be smart? You could change to be a different way because what you were changing wasn't the real you."

As tortured logic went, that wasn't bad. I couldn't argue with it, at least, even though I had no idea where he was going with this. "I guess if someone was trying to shed a façade, then that kind of change would be possible."

Stefan nodded his approval and smiled, obviously pleased by my answer. "Maybe it just takes the right set of circumstances for a person to change."

"Maybe." I didn't know what to say because anything I believed about people changing went completely against his positive ideas about the subject. I'd never seen anyone really change. Not for anyone or anything. Not even for love.

Looking out at the water, I moved to change the subject. "I like it here. It's quiet. After all the noise from the bar each night, this feels so relaxing."

He ran his finger through the sand toward me and lifted a handful of it up, dumping it out on my thigh. "You know what I've always wanted to do? Bury someone in the sand."

"You're creeping your new friend out, Stefan."

Scooping up another handful, he poured it out over my knee and smiled up at me like he was proud of his handiwork. "I'm not trying to kill you, Shay. I'm just saying I think it would be fun to bury someone in the sand like they do in the movies. Haven't you ever wanted to try that?"

I brushed the sand off my leg and onto his arm. "No. I have a deathly fear of being trapped in anything, even sand. Small enclosed spaces, elevators, even those tiny Italian cars freak me out."

Even as I sat there explaining how I dreaded the very thing he wanted to do, he scooped up another handful of sand and then another, dumping both on my shin and nearly covering it. "Sounds like you have a fear of being out of control, if you ask me."

I kicked my leg and sent sand flying everywhere. "Thanks, Dr. Phil. I'm thinking in a past life I was trapped in some enclosed space, like a mine shaft or a box, and smothered to death, so I'll thank you not to cover me in any more sand."

Brushing myself off, I stood to move away from him, but he grabbed me by the ankle. "Don't leave. I promise not to bury you in the sand, okay?"

I looked down at him as he gave me those puppy dog eyes that never failed to soften my heart and smiled. "Promise?"

He grinned up at me, like he was having fun. "I promise. Scout's honor. But I still want to do the whole bury someone in the sand thing, so what about if you covered me instead? I don't have any fear of being trapped by a few grains of sand."

"You want me to cover you with sand?"

Jumping up, he unbuttoned his pants. "Yeah, but not in these. Give me a second." And with that, he stripped them off and threw them over the back of a beach chair before he turned back to face me wearing only his boxer briefs. "Okay, I'm ready. Let's do this!"

I watched as he sat back down and lay flat on the sand really wanting me to bury him. I'd never seen him like this. He seemed genuinely happy—not like he was at the club, usually because he was up to no good there but happy, like he didn't have a care in the world and playing in the sand was the best thing he'd ever thought of.

"For the record, even burying someone in sand sort

of creeps me out," I admitted as I sat down next to him.

He picked up some sand and threw it on top of his knees. "I'm a willing participant, but if it makes you feel more comfortable, only cover up to my waist. Sound good?"

The real sense of fear that had been building inside me since we'd begun this conversation ebbed a bit at the thought that at least most of him wouldn't be trapped. Scooping up a tiny handful of sand, I tossed it onto his muscular thigh next to me. "Okay, that makes this a little easier. This still seems silly, though."

As I began in earnest to pile the sand on his legs, he leaned back and crossed his arms behind his head, totally relaxed about being immobilized at my hands. "What's wrong with something being silly? Life is too fucking serious, Shay. You have to enjoy yourself."

"I enjoy myself. You make it sound like I don't," I said as I finished covering his ankles.

"I'm just saying life is too short. Take all that school you've done. If the world ended tomorrow, what would it matter?"

His condemnation of what I'd devoted so much of my life to, even if he was just joking, bothered me. Turning to face him, I tried to force myself to keep my words light like his, but I couldn't. He'd picked the wrong topic to tease me about.

"If the world ended tomorrow, I'd be proud of the work I'd done. My research might someday help cure disease and save lives. What have you done that can measure up to that?"

Instantly, the hurt from my words showed in his eyes. I hadn't meant to be such a bitch, but there it was. Regret surged through me, but before I could apologize, not for the meaning of my words but the delivery, he laughed. "You're that same person who put me in my place the first time I met you. Fair enough. I haven't done much of anything that can measure up to the important work you've done. You're not wrong."

"I'm sorry for saying that, Stefan. That wasn't fair. I should be able to be proud of my work without looking down on yours. I'm sorry."

Touching my hand, he shook his head and smiled. "No, you're right. I run a nightclub. Not much of anything to change the world there."

"I didn't mean it like that. I guess I'm just touchy about my work. I don't mean to be a bitch either. I know I was the first day. One would think after all the time I've spent in clubs that I'd be more easygoing with that kind of stuff."

"You are who you are, Shay. And I'm who I am. That doesn't mean we can't have fun, though, so get back to covering me in sand before the sun comes up."

His easy dismissal of my defensiveness made forgiving myself easier, but as I got back to the task of burying him in the sand, I couldn't help feel that he'd forgiven me too easily. Whatever thoughts I had about that, though, disappeared as I reached the tops of his thighs and saw the outline of his hard cock pointing up toward his stomach under his boxer briefs. I felt his stare on me as a rush of heat flooded my cheeks.

"Almost there. Just a few inches more and I'll be completely buried."

I turned to see him grinning at me. "Enjoying yourself?"

"Immensely." His gaze traveled to his cock and he winked at me. "And I can't wait to see what you do with that."

"You should be worried that you might get sand in your junk, Stefan. I can't imagine that would feel good."

His face twisted into a painful grimace. "Oh. That

sounds bad. How about you just avoid that whole area?"

"Just like a friend would," I joked as I piled on more sand, carefully working around his hard-on.

By the time I'd finished, we were back to joking and laughing, and as I stood up to take a look at my accomplishment, I couldn't remember having a better time with a man. How strange that it should be with the one I'd been so sure I could never like at all.

"All done, so now you can check off buried in sand on your bucket list," I proudly announced as my gaze trailed over his half-covered body. "You look like some weird merman."

Sitting up, he nodded and laughed at my joke. "I think it would be a sandman, but that name is taken already. You're the one with the brains, so what should we call this?"

I had no idea what to call him, but what I did know was that except for those few minutes I felt bad about what I'd said to hurt his feelings, I'd smiled more in the past couple hours than I could remember in a long time. "I have no idea. It's silly, though."

His hand shot out and grabbed mine, pulling me down on top of him and crushing my chest against his. Stunned, I didn't even struggle to get free. Those brown eyes of his stared into my eyes, and I felt myself get lost in them as he said, "How am I doing with this friend thing so far?"

It took me a second to process what he'd said. Lying on top of him didn't help to make my thinking clear, and his mouth mere inches away from mine made things much worse. Finally, I croaked out, "Fine. You're doing fine."

Stefan leaned forward and pressed his lips to my cheek in a soft kiss. Pulling back, he stared into my eyes and whispered, "Good. I think it's time I got you home, though. We can practice our friend thing another time. Sound good?"

All at once, the reality that I was still on top of him rushed back into my brain and I scrambled to my feet to get my wits back. "Sure. That sounds fine."

It took him less than a minute to undo all my fine work, and then he was standing next to me slipping his pants back on. Even though I'd told myself over and over that anything that happened between us would lead to nothing good, I couldn't help want to touch him, to run my fingertips over his chiseled abs up to his strong shoulders. He knew it too, or at least I believed he did when I caught him watching me stare at him.

Quickly, I brushed away the sand that clung to my shorts to distract me from him standing so close. "Time to get going."

He gave me a smirk and nodded. "So this is what friends do, huh?"

"Sort of, although the burying you in the sand thing was new for me."

"Want to do this friend thing tomorrow night?"

Before I thought his offer through, I answered, "Sure. Same place and time?"

"You're scheduled to work, so same time, but I think we should do something different next time. Maybe get a bite to eat."

We began walking back toward the house, and I said, "That sounds suspiciously like a date, Stefan."

Shaking his head, he looked at me. "Date? Nah. No such thing. Just two friends eating something together. Happens all the time with friends, doesn't it?"

His grin told me he knew we weren't acting like friends, but I didn't care. It was cute. "Yeah. Happens all the time."

SEVENTEEN

♭ STEFAN

Every night for two weeks Shay and I hung out doing the friend thing, even though I knew she didn't think of me as just a friend any more than I thought of her as one. One night we gorged ourselves on the best Mexican food to be found at three a.m., and another night we drove around for hours with Shay's arms wrapped tightly around me as I teased her by going too fast and she tried to explain to me what she did in her research.

Never before in my life had I enjoyed being around someone and not made a move on her. Not that I didn't want to. God, I wanted to. Every minute I spent with Shay I wanted to take her in my arms and kiss her. Not a night went by when I didn't want her in my bed, but until she saw me as more than just a player, friends would be all we could be.

It was strange, but part of me wasn't in any hurry for that to end. I could be myself around her. If I felt like acting stupid, I did and she laughed at my stupidity. When I decided to be serious, she let me be that without asking if something was wrong or if I was mad at her like other women did when I wanted to be something other than Stefan March, owner of Club X. There was no posing or pretending with Shay.

Just thinking of spending time with her put me in a good mood, even when I had to attend one of the weekly owner meetings or had to deal with Kane or Cash reading me the riot act for one thing or another I'd done. On the outside, I was the same Stefan, but underneath that façade, I got to be the person I was with Shay.

Even managing the club became something it never had been for me before. I'd always accepted my position there. Cash was the face the world saw of Club X. Kane was the hidden part, something that fit him to a T. I lived somewhere in the middle. The man members saw as the manager of the nightclub, I'd always been expected to be the life of the party, and for a long time I'd played that role easily. Drinking and chasing women helped solidify my reputation within a few months of the club's opening, but it didn't take long before both had become routine and too often boring. Now, though, I enjoyed meeting people and working with my staff, not because I wanted to sleep with any of them but because I was good at showing members a good time.

That didn't mean things had gotten any better with my brothers. In fact, they'd gotten worse. Kane especially seemed to need to remind me on almost a daily basis how important Lola and her father were to our continued success, as if I didn't already know that. Shay's knack for understanding the people around her, including me, had begun to rub off on me, but no matter how much I wanted to see Kane's point of view, I couldn't.

I knew what I had to do. Why did he think I needed

to be reminded constantly?

As I thought about all this, I heard someone walk up behind me. Turning around, I saw him approaching me with that same angry look on his face he so often wore in front of me. I was looking forward to another great night with Shay after work. I didn't want him ruining it.

"Hey, Kane, what's up? Before you bring up the whole Lola thing, I know. I have to make sure she's happy."

"That's good, but I'm more curious about our bet, little brother. You leave every night with Shay, from what I can see. At least you're trying to be sly about it and not let Lola see, but I'm wondering why I haven't heard you gloat about taking over my part of the club in nearly two weeks."

"Nothing to gloat about. We're just friends."

I rarely saw shock on Kane's face, but there it was. I'd succeeded in stunning him.

"Friends? Stefan, she's a female. Unless you've lost your dick, you can't be friends with a female. It's impossible."

"For you maybe. Not me. I haven't made a move on her in weeks, even though we spend every night together."

Kane gave me one of those throaty laughs he did when he found something really amusing. "Me? I could be friends with a hundred women. I practically am upstairs. But even I would have to dump the friend thing if I was spending every night with the same woman. You, on the other hand, are a dog. You're Cassian March's son all the way, so don't try and feed me that friend bullshit. You're playing an angle, and you know it. I'm just curious how it's going."

I turned away to avoid the judgmental look in his eyes. "Not this time. I admit I've been a bit of a man whore in the past, but Shay's different. We're just friends, and no, I'm not playing any angle."

Kane walked around me and stood at my side so I couldn't evade his stare. "A bit of a man whore in the past? Stefan, you're a man who's made it his life's work to sleep with every woman who passes in front of him. And when you aren't sleeping with a woman, you're figuring out how to get in her pants. So now, I'm supposed to believe you've found what? A conscience? God? A love of rejection?"

Jesus, he was a ball buster! Shaking my head, I tried to explain how things were between Shay and me. "We're just friends, Kane. Do I want more? Fuck, yeah. But I'm not going to get more if I do my usual thing, so I'm content to be friends."

"So this is some game. I knew the real Stefan was in there."

"No. No game. I'd say the same thing if she was standing right here next to me. I'm into her, but if friends is all I can have, then that's what I'll have to settle for."

"And you'll stand by our deal and lose your place for a year, along with your bike forever? That's a pretty steep price for friendship."

I'd all but forgotten about the terms of my bet with Kane, and the mention of losing not only my place but my bike did unnerve me a bit. It didn't matter, though. When I made that bet, I was a different person, but I'd have to live up to my word anyway.

"I'll tell you what, Kane. I give up. You win. Tell me when you want to move in and I'll get my stuff out of my condo."

"And the bike?"

I swallowed hard as the thought of losing my bike settled into my brain. "Yeah. It's yours. You win everything," I choked out.

"Holy fuck, Stefan! I'm stunned. I don't know what to say. I'm going to have to think about this and get back to you."

"That's fine," I said with a shrug. "Just let me know."

Kane said not another word and walked back to Cash's office looking like he was in a daze. At least there was that. I may have lost my place and bike, which meant I needed to find another condo and transportation, but I'd found a way to shut him up, so maybe it was all worth it.

And he hadn't given me his standard "You have to make Lola happy" lecture, so all in all, my day was going pretty well. Now I just had to find something fun to do with Shay later on that night and my day would be made.

X

At seven sharp, I gathered up all the bartenders and servers for our nightly meeting, but Shay was noticeably absent. Figuring I'd wait a few minutes for her, I announced, "I forgot something in my office, so everybody hang out and we'll get going in a few."

I'd never wondered where a bartender was before. I'd certainly never wondered where a woman was ever before. But Shay was no ordinary woman or bartender.

Closing my office door behind me, I checked my phone to see if she'd texted or called, but there was no message. Maybe she was just running late. I resigned myself to give her some time and took a seat behind my desk. Someone knocked on my door a minute later, and thinking it was her, I yelled, "Come in! You're late!"

The door opened and instead of Shay I saw Lola's head peek in. "Hey, Stefan. Can I come in?"

"Sure, Lo. What's up?"

She walked in slowly, almost as if she didn't feel welcome, and closed the door. "I wanted to talk to you about something."

"Take a seat. I'm giving Shay a few minutes, so we have some time to talk."

For a second, she frowned just a little, but then her expression returned to her usual sweet smile she wore when she was around me. "Oh. Okay." She sat down in front of my desk and hesitated a moment before she spoke again.

"Stefan, my father told me what he does to help you guys with keeping the cops off your backs. I didn't know when I got this job, you know?"

"He helps us a lot, Lo. We'd be lost without him, so please tell him thank you for us."

She flashed me a cute smile and nodded. "I will. The thing is, though, I'm not sure he'd want to do that if I wasn't working here anymore."

"Why wouldn't you work here anymore? You planning on leaving me, Lo? You know you're one of my best behind the bar."

"I don't want to, but I get the feeling I'm not really appreciated around here much anymore. You know what I mean?"

Those big blue eyes of hers didn't look so sweet or innocent anymore. Her intention in coming to see me couldn't have been clearer, and I understood the threat all too well. Every warning Kane had given me echoed in my mind.

You have to make sure Lola's happy, Stefan. For all of us.

"Not appreciated? No way. You know I'd be lost without you, Lo. Who's going to man the front bar like you?"

"Shay could. You seem to think she's pretty good.

Don't you?"

As great as I thought Shay was behind the bar, now wasn't the time to sing her praises. To make Lo happy, I had to lie. Thankfully, lying was one of my better skills.

"Lo, Lo. No way. You're my number one girl behind the bar. Don't give it another thought. You'll always be my favorite out there."

"Really? I had a feeling that you liked Shay more. I mean, I like her a lot, but she's not committed to the club like I am."

"No way. You're my girl, Lo. The members love you. I'd be crazy to lose you. Don't even give it another thought."

Lola's face lit up from her broad smile, and she stood to leave, obviously satisfied that she'd gotten what she came for. "Thank you, Stefan. It means so much that you appreciate me, and I know it will mean the world to my father. I can't wait to tell him."

I stood to add the finishing touch to my lie. Opening my arms, I walked toward Lola to hug her. "Come here. You know how much I need you here, Lo. Right?"

She wrapped her arms around me and rested her head on my chest, hopefully content with what I'd said to her. "I do, Stefan. I do. I guess I was just feeling insecure."

Tilting her chin up toward me, I flashed her my warmest smile as I stared down into her blue eyes, which once again stared sweetly up at me. "We okay?"

She nodded. "We're okay. Thanks, Stefan."

"Good. Now get out there and show everybody how it's done."

"Okay! See you out there in a minute? It's getting late. I'm sure Shay can catch up when she gets here."

"You got it. Just let me finish here and I'll be right out. Do me a favor and round up everyone for me, okay?"

"I'm on it!" she chirped out, happy to have a hand in helping me.

Lola closed my office door, and I took a look at my phone again. No message or text from Shay. Where was she?

I gave her ten minutes more and headed out to the bar to hold my meeting. Lola had gotten everyone together, just as I'd asked her to, and there in the back standing alone was Shay. Something about her seemed off. I couldn't put my finger on it, but she didn't look right.

"Okay, everyone! Sorry about the delay, but I'm sure you didn't miss my nightly talk much, right?"

Kerry spoke up and joked, "You know we love these little get-togethers, Stefan. We adore our boss."

"Yeah, yeah. Listen up, everyone! Lola and Mika are at the front bar tonight."

I'd barely gotten the words out and I felt Shay's glare from all the way across the room. Quickly, I added, "And Mika, Lola's your boss in this. I hear one problem and you'll be gone. Are we clear?"

Mika nodded and forced a smile, which made me think that right at that moment she was fantasizing about stabbing me in the temple with the nearest sharp object. Lola beamed at my warning to the woman who'd not only been her competition behind the bar but in my office also. But when I looked over at Shay, her face showed that same strange look she'd worn since I came out of my office.

"Kerry and Jana will be at the back bar, and Shay will handle the fourth floor. Everyone else is status quo. Anyone has any questions, come see me. Let's have a good night!"

The crowd dispersed, but Lola quickly moved

toward me to let me know she didn't think pairing her with Mika was a good idea. I calmed her and explained I didn't intend on having any more problems with Mika, no matter what she thought would happen, but she clung to me long enough that by the time I'd finally calmed her down enough for her to work, Shay had disappeared to the fourth floor.

Something in the way she looked at me from the moment she laid eyes on me tonight said something was wrong. Not that her not stopping to talk to me before heading upstairs was strange. Shay didn't need me to hold her hand to do her job, but my gut told me there was a problem.

Of course, every member of the bar staff had some problem of their own I had to personally deal with, so by the time I could get to Shay and see what was wrong, it was after two a.m. As I hit the fourth floor, I saw her talking to Kane, instantly making a surge of jealousy course through me. It didn't matter that my half-brother didn't seem to want women in his life or bed, even on a temporary basis. Seeing him talking to her bothered me.

Maybe it was the idea that even though he was no rocket scientist, I had a sense she might think he was smarter than I was. Maybe she'd want someone like him, even with that dark, spooky thing he sported more often than not.

They stood there talking like they'd known each other for years, Kane leaning over the bar laughing at something she said and Shay cleaning up for the night but full of smiles for him. I felt like an intruder on some private moment I wasn't welcome at.

Kane finally noticed me standing next to him and chucked me in the shoulder. "Hey, Stefan, what's up baby brother?"

"Nothing, Kane. Just here to see how my bartender

is doing tonight."

"Your bartender. Hmmm...I think that's my cue to leave." He turned to face Shay again and smiled. "Have a good one. I'm glad I could help with your problem."

"Thanks, Kane. I appreciate it."

"Always. Just give me a holler if you need anything else, but I think you'll be fine in Stefan's capable hands."

Shay flashed him one of those smiles I thought she only gave me, and I felt my face twist into a scowl as I watched him walk away with that smug look on his face I knew was meant to irritate me. I'd basically told him I was into Shay. Why was he butting in where he didn't belong? And what the hell made her all lovey dovey with him?

"I'm done here, Stefan, and Kane told me there aren't any more members in rooms on this floor, so I'm going to head out. Have a good one," she said in a flat tone as she rounded the corner of the bar to leave.

"Where are you going? What's going on?" I asked as I caught her by the shoulder to stop her.

"Home."

"Why? You don't want to do anything tonight?"

"I don't think so. Good night."

She pulled away from me with a look of disgust on her face and headed toward the stairs, so I jogged up behind her to find out what had changed between us to make her so cold. "Hey, wait up! What's wrong, Shay?"

Stopping, she looked up at me and shrugged. "Nothing."

"I don't understand. We've hung out every night for two weeks, and now you're acting like we barely know one another. What's wrong?"

"Do I know you, Stefan? I thought I did, but then I showed up to work tonight and there was Lola coming out of your office."

She was jealous. I couldn't help but smile at how cute she looked all angry at me, but that didn't help matters any and she stormed away even more furious than before.

"Shay, come back."

"You think this is funny?" she asked as she spun around to face me. "You know, maybe if I thought you were ever really my friend, I wouldn't feel so betrayed, but it seems that you're that same guy I've thought you were all along and I've been fooling myself."

"Shay, nothing happened with Lola. I haven't been with her in nearly a month. I haven't been with anyone since we started hanging out."

"Whatever, Stefan. I can't be around you right now."

She moved to leave, but I caught her by the arm to hold her there, needing to let her know I wasn't the person she'd condemned. Stunned, she pushed against me with such anger that I held her tightly to me, afraid if I let her go without proving to her how wrong she was I'd never get the chance again to see her laugh at my jokes or roll her eyes at me as I said something stupid.

"Let go of me!"

"No, not until you listen to what I have to say."

I pulled her back as she fought to leave, nearly falling into one of the fantasy rooms before she slapped me hard across the face. "I don't want to listen to what you have to say. You're that same player I knew you were the moment I met you. How could I ever have let myself believe the way you've been for the past two weeks was anything but some game? I don't ever—"

Each word out of her mouth hurt more than the last, and before she said she never wanted to see me again, I covered her mouth with mine in a kiss filled with all the pain I felt at the thought of Shay absent from my life. I may have been that person she thought I was for more years than I could remember, but with her I wasn't that man. I didn't want to be him anymore, and that was because of her.

But if she left me, I didn't know if I could stay the person I was with her. I didn't want to go back to who I used to be. I needed her, whatever way I could have her in my life.

Shay pushed away from me and shook her head. "What are you doing? I'm not one of your whores from downstairs. We're supposed to be friends, nothing more."

"Stop pretending, Shay. You no more want me to be just a friend than I want you to be just that. If all you wanted from me was friendship, you wouldn't care who I fucked."

She closed her eyes, as if what I'd said hurt her, and mumbled, "I don't care. Fuck whoever you want."

"Stop lying to yourself! You do care. When you saw Lo come out of my office, you were jealous. Admit it."

Her eyes flew open and I saw pure anger in their green color. "Don't flatter yourself. I wasn't jealous. I just don't like being lied to."

"You were jealous, Shay! Why can't you admit it? What harm comes from admitting you don't want me sleeping with other women?"

Her face twisted into a grimace as she struggled to hold back the tears. Finally, she shouted, "Fine, you're right. Does it make you happy to know that the idea of you being with Lola or anyone else makes me jealous?"

"Yeah, it does because just seeing you talk to Kane makes me want to kill someone I'm so jealous, so yeah."

Shay flailed against me and turned to leave. "I can't do this with you, Stefan."

"Do what? Admit you want me like I want you? Why not?"

She stopped just as her hand grabbed the doorknob and hung her head. Silent for a moment, she began to softly cry. "This is a mistake."

I touched her on the shoulder, and she turned around. Her face was wet with tears, so I wiped them away with the pad of my thumb, gently drying her cheeks. "Why? We've hung out every night for weeks and I know you want me like I want you. Why does it have to be a mistake?"

Shay sniffled and looked down toward the floor. "Because you're going to hurt me when the player comes back."

"Is that what you think? That the person I've been when we've been together all these nights is just some act—that once I get you to sleep with me again I'll go back to who I was?"

She said nothing and didn't even look up at me. Instead, I saw her give me a tiny nod. Hurt by what she thought of me, I backed away. "I guess you think I deserve that. Maybe you're right. Maybe I do. But you're wrong. I haven't been playing some game just to get you back into bed. I don't know how it happened, but you made me want to be the person I was all those nights. I'm not going to deny that I wanted you. I did, but if all I could have was friends, I would have been okay with that, hoping that someday you'd want me like I want you."

She looked up and frowned. "I didn't know...I saw Lola come out of your office when I got here tonight and I couldn't help myself. I was so jealous I could barely see straight. Then you didn't even come up to see me until the bar was closing, and by that time my anger had grown so much that I wanted to hurt you. All those feelings were so confusing. I believed it when I said I just wanted to be friends, but just the thought of you with someone else made me realize that was a lie I kept telling myself to avoid being hurt."

"I think you were right, Shay. This is a mistake," I said, hating the words as they left my mouth. Pushing past her, I swung the door open to get the hell out of that room. And her.

"Wait!" she cried as she clung to my arm. "Don't go. Please."

I didn't know if staying was the right thing to do, but something inside me screamed not to let my hurt feelings ruin what we could be. I spun around and took her in my arms. "No more games, Shay. We do this or we admit this can never happen. No turning back."

She pulled me by the neck and kissed me hard as her body arched into mine. My hands slid down her back to her ass, and I tugged hard on her shorts, desperate to get to what awaited me under them. Shay moaned into my mouth as I made quick work of her thong, tearing it off as her fingers fumbled with my zipper to free my cock.

Taking her hand in mine, I opened my pants and placed her hand back on my cock. Already rock hard, it swelled even more when she wrapped her fingers around it and stroked me from base to tip, staring up at me with a look in those beautiful green eyes I hadn't seen since the first time we were together.

"Hurry, Stefan. No more waiting," she pleaded.

I lifted her just above my cock and slowly slid into her, loving the feel of her tight cunt as it swallowed my cock inch by inch. So hot, so wet for me. When she'd taken all of me, I groaned, "Wrap your legs around me. Hang on, princess."

Shay's heels pressed hard into my back, even as my hips pulled back to let me plunge back into her, and her hands threaded behind my neck pressed hard against my skin. With each thrust, I claimed her body as mine and tried to push away the jealousy I'd felt just minutes before. I wanted her as mine, even though I'd never wanted that before with a woman.

"Stefan...faster...please, don't hold back."

My hands tugged her hair, pulling her head back so she had to look at me as I fucked her. "No holding back. You're mine now and from this moment on."

I pounded into her until our bodies were slick with sweat and my legs ached, but I could have held her there on me forever listening to her pant and moan my name as each thrust inched her closer to coming. Her pussy tightened around my cock and she scratched her nails across the back of my neck as her orgasm ripped through her, taking me over the edge with her.

When her body finally ceased its trembling, she pressed her forehead to mine and whispered, "Stefan, what did we do?"

"Shhh. No regrets. Okay?"

Shay pulled me close and hugged me. "Yeah. No regrets."

EIGHTEEN

🌸 SHAY

The morning sun streamed in through my window, waking me after far too few hours sleep. Groggy, I squinted and rolled over, smashing into Stefan's side. The man slept like the dead compared to me and barely flinched but mumbled some garbled words as he turned away from me and the unwanted morning light.

My alarm clock announced in bright red numbers that it was barely nine o'clock, way too early for night owls to be awake, so I pulled the blanket up over my head and hoped I could fall back to sleep.

"You know, there are things called shades. Some of them are even room darkening," Stefan whispered as he snuggled up against my back. "This room is desperately in need of them."

I turned my head and looked to see him smiling at me. God, he was even sexy first thing in the morning. "Yeah? I'll get on that right away."

He groaned and pushed his hips forward, grazing my ass with his hard cock. "Good. Get on that."

Rolling over to face him, I tapped him on the tip of his nose. "You're pretty demanding in the morning. Do you know that?"

Stefan opened his eyes and smiled so sexy I couldn't help but be turned on. "Not demanding at all. Just observant." He nuzzled my neck and kissed me just below my ear, instantly making me want him. "If you want demanding, I have a few ideas about what we should be doing instead of talking about your room's location on the surface of the sun."

My head felt like it was swimming. Closing my eyes, I moaned, "Oh, God…mmmm…like what?"

"Like you climbing on top of me and straddling my hips to take advantage of this hard on that's so nicely shown up just for you."

"I like the way you think."

Stefan rolled onto his back and pulled me on top of him in one fluid motion. Sliding his hands down my back, he cupped my ass and thrust his hips up so his cock slid through my already wet pussy. God he felt good!

Leaning down, I ran my tongue lightly over his pierced nipple and rolled my hips so his cock hit my clit perfectly. He tugged my head up and lifted his hips off the bed. "You're so wet. I love that."

I rolled my hips again, this time taking just the head of his cock inside me, and sat back on my heels, teasing him as I slid my fingers up the length of his shaft between my legs. "I like this."

Stefan opened his mouth to speak, but the sound of his cell phone ring interrupted us. Looking down at his phone resting on his clothes that lay in a pile on the floor, I saw Cash's name come up on the screen. "It's your brother. Want me to grab it?"

"The only thing I want you to grab is my cock. Whatever my brother has to say to me can wait. Now, where were we?"

He lifted his hips again and slid the head of his cock over my clit, making my eyes roll back in my head. I'd had enough of teasing and foreplay, so I rolled my hips to take him inside me, but his phone rang again with his brother calling.

"You sure you don't want to get it? It's Cash."

A look of pure frustration came over him. "Yeah, I better get it. He'll keep calling until I answer. Can you reach it?"

Disappointed at the interruption, I leaned over and grabbed his phone as it hit the third ring. "Tell him I said hi and thanks for ruining a great wakeup," I joked as I handed it to him.

Stefan swiped the screen and put the phone to his ear. "Cash, what have I told you about calling me before noon?"

His expression grew dark immediately as the person on the other end of the phone began speaking. "Olivia, when did it happen? Where is she?"

Listening closely, he nodded and the corners of his mouth turned down. "I'll be right there. I'm not far away."

He pressed END on his phone and threw it off to the side. Worry filled his brown eyes, and he said, "I have to go. My mother's in the hospital. Olivia says they think she had a heart attack."

I quickly climbed off him and sat there watching him racing to get his clothes on. "I'm so sorry, Stefan. Do you need anything?"

In seconds, he was fully dressed and leaning over to kiss me goodbye. "I'll call you when I find out more."

"Okay. If you need me, I'm here."

He nodded, and I saw the sadness settle into his face. I wanted to help, but I wasn't going to push. We were too new for that.

Hours later, I lay there in bed wondering if his mother was okay. I still had both my parents, so I could only imagine how awful it was to lose one, and Stefan had already lost his father. And he was close to his mother too. My heart hurt for him, but I stopped myself from calling or texting, wishing we were closer so I could at least be a shoulder to cry on.

After calling my mother to tell her I love her and reassure her I wasn't dying or I hadn't run off and gotten married without telling her, I had to get up and do something. I couldn't stay in bed all day worrying. I'd never met Mrs. March, but somehow after spending that night on the beach at her house listening to Stefan talk about how close they were, I felt like I knew her in some small way and I wanted to know more about her.

A shower made me feel a little better, although all I could think of standing naked under the water was how my body had felt against Stefan's as we'd made love, first at the club and then when we'd gotten back to my place. All this time fighting what I'd wanted seemed silly now that we finally gave in and enjoyed one another without thinking of what would happen later on.

I didn't know what we'd ever be, but if all we were ended up to be just fun, I liked that idea. Dressed for the day, I checked the time and saw it was just about noon. Until Stefan called with more information on his mother, I planned to keep myself occupied one way or another. Carrie had been after me to have lunch for days, so I called her hoping she could take my mind off what might be happening at the hospital.

"Hey, Shay! Tell me you're calling me for that lunch. I'm dying for a hamburger and fries."

"I guess. Give me a few minutes and I'll fly by and pick you up."

"Everything okay, honey? You sound upset."

"I'm worried about a friend. I'll tell you about it when I see you. How's fifteen—" My phone buzzed from a text. "Hang on, Carrie." I check my phone and saw a text from Stefan.

I need you. Can you come to Tampa General?

I read over the first part of his text. *I need you.* Had she taken a turn for the worse? I quickly texted back *I can be there before one* and waited for him to text back, but I remembered Carrie was still on hold. "Carrie, let me call you later, okay? Something's come up."

"Okay. Call me if you need me."

Stefan texted back *I'll meet you at the front entrance. Thnx* and I grabbed my purse and keys, hoping everything would be okay.

X

He stood waiting for me at the front doors of Tampa General, and we walked to the cardiac ward and his mother's hospital room. Her heart attack had been relatively minor, but she'd have to stay for a few days for observation because one of her arteries had been totally blocked. Stefan looked like the weight of the world had been lifted from his shoulders, and he was back to his old self by the time we got to her room.

I stopped just before the doorway, suddenly feeling out of place. I'd never met his mother, and now I was visiting her in her hospital room after her heart attack. That seemed inappropriate.

Stefan picked up on my uneasiness. "Don't worry. She's up and acting like herself already. Cash and Olivia are in there, but they'll be leaving soon so it will just be us."

Peeking in, I saw Olivia smile at me. Turning toward

Stefan, I asked, "Are you sure? I'm a total stranger to your mother."

Those deep brown eyes looked down at me, making me feel like I wanted to do anything to make him happy. "It's okay. I told her I wanted to have you here with me. She knows you're coming."

"What did you tell her about me?" I asked, unsure what he could have said to his mother since all we'd been was sex and a couple weeks of pretending to be friends.

"I told her you and I had hung out on the beach at the house and you'd buried me in sand. It made her laugh for the first time all day. So don't worry, okay? I'll be right there with you."

I took a deep breath. "All right. I'm just glad she's going to be all right. You looked so worried this morning I was afraid it would be bad news."

Stefan leaned down and kissed me softly. "I hope we can pick up where we left off soon."

Knowing his mother, Cassian, and Olivia were just a few feet away made me blush at Stefan's reference to us having sex again and I rolled my eyes. "Nice. Now I'm going to be all red when I walk in."

"Don't worry. I'm just like my mother, so you know what to expect."

He took my hand and squeezed it, and a soft female voice from inside the room said, "Stefan, are you out there with someone? Don't make her stand out there in the hallway. Come in."

Now I had no choice. I had to go in to meet her. I swallowed hard and put my sweetest smile on as I headed in to meet the mother of the man I'd just begun sleeping with. No pressure or strangeness.

Right.

I tagged behind Stefan, gripping his hand tightly, like

a nervous child going to school for the first time. Olivia and Cassian stood at her bedside next to an enormous window, and for a moment I wished I was anywhere outside in the distance than there in that room. Oddly enough, even though I'd spent years studying all facets of organisms found in the human body, I found basic sickness something I'd never been comfortable with. Added to that the pressure of meeting someone's mother for the first time and I was a nervous wreck.

He stopped at the foot of her bed and said, "Mom, this is Shay." Looking down at me, he smiled. "Shay, this is my mother, Alexandria March."

Alexandria March sat upright in a hospital bed, her stark white sheet and blanket neatly folded across her lap. She wore a satin blue nightgown like my mother wore when we had guests at our house — far fancier than anything I ever wore to bed. It hid most of her shape, but I could tell by her face and neck that underneath all that fabric she was thin.

Her eyes were the identical deep brown color of Stefan's, and in many ways, she looked like her younger son, right down to the brown shade of her hair. I had no idea how old she was, but she had a young look to her face, especially when she smiled. Instantly, she made me feel at ease, even though I stood there in her hospital room a near perfect stranger.

"Shay, it's very nice to meet you. You must be the second shift since Cassian and Olivia are leaving."

"It's nice to meet you too, Mrs. March."

She giggled and looked over at Olivia, who hadn't taken her eyes off me since I'd entered the room. "Oh, she's just like you with the Mrs. March business." Smiling at me, she continued, "Please feel free to call me Alexandria."

Cassian spoke up and moved to his mother's side.

"Mom, we'll leave you with Stefan and Shay. Olivia and I will come back later and make sure you don't need anything." Leaning over, he kissed her on the cheek and Olivia did the same.

"Feel better, Alexandria. I'll bring you those magazines later so you have something to keep yourself busy."

"Don't worry about me, you two. I'll see you later."

Olivia winked at me as she left, like she knew more about me than I could imagine, and then Stefan and I were left alone with his mother. He moved around her bed to drag a wooden chair over for me, and I sat down next to her bed near the nightstand. Behind me, I felt his hands on the back of the chair, making me feel like I was truly with him there.

"Stefan's told me a lot about you, Shay. A scientist. That's impressive. What kind of science?"

"Microbiology."

"Interesting." She moved her gaze from my face to Stefan's above me. "Honey, will you go to the gift shop and get me something to read?"

The confusion in his voice was clear after hearing what Olivia had just said. "You don't want to wait until Olivia brings you the magazines?"

"I'll need something to do until the next shift comes in after you two leave, so pick me up Time and The Enquirer." She looked at me and smiled. "I like to be in the know, but I can't help but be curious about what Hollywood stars are doing. Do you know who I love? That Robert Downey Jr. There's a success story I love!"

"Okay, Mom. Shay and I won't be long."

A slow smile spread across her lips. "Shay can stay here with me so we can get to know each other. Take your time."

Alexandria March obviously didn't feel the need

to be subtle. I looked back at Stefan and bit my lip nervously. Smiling down at me, he said, "You okay hanging out here?"

"I'm fine. I'll bore your mother with talk of all things microbiology."

His hand rested on my shoulder for a moment and then he turned to leave. "I'll be back in a few. Don't tell Shay about any of my more embarrassing childhood stories, okay Mom?"

Alexandria winked at him. "I make no promises."

I listened as Stefan's footfalls disappeared out into the hallway and watched his mother as she seemed to study me. Obviously, she wanted to be alone with me, but why?

Nervous, I blurted out, "Stefan takes after you. You have the same brown eyes."

"He does," she said with a genuine smile. "Cassian looks just like his father, but Stefan is definitely my son."

I sat there waiting for her to say something else, but she didn't and all the anxiety I'd had about coming to see her rushed back. Bracing myself for whatever she might say, I was surprised by her next words.

"Stefan likes you, Shay. I'm sure you know that. You're an intelligent girl. Some people might ask what someone so intelligent would see in him, but I have a different question for you. Do you think he's just what you see on the outside?"

"We're not...I mean, we're just..." I didn't want to lie to the woman, but I couldn't tell her the truth that all we'd really been, other than pretending to be friends for a few weeks, were two people who'd slept together a couple times.

"I bet you think I don't know what my son is, or at least what most people, including his brother, think he is. I do. I just think he's so much more."

"I'm not sure what you mean," I said, coming dangerously close to lying since I had a feeling she was referring to his reputation as a player.

"Stefan may look like me, but he's a lot like his father. Cassian never paid much attention to Stefan. He was always only interested in the son who was his namesake. That didn't mean Stefan loved him less, though. I'd hoped that because he looked like me that he'd be more like me, but it became clear by the time he was a teenager that he was his father to a T. His father certainly loved women."

I didn't know what to say at that moment. His mother had just admitted her son was a man whore. What was the appropriate response to that?

"I'm not forgiving anything about Stefan's behavior, Shay. I just think there are reasons people act the way they do. Stefan's father had women all over town. Besides the two sons he had with me, there are three other children he had with those women. You work at the club so you've met one of them. Kane."

She stopped talking for a moment, and I wondered if I should suggest we change the topic so she didn't get upset. She had just had a heart attack. I doubted she needed to be discussing something so difficult for her, but she continued telling me what she obviously thought I should know about her son.

"So you're okay with Stefan and Cassian running the kind of club they have?"

Alexandria nodded her head. "Everyone involved is a consenting adult. I judge people based on things other than their brand of sex."

I couldn't help but like Stefan's mother. He'd been right when he described her as just like him. She had a carefree way about her that drew me in, just like her son had.

"I hated those women and their children for a long time. I know. I should have hated my husband, but I couldn't bring myself to do that, so I hated the others. I walked around with that hate in my heart, the very heart that seems to not be working as well as it used to. Then one day I saw Kane. He was about nine or ten the first time I saw him, and I knew the moment I looked into his face that he carried the same hate in his heart. He looked so much like my son Cassian, but where my son had gentleness in his face, all that boy had was hate and hardness."

I knew exactly what she meant about Kane. Compared to Stefan and his lightheartedness, Kane was dark and hard.

"I couldn't walk around with all that hate inside me. I didn't want to look like that angry child, so I worked every day to forgive my husband. Then when Stefan became a teenager, I saw he was just like his father. Females came and went—have for years—but he's not just like his father. There's me inside him too, and that part makes him want more than what he's gone after all these years."

"I'm not sure I know Stefan well enough…" I stammered out, now completely lying to her.

"Yes, you do. You're a smart girl. You know what he is. I'm just wondering if you know what he could be with the right person."

"I'm not sure anyone knows what another person could be." She looked unhappy with my answer, so I added, "I can say this. Stefan isn't just the player man whore I thought he was."

My blunt admission made her eyes widen for just a moment, and I thought I'd offended her, but then she flashed me a big smile. "I like hearing that. You know, his brother has always been easier, even though he carries his father's name. I always knew Cassian would settle down and be happy. That he married wrong the first time didn't matter. I knew he'd find someone like Olivia. But Stefan I wasn't sure about. I didn't know if anyone would take the time to see what's underneath the façade."

"Alexandria, I don't know what he told you about me. I'm leaving in a few months to study in Europe for a year."

Her expression fell slightly, like what I'd said disappointed her. "He didn't tell me that. Does he know?"

"Yeah, he knows."

"Well, I still think you're good for him. Do you know he's never told me about any girl ever before? You're the first."

Smiling, I said, "I'm honored to be the first. Stefan's a great guy."

"What do you plan to do after your time in Europe? Will you come back?"

"I'm not sure where I'll end up. I want to continue my research, but I'm not sure there's anything here for me with that."

I saw by the look in her eyes that my answer wasn't what she wanted to hear, but I didn't have a better one. I didn't know what the future held after Copenhagen. If my research led me away from Tampa, that was the way it had to be. I'd devoted too many years to my dream to discard it.

"Do you know I was a nurse when I married Stefan's father? I loved being a nurse. I worked right here in this hospital. It's probably the reason they're nice to me, although more likely it's because I'm on the board of directors," she said with a chuckle.

"I had no idea you were a nurse. What made you

stop working here?"

"I had Cassian and became very sick after giving birth to him. When I recovered, I chose to stay home with him and two years later I had Stefan. By that time, my husband's businesses had grown to where I didn't have to work."

She stopped talking and I didn't know what to say. The wistful tone in her voice told me she might have regretted giving up her career for the men in her life. I couldn't do that, even if I loved someone. I didn't want to be like her in thirty years and look back on my life with regret like I suspected I heard in her words.

I heard a noise behind me and turned to see Stefan with an armful of magazines, books, and newspapers. He wore the grin of a doting son as he deposited the goodies on the table near the window. "I thought you might want more, just in case you got bored."

"My son spoils me, Shay. Can you tell?"

"Just a little," I said with a smile as I looked at Stefan arranging enough reading material for a month.

"Do you need anything else, Mom?" he asked, his brown eyes wide with concern.

"No. I think it's time you and Shay go, though. I'm getting tired and the doctors will be furious if I don't follow their silly rules."

He leaned down to give her a kiss goodbye. "Okay. Call me if you need anything. Anything at all."

Cradling his face in her hands, she smiled up at him. "Thank you, Stefan. Don't worry about me. Everything will be okay."

"Okay, Mom. Love you. I'll see you later."

I stood from my chair and held my hand out to shake Alexandria's, but she gently pulled me into a hug and whispered low in my ear, "It was so nice to meet you, Shay. Think about what I said."

When she released me, I saw Stefan come to stand behind me. "I hope you feel better soon."

"Come back to see me again and next time I'll tell you about the time Stefan and Cassian thought it would be nice to surprise me for Mother's Day and nearly demolished my kitchen."

Stefan shook his head and laughed. "We were just trying to do something nice. Now we know that flour makes a mess when two boys get into it."

"He told me about how much he loves your meatloaf," I said with a smile.

"He did?" she said looking up at him with a look of pure motherly love. "He's the only person in the world who even likes my meatloaf, Shay. Maybe someday I can make it for the two of you and I can get another fan."

"That would be nice. Thank you, Alexandria."

"You'll be coming to Cassian and Olivia's engagement party, won't you? I don't know if Stefan showed you the inside of the house when you were at the beach, but I'd love for you to see it."

"She's coming, Mom. You'll get to show her the scene of the great flour crime of 1996."

"Good. Now you two get going and do something fun."

Stefan and I walked out of the room and when we were far enough away from the door for her to hear what he had to say, he stopped and turned toward me with a look of worry on his face. "I hope she didn't say anything to make you not want to be around me."

"Not at all. She's your biggest fan."

"That's good. I was worried she'd give you a rundown of every girl I've ever dated since the seventh grade."

"That would be a long list, I would think," I said

jokingly. "We'd be in there for days talking."

"Funny, but something tells me I shouldn't have left you in there alone with her."

I poked him in the side and smiled. "I wouldn't worry. It was just the woman who knows more about you than anyone else talking to the woman you just began sleeping with. What could go wrong?"

NINETEEN

✾ SHAY

By the time I arrived at the club that night, I'd thought about my conversation with Alexandria about a hundred times and come up with dozens of conclusions and even more questions. Had Stefan told her we were serious? Or had she just assumed that when he brought me there with him? Why had she told me about his father, another notorious man whore, if the stories I heard were correct? Didn't she worry I'd think he was as bad as his father and want to run in the other direction?

Regardless of anything she'd said, I couldn't help feel good about being there for Stefan. He practically beamed when he first saw me at the hospital, and after leaving his mother's room he couldn't thank me enough for coming.

Whatever we were doing together, it was all happening so quickly. My first instinct told me to slow down with him. So carefree, he had a way about him that took hold of you and didn't let go, taking you along with him. I had no idea where all this with him would end, but in my heart, I knew it would someday end.

I just prayed that it ended because of my leaving and not something he did.

The club appeared empty as I set myself up at the front bar and began to prepare for the evening, but within minutes Cassian and Olivia walked out of their offices in the back. For the first time since I'd begun working at Club X, they stopped to speak to me, likely thinking Stefan and I were far more serious than in reality we were.

Always professional, Cassian March had an air of coolness that his brothers simply didn't possess. His blue eyes, like Kane's, were so different than Stefan's deep brown eyes that always gave the impression that he was always on the lookout for fun. Cassian's eyes looked like he was studying you and behind them his mind was choosing whether or not to like you. The few times I'd seen him out in the club, he didn't intimidate me so much as make me wonder how someone so attractive could be so aloof. The idea of him hitting on me or any other bartender seemed preposterous, yet Lola had told me all about the story she'd heard from one of the other bartenders that Olivia had been his assistant before she and Cassian became involved and supposedly their romance had begun up in one of the fantasy rooms.

The idea that the very sweet yet very businesslike Olivia had gotten freaky with her boss made her all the more likeable to me. Maybe it was because I was screwing around with one of the owners, but after seeing her at the hospital earlier that day, we seemed to have more in common. I imagined she thought so too since she stopped for the first time as they walked out tonight.

Cassian saw me standing behind the bar and made

a point to speak to me. "Shay, I wanted to thank you for visiting my mother this afternoon. That was very nice of you."

"I was happy to, Cassian. She's a lovely woman."

"Well, I spoke to her a short while ago and she couldn't say enough about you. It seems you made quite an impression on her."

I chuckled at how gossipy the March family was. "We had a very nice talk. She promised to show me the scene of the crime from when you and Stefan blew up her kitchen with flour."

For the first time, Cassian's deep blue gaze softened as his smile went all the way up to his eyes. "Ah, she told you about that."

"I love that story!" Olivia said and kissed Cassian on the cheek. "She loves to tell that story. It's so cute to think of Cash and Stefan as little boys trying to make their mother something special for Mother's Day. What were you trying to make again?"

"Pancakes. I was ten and Stefan was eight. Needless to say, it didn't turn out well."

"Well, you meant well," she said with a giggle.

Cassian smiled and said his goodbye, but Olivia hung back for a moment and I saw she had something to say. Leaning over the bar, she whispered, "Stefan told me he liked someone, but I had no idea it was you."

"I'm not sure it was me. You know what they say about him."

Knitting her brows, she frowned. "I know, but I think there's more to him than that."

Olivia was very much like her soon-to-be mother-in-law that way. "Well, we aren't anything super serious like you and Cassian, so don't have us walking down the aisle just yet. We've just been hanging out. That's all."

"I understand, but both Alexandria and Stefan made sure to tell me to put you on the list for invitations to the engagement party. You might be just hanging out, but they like you."

"You know I'm leaving at the beginning of next year, right? When is the party?" I asked, pretty sure she knew when I was scheduled to leave. Olivia gave me the impression that she knew far more than she let on.

"December 6. I know you're leaving right after the holidays, so I hope to see you there. Not only would it mean a lot to Stefan and Alexandria, but it would mean a lot to Cash and me too."

"Well, then. Seems all the Marches and future Marches want me there, so I'll be there."

"Less than a month and counting," she said with a smile. "I have to catch up with Cash, but it was nice talking to you, Shay. Come back and see me sometime. My office is right next to his."

Olivia walked away, and I couldn't help but feel like everyone thought this thing between Stefan and me was much bigger than what I thought it was. Not that I didn't enjoy being with him. The funny and sexy sides to him were definitely parts I liked, but what about the player part? The memory of that side to him never left me.

"Hey, you look a million miles away. What's up?"

I shook myself out of my thoughts and saw Stefan standing in front of me. Quickly, I wondered if I should bring up what everybody thought. Maybe he'd said something about us that I should know. As this idea trudged around my brain, I couldn't help but think that I should just enjoy myself and let this thing between us go wherever it was meant to.

"Just daydreaming. How are you? Everything good with your mother?"

"Yeah. She's feeling better. The doctors think she might be able to go home tomorrow or the day after."

"At least you know she has something to read," I teased, receiving a smile in return.

"I know. I went a little overboard. I tend to do that with people I care about."

"It's nice to see a man who treats his mother well. They say you can tell how a man will treat a woman by the way he is with his mother."

I knew Stefan's history belied everything I'd just said, but seeing how he was with her had impressed me.

"Then that's a good thing for me. Maybe that will cancel out the other things you don't like so much about me."

"Maybe. You better get going. Something tells me we're giving off a couple vibe here, and if Lola sees that, she's likely going to interrogate me the entire night."

Stefan's brows knitted in anger. "You do realize I own this place and she's my employee, right?"

"Yes, but she already sees me as competition, so adding fuel to that fire can't be a good thing for your business. Or for me."

"Did she give you a hard time the other night? Is that why you wanted to be up on the fourth floor?"

I couldn't hide my disappointment at losing the only friend I thought I had at Club X. "Yeah," I said quietly. "She's very territorial about you, and I guess she felt like I was intruding on her property. I thought we were friends, but I guess not."

Stefan's frown deepened. "Then maybe it's time she spends a few nights up on the fourth floor to get that idea right out of her head."

Reaching out, I squeezed his hand resting on top of the bar. "You don't have to defend me, Stefan. I'm a big girl. I can handle myself."

"Maybe I want to defend you."

"I just don't want you to do anything that would create a problem here. She's your head bartender and losing her over this would be foolish."

"Over what? You? I don't think that would be foolish, Shay. You're an even better bartender than she is, so if Lola decides to leave, the club won't suffer."

"I'm not going to be here forever. It's best to keep that in mind when you make decisions regarding her."

I watched as his eyes filled with hurt at my allusion to leaving and felt bad, not because I had to leave but because he clearly didn't even like hearing about it.

"Right."

"And we agree we should keep whatever we're going together on the down low?" I asked with a chuckle. "I mean, if you can't really explain what you're doing with someone, maybe you shouldn't make it obvious."

Somehow, I'd become a blabbering idiot in the past few minutes, but I had a vibe that if Lola found out Stefan and I were together in any way, she'd make our lives a living hell. No longer my friend, she likely wouldn't see any reason to keep the peace.

"What if I don't want to keep us on the down low?" he asked defensively.

"Stefan, there's nothing wrong with keeping your private life private. It won't take away anything from what we're doing if no one but us knows. It actually will make it more special, like a secret only we share."

He looked unconvinced, so I said, "What if I ask you to do this for me?"

His eyes softened and he smiled. "You already know my weakness, don't you? If you ask me to pretend like we aren't together, I'll do it, but I don't want to hide being happy."

"I don't want you to hide your happiness. Just that it

comes from anything involving me."

Stefan hung his head for a moment and then looked up at me with that puppy dog look I couldn't help but fall for. "Okay, but in return for doing this, I want you to come to my place tonight. Those are my terms."

He was so cute. Trying to stifle a smile, I said, "I didn't realize we were negotiating, but okay. I agree to those terms."

"Good. Be ready to leave after the bar closes. Until then, I promise to look like the same guy I've always been."

Stefan flashed me a sexy smile and winked before turning and heading toward his office. Almost as if we'd gotten lucky, Lola walked in just as he closed his office door. Her eyes lit up when she saw me like they always had, but now I knew I had to suspect her every move since she'd decided I was the enemy as much as Mika.

"Hey, Shay! You're here early tonight."

"Just wanted to get a jump on the night. You know how it is."

I intentionally busied myself with arranging glasses and prep to avoid speaking to her as much as possible, but once Stefan emerged from his office, there was no way I could avoid her. His version of keeping us on the down low actually drew more attention to us, not less. While I tried to keep my eyes off him, his gaze seemed glued on me, which didn't escape Lola's attention. At times, it felt as if his stare was burning a hole in my side, and after about an hour of him acting like that, I wasn't surprised when she finally gave in and asked me about it.

"Did something happen between you and Stefan, Shay?"

I served the member who'd ordered a gin and tonic and steeled my expression before turning to face her.

Squinting, she wore the look of someone who suspected her man had been cheating on her. "Something happen? What do you mean?"

Lola's body twisted into a defensive pose as her right hip shot out. "He can't take his eyes off you tonight. I've been watching him since he came out of his office, and he hasn't stopped looking at you."

"How do you know he's not looking at you? We've been standing right next to each other since you got here," I offered, silently praying that my deflection worked.

No such luck. "He's looking at you. What's going on? Did you two sleep together?"

My mouth fell open in genuine surprise. Christ, she didn't pull any punches when she thought someone was stealing her man. "Sleep together? Jesus, no!" She continued to glare at me, and something made me want to be spiteful. Not that being that way was ever a good idea.

"I'm not like Mika or Kat or Jana. I know better than to sleep with a man whore. That's a road to nowhere."

My mother's repeated caution when I was a child not to spite my face by cutting off my nose rang in my ears as Lola's eyes flew open in shock that I'd basically just indicted her along with the other women at Club X who foolishly slept with Stefan believing he would someday choose them and them alone. She may never have admitted to me she'd been sleeping with him, but we both knew what had been going on. I didn't need to be defensive about her questioning or her sleeping with him, but I couldn't help it. Something about the way she acted like Stefan was all hers bugged me, and if I couldn't say anything outwardly about it, I'd take whatever opportunity I could to slip in a dig or two.

She worked quickly to regroup and contain her

anger at my comment. "I know. It's ridiculous that they think he cares about them. I wonder why he's looking at you then."

"I have no idea. I'm sure if he has a problem with me, he'll let me know. It's not like Stefan ever holds anything back. Remember how angry he was with me about the Mika thing?"

Lola nodded and appeared to consider the truth in my statement. "You're right. I was probably just seeing things."

I looked toward the door as a steady stream of members made their way into the club. "Let's hope so. I don't need him yanking me out from behind the bar tonight. Looks like we're going to have another great tip night. I don't want to miss that."

My enthusiasm for making money seemed to put to rest her concerns that Stefan had taken a shine to me, but something told me this wouldn't be the last time I'd have to deal with her suspicions.

X

One step into Stefan's condo and any ideas I had that he was just any other guy flew right out the penthouse window. A nearly 360 degree view of the bay may have been the selling point for the place, but the inside of the condo was nearly as spectacular. Impeccably furnished, his place could have been a showcase for contemporary design. Unlike most apartments I'd been in with that style, though, his had a warmth to it instead of a sterile feeling.

Throwing his keys on the kitchen counter, Stefan spread his arms and smiled. "Welcome to Chez Stefan. What do you think?"

I sat down on one of the barstools lining the island. "It's gorgeous, but I'd expect no less. You're a man who likes to enjoy life, and this condo shows that."

"You make it sound like I'm some billionaire playboy, Shay. I'm just a bar owner. That's all."

Raising my eyebrows, I chuckled. "Going for the humble thing now? I'm not sure you can pull that off, Stefan."

"I figured it was worth a try. Come with me. I want to show you something."

I followed him out through the glass doors that led to the terrace and stopped dead at the sight of the view he had. It nearly took my breath away. The bay looked like it went on forever and from where I stood it seemed like I could see the entire world.

Turning toward me, he grinned. "What do you think? Pretty nice, huh?"

"It's stunning. Utterly breathtaking. I can't imagine having this right outside my window every day. I'd never leave home."

His eyes filled with pride. "I thought you might like it."

"Like it? I love it! It's so gorgeous I could stay right on this spot forever."

He stayed silent for a long time as we looked out over the water and then moved behind me to wrap his arms around my waist. Leaning down, he rested his chin on my shoulder. "About that. We're still doing the truth thing, right?"

I turned my head and his lips softly grazed mine. "The truth thing, as you call it, is probably best for whatever we're doing, friends or otherwise."

Stefan gently turned me to face him and kissed me, his tongue sliding into my mouth to playfully tease mine. He pulled away after a few moments as a jolt of need tore through me straight to my core, but I saw in his eyes he had something he wanted to tell me.

"So about that truth thing…I have to tell you about something that you might not like," he said in a quiet voice.

"Like what?" I asked, worried that what he was about to tell me would ruin everything I felt for him already.

"Maybe I should give you a little background so you can see this in the proper light. Kane and I have a love-hate relationship. Well, sort of. We used to be really close when we all got together to run Club X. He's always been a little moody, but we had a good time."

"Chasing after women and having a good time?"

"Well, for me, yeah. Him not so much. Kane never chases after women. I don't know why or what the hell happened to him, but he's never really had many women in his life. Other than how he is with you, which drives me out of my fucking mind with jealousy, he really only talks to Olivia and his dancers, but he never touches them."

"Which must confuse someone like you since you'd probably be all over those dancers," I said with a smile. I knew what Stefan was, and in some ways, I had to agree with Lola. He loved women. Not in the way they usually wanted him to, but in a way that showed he enjoyed them.

"The old me would have. That's sort of what I'm getting at. The old me and Kane were close but not so much recently. He likes to bust my balls, which pisses me off. See? Love-hate. So that first day I met you right after your interview he was busting me about not being able to get you—that you were out of my league. And I…"

Worry settled into those brown eyes of his and made

me nervous. What had he done? "And you...?"

"I made him a bet that I could get you to fall for me." The words came out so fast that my brain took a few seconds to process what he'd said. By then, he had launched into damage control mode. "The bet wasn't just for sex, though. I had to make you fall in love with me or I'd lose."

"Lose what?" I bit out. "Money?"

"No. I'd lose this place for a year and my bike forever."

"You're pretty damn confident in your abilities, aren't you?"

A smile lit up his face for a moment. "Well, yeah."

"And you're telling me this why?"

He looked out over the balcony's edge and frowned. "Because I lost this place and my bike when I told Kane that we were just friends. I gave in and admitted he'd won because I didn't want to be betting on us anymore, so he gets my condo for the next twelve months and my bike. So don't get too attached to the view here."

I nudged his chin back toward me so he had to look into my eyes when I spoke. "You know, you two are really childish. Was that the reason why he's been so nice to me?"

"I don't think so. I think he likes you. Not the way I feel about you but as a person. He's like that with Olivia too."

"Why are you telling me this? I probably never would have found out, Stefan. I doubt Kane would have told me."

"I know. I just didn't want to carry that around anymore. I like being able to be honest with you. I'm not trying to sound like an asshole, but I've never been honest with a female in my life. Well, other than my mother, and that's only about some things."

"Don't worry. She knows exactly what you are."

"Does she? How do you know?"

"That's what she wanted to talk to me about the other day. She hopes I'll see past the man whore thing and realize that the guy underneath is pretty decent."

"Any chance that can happen, especially after what I just told you?"

Pressing my forehead to his, I closed my eyes and smiled at how cute he could be. "I think you're a decent person, Stefan. Even if I still can't believe it, I like you, probably more than I should."

He cradled my face in his hands and kissed me gently. "I was so worried you'd get angry and storm out after I told you about the bet. I swear that was the old me. That guy doesn't exist anymore. Only the one who loves spending time with you and misses you when you're not around exists."

"So the leopard has changed his spots?"

Stefan shook his head. "Nope. The tiger took off his leopard coat. It was all a façade."

Even though I should have been furious with him for betting he could make me fall for him, I couldn't stay angry at him. Not when he stood there being so cute and giving me that look that made me practically melt. I didn't tell him, but he was very close to winning that bet. All it would take was letting myself go.

TWENTY

🍾 STEFAN

I felt like the weight of the world had been lifted off my shoulders when I saw Shay smile after I told her about my bet with Kane. As I stood there with her on my balcony looking out at the lights shining off the water, I wished I hadn't made that stupid bet. Sure, Shay had taken it well, but I was losing my home and my bike, and she'd really been impressed by my place.

Jesus, the old me was really an asshole.

"So, when do you have to move?"

"I don't know. When I told Kane, he was so shocked to hear me admit I'd lost that he was speechless. I'm sure when it settles in, he'll let me know when I should have my things packed and ready to go."

Shay wrapped her arms around my neck and looked up at me playfully. "That's too bad. I like this place."

I nuzzled the soft skin just under her ear. "Then we better take advantage of it while I still have it."

"Got anything in mind?"

"Yeah, I do."

Lifting the black Club X t-shirt over her head, I kissed

my way from her mouth down to her perfect breasts waiting for me, barely hidden in her black lace bra. Just enough for my hands, they were exactly what this breast man loved. As I kissed and nipped at her skin, I unhooked the bra and threw it off to where her shirt had landed a few feet away.

She ran her fingers through my hair, tugging gently to urge me on. "What if your neighbors see, though?"

"It's the middle of the night," I mumbled against her soft skin. "They should be asleep or at least not peeking out their windows. Either way," I said low as I slid my finger under her shorts to tease her clit, "I don't care. Let them watch."

Moaning softly, she unbuttoned her shorts and slid them down her legs. Now only a thin cotton barrier remained between my tongue and her pussy. First, though, I had other areas to attend to.

I pulled the chair over from the corner of the balcony and sat down, pulling Shay onto my lap so my mouth had perfect access to her delicious dark pink nipples I could spend hours sucking on. Taking one between my lips, I flicked my tongue over it and felt it harden in my mouth. I loved Shay's body, but especially her breasts.

A needy moan escaped her lips telling me she loved my attention there too. I bit down gently on the base of her nipple, knowing she enjoyed a little pain with her pleasure, and felt a hand tighten into a fist in my hair.

"Oh, God…I love when you do that," she whimpered above me.

I looked up at her and saw her watching me. Grinning, I opened my mouth and slowly bit down again as her eyes closed in ecstasy. I couldn't let the other one feel neglected, so I moved over to her left nipple and sucked it hard into my mouth, loving the sound of her moan as it filled my ears.

Shay's hands fumbled with the button on my pants and then my zipper as she scrambled to move our lovemaking to the next level. I liked foreplay, but if she wanted to kick it up a notch, I was all about that too.

She slipped my cock out and stroked me from balls to tip, sending my body into overdrive. Her nipple still in my mouth, I bit down hard and heard her squeal above me, "Ooohh!"

Yanking my head back, she stared down at me with a look of pure need in her eyes. "I need you inside me. Now, Stefan."

I tore her panties off and grabbed her hips hard in my hands. Lifting her off me, I thrust my hips off the chair and rammed my cock into her wet and waiting cunt, loving the feel of her around me. Shay moaned and kissed me long and deep as I began to move her up and down on me.

Suddenly, her eyes grew wide and she shook her head as she pushed down on my hands to stop her movement. "You're not wearing a condom. We need to stop."

"I don't want to stop," I said as I moved my hands back into position on her hips. "Whatever happens, we're together."

She shook her head again. "No. I can't risk getting pregnant."

I sat there with my cock still inside her and knew she was right. She was leaving and nothing could change that.

Even if all I wanted to do was change that fact.

Nodding, I gently lifted her off me and sat there as she picked up her clothes. She turned to me and held out her hand. "Come on. We can pick up where we left off inside."

I straightened myself and took her hand as she led

me to my bedroom. Still rock hard, my cock stood ready to go, but the rest of me couldn't shake the truth of her leaving. I'd ignored it best as I could, but I couldn't anymore. Shay and I were on borrowed time, and in less than two months the happiest time of my adult life would be over.

"Stefan, I know what you're thinking. Don't. We were always just supposed to be about having a good time, remember?"

I tried to force a smile, but I couldn't. I didn't want just a good time anymore. "I know. It's just that things changed. I don't know when or how, but I want more than that."

Shay pulled me down onto the bed and kissed me, making me wish I could stop time right at that moment. "And across the city hearts just broke."

I looked down into her green eyes and told her what I'd never said to any other woman before. "I don't care about any of them. It's all you. It's been all you since that night on the beach."

She cradled my face and smiled. "Don't think about the future. Think about right now the two of us here together."

I tried to do that as I made love to her, giving her everything I had of myself, but for the first time ever I wasn't able to use sex to push away thoughts of something bad. Now all sex did was make me realize how much I cared about her and how much it was going to hurt when she left.

Shay lay her head on my chest and silently traced her finger over the tattoo across my ribs, but I sensed there was something on her mind. My fingers stroked her long brown hair, and I leaned over to kiss the top of her head. "What's up, princess? I get the feeling you have something to say."

Shaking her head, she murmured, "Uh-uh," but I didn't believe her. There was a problem.

"Tell me. Remember? The honesty thing between us?"

She craned her neck to look up at me. "I'm just wondering how many women have been here before me." Burying her head in my chest, she whispered, "I'm sorry."

"I deserve these questions. I know. The way I've lived my life makes them valid questions. The answer is none. I've never had anyone here before you."

Rolling away from me, she looked up at the ceiling and frowned. "Don't lie. It makes it worse."

I slid over next to her and gently turned her head toward me. "I'm not lying. I have an office at the club, remember?"

"No one? Ever?"

"No one."

Her green eyes wide with curiosity, she asked, "Then why did you ask me to come here tonight?"

"I wanted you to see my place before I lost it. I wanted to impress you."

Shay blew the air out of her lungs and looked up toward the ceiling again. "That doesn't sound like a very good lie."

"No lie. Trust me. I'm much smoother than that. If I wanted to lie, I'm pretty good at it. I could have thought of a good one."

She knitted her brows and turned toward me. "You shouldn't tell me you're a good liar. Why would I believe anything you say?"

"Because we've got that trust thing between us. I like telling you the truth, Shay. You never pull your punches, but you show me your respect even when you're telling me I'm doing something stupid or you disagree with me. I like having that in my life. I don't want to lose that. I don't want to lose you."

"I don't know what to think about you. You've been nothing but a man whore your entire adult life, and now you tell me you aren't that person anymore because of me. But I didn't do anything. I didn't tell you to change. I didn't insist you be anyone but yourself. Why would you be different now?"

"Because of you. It's as simple as that, and trust me, I'm a master of simple. I've been that all my life."

"There's nothing simple about you, Stefan March. You seemed to be one thing, and I knew how to think about that person. Then we starting spending time together, and I found out you were entirely different than I thought. But somewhere deep in my mind I still wonder if all of this is a façade you'll shake at some point, and I'll be left hating myself for believing you were anything but that person I met that first day."

I pulled her close to me and held her. "I guess you're going to have to take a chance and believe the leopard skin was just a coat and underneath is just a sexy tiger."

"These animal metaphors are getting confusing," she said with a tiny smile.

"Then just trust your gut, or if it's telling you to leave and never come back, trust your heart. That's what I'm doing."

Shay snuggled up against me and hugged me to her. "I'm never going to forgive you if you turn out to be that guy. Just so you know."

I kissed the top of her head, closing my eyes to listen to the soft sound of her breathing in and out. If she needed more convincing to believe I wasn't that old Stefan anymore, then that's what I'd have to do. As she fell asleep on my chest, I thought about her never forgiving me if I let her down and hated the empty feeling I got inside.

I know, Shay. I know. I won't let you down.

X

After taking Shay back to her place to get her bathing suit because she refused to let me buy her one, we headed down to the water for a few hours of jet skiing. I hadn't ridden in nearly three weeks, but as soon as I got on the water I realized how much I'd missed it.

Like on my bike, Shay wrapped her arms around me, but she held on a little too tightly. Turning around, I saw the fear in her eyes. "Hey, what's wrong?"

"I've never been on one of these," she admitted.

"It's just like my bike. Just hold on. I won't let anything hurt you."

"It's not that." Shay bit her lip nervously and knitted her brows. "I don't know how to swim. Even though I have this life jacket on, this is scary."

"Why didn't you tell me?"

Shay lowered her head. "I didn't want to be boring."

"Princess, you're never boring. If you don't want to do this, just say the word and we can do whatever you want today."

She shook her head and looked up at me. "No, I want to. I've lived here all my life and never gone out on the water."

"I'll take it slow at first, and when you're ready, just let me know, okay?"

Taking a deep breath, she let it out slowly and nodded. "Okay. If I hang on too tight, just tell me. Water just freaks me out."

"Shay, we don't have to do this."

She forced a smile and squeezed her arms around

my waist. "I've got my sunscreen and life jacket on, so I'm ready. Let's do this!"

I took it easy, but from the moment the engine started, her cheek was pressed to my back and her arms locked tightly around me. For the first few minutes, her hands trembled against my stomach, but then slowly her hold on me eased and before long I heard her giggling behind me.

"This is so much fun! I had no idea!" she squealed in my ear.

I sped up and yelled back, "Hold on!"

"Don't go so fast! Stefan! Not so fast!"

I covered her hand on my waist with mine and squeezed gently to let her know she was safe. "It's okay. I'm here. I won't let you get hurt. Don't let go!"

We soared across the water, bouncing against the waves and one another for hours, and her fear gradually evolved into trust for me. When she got frightened, she yelled and squeezed me tighter so I slowed down. After a while, she didn't even have to say anything. I knew a squeeze meant slow down, so I did.

Pulling up to the dock, I let her off and took the jet ski back to where I kept it before meeting up with her to take her home. I'd had a great time, but she stayed quiet as we walked to my bike. I had pushed her past her limits a few times, so maybe it had been too much?

"You okay?" I asked as I reached out for her hand.

She looked down as my fingers weaved in between hers and shook her head. "Yeah. That was fun."

"We can do it again, if you like."

Shay stopped and turned to face me. "I'd like that."

"Good. It's a date."

"A date…"

"We can call it that now, you know. That's sort of what we're doing together."

Shay smiled up at me, making me feel like the luckiest guy in the world. "Dating, huh? The women of Tampa will never believe it."

"Funny. I don't care what they believe. All I care about is that you believe in us." I stopped in front of my bike and took her in my arms. "Tell me you believe in us. I need to hear it from you, Shay."

She hesitated for a few moments and then finally said, "I believe you want me to see the best in you, Stefan. I believe all this has happened so fast that I'm scared of what we're doing even more than I am of being in the water. But I believe I've never been happier with anyone in my life, so I'm trying to forget about my doubts and fears."

I cupped her face and kissed her softly, wishing we were back in my bedroom with me buried deep inside her. "You'll see. I'll put all those doubts and fears to shame. Then all you'll have is that happiness."

My phone vibrated, and I looked to see a text from Cash. *Need to talk this afternoon.*

"Duty calls. Time for me to go meet with my brothers. Let me get you back to your place."

X

Cash and Kane sat in their usual places around Cash's desk when I walked in feeling like I was bouncing on air. Unable to keep the grin off my face, I asked, "What's up, big brothers?"

"Stef, you look different today? What's going on?" Cash asked, immediately suspicious of my happiness.

"Just off a midday quickie in your office with the flavor of the week?" Kane added in his usual ballbusting way.

I sat down and laced my fingers behind my head. "About that. I'm dating Shay. Feel free to be jealous, Kane."

"I'm happy for you, Stef," Cash said with a smile I knew was genuine. "I figured as much when I saw you two at the hospital. She's not your usual type, though, little brother. Does this mean you're finally growing up?"

"I'm a changed man, gentlemen. The man whore is gone, replaced by the man you see in front of you, happy with one woman."

"No way," Kane said with a sneer. "I don't believe it."

"I can understand your jealousy. Shay's got it all — looks, brains, a great personality."

"A great personality? When the hell have you ever cared about a great personality? And what happened to you two just being friends? I knew that was total bullshit. Even more important, does Lola know?"

"We didn't want to be just friends. And I have no goddamned idea what Lola knows."

Cash cleared his throat and both Kane and I stopped our sniping at one another to look at him. "You and your love life are sort of what this meeting is about. Shank seems to be more and more miserable every time I speak to him. He called me this morning and between the veiled threats and his tone of voice, I get the feeling Lola already knows you're off the market and has told Daddy. I don't begrudge you happiness, Stef, but this thing with Lola is getting away from you."

"Have you made any progress finding anyone else who can help us? There's got to be someone in this town who's willing to help us with more power than that scumbag Shank. We've got politicians and businessmen as members here. Can't they help?"

"I'm working on it, but this kind of thing takes time. I can't just meet with someone and ask them if they want to help us keep the illegal activities of the club under wraps so the cops don't close us down. It requires a little more finesse than that. I've got a councilman I think might be able to help, but I need more time."

I looked at Cash and Kane and shook my head. "I'm not fucking up what I have with Shay over this."

Cash quickly put up his hands to calm me down. "We're not saying you have to ruin anything, Stefan. We just need to figure out how to handle this. Lola isn't happy, and now her father isn't happy."

"Well, then we need to think of something else because sleeping with Lola isn't an answer anymore, Cash. I can't do that to Shay."

"We'll take care of it. We always do, don't we?" Cash said, trying to reassure me. "I think I speak for Kane too when I say we wouldn't ask you to hurt someone for us or the club."

I looked over at Kane and searched for the truth in his face. Did he agree with Cash or would he be that same guy he'd been for so long when it came to me?

Kane nodded. "Cash is right. No matter what I think of the mess with Lola, I don't want to see you hurt Shay because of your past mistakes. She's the only woman you've ever been with that didn't disgust me."

"I'll make sure to tell her," I joked. "I'm sure she'll love the compliment."

"But that doesn't change the fact that the minute you and Shay let the rest of the world know you're together, Shank's days of helping us are over."

"We've already decided to play it cool. No public displays of affection at the club here. No acting like we're a couple."

"I bet that was Shay's idea," Cash said with a chuckle.

"It was. In my opinion, I should be able to date whoever the fuck I want, but she didn't want the rest of the staff to know and give her grief for it. Another one of the great parts of her — her brain."

"I don't think it matters if you put your relationship of display or not, Stefan," Kane said somberly. "You're not sleeping with Lola, which no doubt makes her unhappy. That will be enough for Shank, if she tells him."

Cash and Kane continued to discuss the Shank problem, but I didn't tell them that Lola had all but warned me that if things didn't go back to the way they were between us before Shay that her father wouldn't help us anymore. I'd been able to handle her that night, but I had to think of something else because sweet-talking her wasn't going to work anymore.

I got up to leave, already sick of dealing with this Shank and his daughter bullshit for the day. "Let me know if you think of anything. In the meantime, I'll try to be as busy as possible when Lola's around so there's no chance of her thinking we could be together."

Cash nodded his head and smiled. "Mom's being released this afternoon. You want to come with me when I go to pick her up?"

"Sure. Maybe I'll hang out at the house until right before work tonight. That way I can make sure she's okay and avoid Lola."

"Good. I'll find you on my way out in about an hour."

I headed out to my office to relax and text Shay until it was time to go to the hospital. I already missed her more than I'd ever missed any woman before her, a new feeling for me but one I liked.

Hey, my mother's being discharged this afternoon & I'm going to hang out with her until work. See you then.

She texted back immediately *Tell her I said I'm happy she's feeling better. Getting her more magazines? LOL*

Never going to let me live that down huh? Better watch out or I won't spoil you like that. :)

Uh oh. I better be nice then. See you tonight. XOXO

I stared at those letters on my screen as my smile grew larger. XOXO.

I heard my door open and looked up to see Shank standing in my office doorway. "Stefan, I'd like to speak to you. I think we need to talk."

"Sure. Come on in," I said as I put my phone aside.

He closed the door behind him and took a seat in the single chair in front of my desk. His greasy hair looked oil-soaked and even his clothes had a grimy look to them as I looked at him now. He really was a scumbag.

"What's up, John?" I asked, forcing a smile, even though I guessed what this visit was for.

Shank rubbed his tongue over his teeth as if he was cleaning them and made a clucking noise. "I like you, Stefan. My daughter likes you even more than I do. You know that, don't you?"

"Lola's my best bartender, John. That's why I made her head bartender over everyone else. I'd be lost without her. In fact, I just told her that the other night."

"She said something like that. She's a good girl, my Lola. A little too trusting, but she gets that from her mother, God rest her soul. Lola had to endure being brought up by me after her mother died when she was just seven. I'd hoped some of my suspicious nature would have rubbed off on her, but it doesn't seem to have."

"The members love her. She's got a great look and when I put her up on the fourth floor all alone last week, she made a killing off a member who took a shine to her."

Shank smiled, and I barely kept my stomach in check as my gaze settled on those disgusting half-rotten teeth of his on full display for me. "That's nice to hear, Stefan, but you know why I'm here. Let's not pretend you don't. Lola doesn't care about any members. She likes you, and until recently, you seemed to like her enough to sleep with her."

And there it was. The truth of why Shank sat there in front of me at that moment. Nothing like pimping your daughter out, dude. I tried to control my expression, but I was sure my eyes were as wide as saucers. "Well, John...I don't know what to say here. Lola is a very nice girl, but I've been warned by our lawyers that I shouldn't fraternize with employees."

Christ, I sounded like Cash. Even I didn't believe the words coming out of my mouth, so it was no surprise that Shank didn't believe them either.

Leaning forward, he tapped his palm on the top of my desk. "Do you think I'm a moron, Stefan?"

I shook my head. "Not at all, John."

Moron? No. Scumbag who thought too much of his own power? Yeah.

Leaning back in his chair, he crossed his right leg over his other knee and glared at me. "I'm not likely to want to help you and your brothers if my daughter isn't happy, and Lola isn't happy right now, Stefan. What do you plan to do about this?"

Had he, in not so many words, told me to go back to fucking his daughter? My shoulders sagged as the realization that he'd done just that settled into my brain. Now was the time for me to take a stand and tell this fuck to take his thinly veiled threats of not helping us and shove them up his ass.

But then the thought of Cash and Olivia's wedding popped into my head. For the first time in years, my brother was happy. How could I do anything to ruin that happiness? How could I be the one to take that happiness from him for the second time in his life? If I could just play off Shank and Lola until the wedding or until Cash convinced that councilman to help us, I'd be able to finally make up for all the pain I'd caused him.

"Don't worry, John. I hear you loud and clear."

He studied me for a long moment and then grinned as if what I'd said made him happy. As if some guy telling you he'll go back to fucking your daughter over his desk was a good thing.

"Good to hear it, son. I knew there was a reason I liked you."

Standing, he extended his hand to shake mine, and I reluctantly touched his skin, sure I should boil my hand immediately after.

"Nice to see you again, John."

Shank headed toward the door and turned around just before he left. "You know what's best about you, Stefan? Where Cassian is principled and Kane is just fucking scary, you're a man I can deal with because you're always looking out for your own hide. You take after me that way. I'll be sure to tell Lola you said hi."

The door closed behind him and I sat back in my chair stunned at his description of me. More accurate than not, it sickened me. But he wasn't wrong. I'd looked out for myself and not given a fuck about anyone else for so long I deserved to be thought of as someone like him.

But now I didn't want to be that person anymore. I had the best reason in the world not to be.

TWENTY-ONE

❀ SHAY

For the first time in my life, I couldn't say I was sure about what I should do. The time Stefan and I had spent together, first as friends and now as so much more, made me happier than I'd ever been with a man. He brought out things in me I didn't know existed. Countless friends and boyfriends had tried everything from pleading to cajoling to threatening to get me on the water, and never once had I been able to push aside my fears and join them. Like my fear of enclosed spaces, my dread of water had been with me for as long as I could remember.

But Stefan had walked in on those fears and before each one of them could make their case so he'd leave and let them win, he took my hand and pulled me out of where they reigned supreme to go with him. He never told me where we were going but just that he'd be there with me. Never before had that been enough.

A voice in the back of my mind whispered now, "Will it always be enough?"

That was the question, wasn't it? Right now, Stefan made me smile and laugh, and if I didn't think about the future, I wanted things to last forever with him.

But they couldn't.

I had to leave soon. But even more — even if I didn't have to leave — could what we were now ever last?

Someone knocking at my door roused me from my thoughts and I wondered if Stefan had left his mother's early. I hurried to answer it and saw Carrie waiting on the other side with a bottle of my favorite wine and two glasses.

"I'm here to celebrate!"

"Did I do something and I don't know yet?" I asked as I stepped aside to let her in.

"Not you! Me. I found out who the thief was and took care of her stealing ass. So I wanted to celebrate and since you've been routinely avoiding my calls, texts, and every other attempt to get together, I figured I'd come over and tempt you with something I knew you wouldn't say no to. Where's the corkscrew?"

"Carrie, I have work in a few hours. I can't drink now."

Giving me one of her trademark pouts, she said, "Not even a glass? Don't be such a philistine. Europeans drink with every meal, or so I hear. You need to get practicing for when you go there."

I rolled my eyes and smiled. "I can do one glass, but that's it. One. No more."

On her way to my kitchen to open the bottle, she yelled back, "Fine. One is enough, and while we're celebrating, you can catch me up on all the things I've missed in your life since you've been avoiding me."

"I haven't been avoiding you," I mumbled, silently acknowledging that since I'd been devoting so much time to Stefan that it probably looked like I was avoiding her. She returned with two glasses of wine and handed me one. "I've just been busy with a few things."

Clanking my glass, she asked, "Cheers! Anyone I know or want to know?"

I took a sip and nodded. "Stefan March and I have been—" I didn't exactly know how to put it. "—dating, I guess."

Stunned at my announcement, Carrie began choking on her drink and spilled half the glass of wine down the front of her shirt. "Dating? He's a player, Shay. They don't date."

"I'm just telling you what he calls it. We're dating."

"Why does it sound like you're reporting the death of someone when you say that?" she asked as she dabbed a cloth on her wine-stained shirt. "Aren't people usually happy to say they're dating someone new?"

"I am. I just don't know if this is something I should be doing right now."

Carrie screwed her face into a grimace. "Why? You said he was great in bed. What's the problem?"

"Do you ever think of anything but sex? You're as bad as a man whore."

"You say that like it's a bad thing. Shay, you're leaving in a few weeks, remember? That was the reason you said you couldn't get serious with poor Elliot. As long as you're having a good time with Stefan, what's the problem? You'll leave right after Christmas and he'll go back to doing his thing after you both had a few good weeks together. Isn't that what you want?"

The thought of Stefan going back to "doing his thing" made my stomach twist into knots. I hated the idea of him being that person I loathed from the moment I met him. That person was so much less than the man I'd seen in the recent weeks. Would he revert back to that man whore once I was gone?

"I guess. I don't know why I'm even thinking about it. We're having a good time, just the way I like it."

"Seems to me you want something more than a good time. I'm just wondering if Stefan March is the right man for that. Leopards don't change their spots, honey."

I took another sip of wine. "Maybe they were just tigers wearing a leopard coat and they really have tiger stripes."

Carrie wrinkled her nose. It's true that statement had sounded better coming from Stefan than it did from me.

"I don't know what the hell that means, but it sounds like bullshit. Leopards are leopards. Period. They don't walk around wearing other animals' coats. I think the wine has gotten to you, Shay."

"Whatever. You're right. We're just two people having a good time while we can, and when I leave for Copenhagen, we'll go back to our separate lives the way they used to be."

"Exactly! Carpe diem is what I say. As long as you're having a good time and no one has any expectations, it's all good."

Then why did I feel like shit thinking about him going back to his life the way it used to be?

X

I got to work by seven, but there was no sign of Stefan in the club or his office. Nobody seemed to know where he was. Lola stood behind the front bar staring at his office door, as if that would make him suddenly materialize, but after the third person knocked and found it empty, she turned to me with a look like I knew something about where he was and was keeping it secret.

"Do you think everything's all right? Stefan's always here for the beginning of the night. What should we do?" she asked, her blue eyes wide with concern.

"You're head bartender. I guess if in the event the owner can't fulfill his duties, it falls to the runner up to step in."

A look of complete confusion crossed Lola's face, and I guessed she didn't get my reference to the Miss America rules. Trying a more direct approach, I said, "Since you're the head bartender, I think you can go ahead and assign people tonight. If Stefan wants to change them when he gets here, he will."

"I don't know. I don't want to get in trouble. I just don't understand, though. My father told me he saw him just a few hours ago. Where could he be?"

I had no idea what Lola was talking about with her father, but the fact remained that Stefan was nowhere to be found and the club would be open in just under an hour. Members didn't need to see bartenders and servers just wandering around because nobody had told them where to go.

"If you don't want to do it, maybe someone should go back and see if Cassian is around."

That suggestion made a look of terror settle into Lola's eyes. "I've never spoken to him since that first day. I don't know him well enough."

"I can do it, if you don't want to tell everyone where to go and don't want to ask him."

"Oh, would you?"

I shrugged, confused by her fear of Stefan's brother. "Sure. I'll be right back."

Cassian's office door was open a crack, so I stuck my head in and saw him working on his laptop. Quietly, I knocked and said, "Sorry to bother you, but we've got a little issue out in the club."

He looked up and smiled, his piercing blue eyes focusing on me. "What's up?"

"Stefan's not here, and Lola doesn't feel comfortable telling everyone where to go tonight."

"Not here? He came back with me after we got my mother settled in."

"Maybe he got sick," I offered, feeling strange about coming up with excuses for Stefan.

"He didn't text you and tell you he'd be late?" Cassian asked, adding, "He told me you two are dating, so I just figured if he didn't tell one of us, he would have told you."

"No. The last time I heard from him was when he told me he was going with you to the hospital. I just figured I'd see him here tonight."

"Do me a favor and text him now. He'll answer you faster than he'll answer me," Cassian said with a chuckle.

Taking my phone out, I typed in *Hey, where are you? Lola doesn't know what to do without some direction here. LOL*

Cassian and I waited for a few minutes, joking about Stefan likely losing track of time, but he didn't reply to my text. I tried again and still nothing.

"Let me try, although if he's not answering you, he's likely in the shower or something." Cassian texted him and then again five minutes later and got no answer either.

"I'll keep trying to get a hold of him, but let me make sure everyone knows where they should go at least."

I smiled, pretending not to be worried, but Stefan's absence from the club and his not answering texts made me concerned. Cassian gave everyone their assignments for the night, and as he left the club to walk back to his office, he pulled me aside.

"Olivia and I have a benefit to attend tonight, but I'll keep trying him until we leave. If I get him, I'll let you know. Olivia has your number, right?"

I nodded and quietly said, "Okay. I'll keep trying too. I'm sure everything's okay. It's Stefan. He lives for this place."

Cassian seemed relieved by what I said, but as he walked away, I couldn't help feel uneasy. Something was wrong.

By two o'clock, I couldn't wait to get to Stefan's place. Even though I'd continued to text him all night, I'd never gotten a reply. Cassian had messaged me right after midnight to say there was no need to worry, but he'd given no other details. But just hearing that there was no need to worry while Stefan refused to answer my texts told me there was every reason to be worried.

I knocked on his door and hoped he'd even answer, convinced by that time that everything I'd feared since the beginning with him had finally happened. I'd let myself trust him, even the tiny amount I'd allowed, and now he'd done something and couldn't face me.

The door opened and I saw him standing there looking like I'd never seen him before. He clung to the door like a dying man to a life line, as if the door held him up. His hair, usually playfully tousled, looked a mess, and his eyes were bloodshot.

"Can I come in?"

He nodded and took a step back to allow me through, but his legs gave out and he slid to the floor still holding on to the door. Laughing wildly, he slammed the door and sat there in the spot where he landed.

"Come to find out where I was, huh? Well, you came to the right place! Come on in!"

"I'm already in. What's going on?"

Stefan struggled to get to his feet and motioned for me to come to him. "I just wanted to have a night to myself to drink myself into a stupor. That's all."

"I've been texting you all night. Why didn't you answer? Cassian said there was no need to worry, so I assume you answered him."

"Come here. I want to feel you next to me, Shay. Come here."

I walked into his open arms and felt his body sag against mine as he hugged me. "Stefan, what's going on? What's wrong?"

He sighed heavily and buried his face in my hair. "You feel so good, Shay. I missed you so fucking much."

"It's only been a few hours since we saw each other. Why didn't you come to work?"

He pushed me away and walked toward the bottle of Jack Daniels sitting on the coffee table. Taking a gulp, he swallowed and shook his head. "I don't want to think of that fucking place. I don't want to think of anything but you and me right here, okay?"

"I thought something had happened. Lola nearly lost her mind worrying, although I have no idea why anyone would worry about their boss not being around if they were head bartender. You should have seen her. She—"

"I said I didn't want to think of that place! No Club X, no bullshit about me not being there! And no fucking Lola!" he yelled so loud I stepped back, stunned at his outburst.

"Okay. I'm sorry. Maybe I should leave," I said quietly as I went for the door, not wanting to go but unable to see how I could stay with him acting like he was.

"Shay, don't go," he said in a voice that sounded desperate. "Please don't leave."

"I don't want to, Stefan, but I can't be with you when you're so volatile. I don't know what's going on, but I can't help if you won't talk to me."

His brown eyes filled with sadness stared at me and I let my hand drop from the doorknob as he said quietly, "Nothing can help."

I couldn't let him stand there so sad without trying to make him feel better, so I walked over to him and took him in my arms. Looking up at him, I said, "Talk to me. Remember the truth thing between us? You can tell me anything."

He kissed me and smiled, but I could tell it was forced. "I heard my father joke one time that I was the spare. You know, the heir and the spare? My mother gave him hell for saying it near me, but he never said he was sorry because he meant it. Cash was the one he wanted. Hell, I think he might have even wanted Kane more. He looks like my father too."

"Don't do this to yourself."

"Do you know what I did? I slept with my brother's wife. I knew it was wrong, and I did it anyway. Cash had never been happier, and I took it all away from him."

I didn't know what to say. He seemed intent on taking this trip down memory lane, but why?

"I'll never forget his face when he caught us. He looked like my father standing there, but his eyes were filled with hurt. I did it in his own fucking bed too."

"Stefan, stop. Don't do this."

"I've been a shit for so long I thought I didn't know any other way. I bet I could get you to fall in love with me, for Christ's sake. What kind of person does that?"

I cradled his face in my hands and kissed him so he'd stop this self-punishment. I didn't know why he needed to beat himself up like this, but it was tearing me up to see him so broken.

"You're not just that person, Stefan. You're so much

more, so please stop this," I pleaded as he hung his head.

"Cash and Olivia's engagement party is just days away. I finally have the chance to make up for the awful things I did, but I can't without fucking everything up. I don't know how to get out of this."

He dropped to his knees and pressed his cheek to my stomach. His arms tightened around me like he was afraid if he let go I'd slip away. I had no idea what he meant by the things he was saying, but I wanted so much to help him get out of whatever he'd done.

I stroked his soft hair and whispered, "Whatever it is, we can get through it. Just tell me what it is and I'll help."

In a voice full of agony, he continued talking. "He just stood there staring for what seemed like forever. Rachel rushed to cover herself and began rambling that we hadn't meant for it to happen, but I never said a thing. I had meant for it to happen. I wanted her and wouldn't give up until I had her. She realized she wasn't going to talk her way out of it, so she ran to the bathroom and slammed the door, leaving me there with him staring at me with those eyes so fucking full of pain. And betrayal. Fuck, his own brother in his bed fucking his wife. And then he finally said to me, 'Someday, Stefan, you'll love someone and the person you are—the fucking soulless, empty shell you are—she'll see the truth and you won't be enough. Your money, your looks won't be enough. I hope I'm there to see that day.' And then he just walked out, leaving me in his bed."

"You're enough, Stefan. More than enough. He was just hurt."

"I don't know how to be enough. I don't know how to get out of this."

I lowered myself to the floor and knelt in front of him to look into those eyes so full of pain. "Out of what?

What we have? Do you mean you don't know how to get out of being with me? What's happened?"

"No! You're the only thing right about me. Why would I want to lose you? If I don't have you, all I am is that empty shell Cash saw that night."

"Then no more talk about this. I'm not going anywhere, and no matter what it is that's haunting you, I'm by your side."

Stefan closed his eyes and pressed his forehead to mine. "I love you, Shay. I know everything you know about me tells you to not believe me, but I do. Don't ever doubt that."

He slumped against a chair and hung his head. I wanted to tell him he'd won the bet, but I didn't. Not like this. It meant too much.

TWENTY-TWO

🍾 STEFAN

Avoiding Cash and Kane's texts all day, I rolled into the club just before seven and immediately headed for my office, hoping to barricade myself in there before any of the bartending staff arrived. I'd spent the day trying to figure out a way to avoid Lola yet still be in the building with her, and that was the best idea I'd come up with. Maybe it was because I was nursing a hangover, but for a moment as I stood in the shower trying to come back to life the idea had seemed like a great one.

I sat behind my desk basically hiding out from the reality that awaited me when I went out into the club, sending Shay messages and hoping by some divine intervention that I wouldn't have to face the Lola issue.

My phone buzzed to alert me to a text, and I looked down to see Shay's message. *Feeling any better?*

She had no idea of the implications of that question. I may have been recovering from too much whiskey, but that was the least of my problems.

Yeah. Thanks for taking care of me last night.

Always. XOXO I'll see you in a few.

I typed *I love you* and stared down at my phone, unsure if I should send the message. I'd said it to her the night before and meant it, but she never said anything in return. Not that I needed her to, but I wondered if I should wait until we were alone and I was sober to tell her for real. Backspacing through the words, I typed *I'll be here.*

The truth of my life. I'll be here.

My gut twisted into knots as I wracked my brain for a way out. There was no way out.

By nearly eight o'clock, I couldn't avoid my life anymore. I had to face whatever waited for me outside my office door. All I knew was this: I couldn't fuck up the great thing I had with Shay.

I headed out into the club and played the role I'd always played. I flirted with Jana, smiled at Kerry, and even did the playful thing with Mika, who thankfully needed a job more than she wanted to sue me. All the while, I felt two sets of eyes on me.

Shay's, as she watched over me, her gaze full of concern, and Lola's, as she waited to make eye contact with me to let me know she knew what her father had said to me the day before and she expected something.

I was so easy to predict. She and her father expected me to act the way I always had. That acting that way meant treating her like dirt didn't seem to bother them, but now it bothered me. I wasn't that man anymore, but when my eyes met Lola's across the bar, it was obvious that whatever change I thought I'd accomplished meant nothing to her.

She made a beeline for me, plastering herself to my side as I stood alone near my office door, and in the voice I'd once thought as cute, said, "Stefan, can we talk?"

"I've got a lot going on tonight, Lo, but how about

later?" I looked down and saw her innocent blue eyes all wide and staring up at me. She played the game perfectly for the old Stefan, but this Stefan could barely stand the sight of her and that feigned innocence she projected.

"After the club closes..." she paused for a long moment before she finished her sentence. "...in your office?"

I gave a slight nod of my head and looked away toward the bar where Shay stood setting up for the night. Somehow not saying the word meant something to me, but Lola pressed me to say it.

"Is that a yes?"

My mouth turned dry, and I swallowed hard, the lump in my throat painful. "Yeah. After the club closes."

"You're the best, Stefan," she chirped before she headed back to stand next to the woman I loved and who had no idea what Lola was capable of.

Yeah. I'm the best.

The night flew by, and each time Shay spoke to me, I became angrier, not at her but at myself. Every moment that ticked by marked another I hadn't been able to find a way to keep her and Cash unharmed by my mistakes. My mind began to spin wildly concocting every manner of excuse why I couldn't be in my office after the club closed, but there was no reason I shouldn't be there. I was trapped.

"Hey, what's up?" she said quietly on her way to the ladies' room just before midnight as I stood staring out at the crowd of people having the time of their lives. "You look so sad. Are you okay?"

"I'm fine," I bit out, sure if I said much more I'd hurt her.

Shay looked up at me with concern in her beautiful green eyes. "I know we said we didn't want anyone here to know about us, but if there's something going on, I'm here for you."

"I'm fine, Shay."

"Okay. What do you say we hit that Mexican restaurant again after work? I could use another meal that makes my eyes tear."

Shaking my head, I forced a smile. "Not tonight. I have work to do and then I'm going to head back to my place."

"Oh, okay. Is everything all right?"

A crowd of people walked by us and I smiled and patted the men on the back like I was supposed to, but once they passed us, I turned toward her and said, "I'm fucking fine. Okay? We can talk tomorrow."

The hurt instantly registered in her expression, but she fought showing me how big a dick I'd been. "Fine. I have to get back."

She marched away back toward the front bar as I stood there hating every word I'd said to her. What the fuck was I doing?

The rest of the night went by in a blur. Even a few shots of tequila didn't take the edge off, and when Shay left right before three in the morning, we barely spoke more than to say our goodbyes for the night, like I did with everyone else on my staff. Somehow I believed that if I didn't treat her any differently than anyone else, even now when I needed her the most, then what I was about to do wouldn't hurt her.

I stood in front of my office door and saw Kane emerge from the top floors like some kind of awful reminder of what I had to do. He walked toward me looking unusually pleased with something and stopped next to me.

"What's up, Stefan? Where's Shay tonight?"

"She's not here. What do you want, Kane?"

The smile slid from his face. "Nothing. I just wanted to say hi. We had a good night upstairs—no fights, no members I had to school on how to behave—so I thought I'd come down here to see how you two are. I figured she'd still be here."

I shook my head and stared off in the distance at Lola as she pretended to work while she waited for the last few bartenders and servers to leave for the night. Kane said something, but it sounded all jumbled and I turned to look at him, confused. "What?"

"Nothing. I just commented on how busy we were tonight."

"Has Cash had any more success with that councilman so we can tell Shank to fuck off?" I asked, desperate to hear anything come from Kane's mouth that even hinted at the idea that I didn't have to do what I was about to do.

"No, nothing yet."

I watched Gabe and Kerry walk past on their way out. Lola saw them too and stopped her pretend work to look over at me and wink. Turning to Kane, I nodded. "Okay. See you tomorrow."

"Everything okay with you? You seem off tonight."

"Yeah, I'm fine. Good night, Kane."

Before I could get into my office, Lola was right there by my side possessively running her hand over my bicep. "Hi, Kane! What's up? We never really see you down here."

"Not much. Had a good night so I figured I'd come down to see Stefan here. You headed out?"

With a big smile, she said, "Not yet. Stefan and I have to have a meeting first, but then it's straight home to bed for me. A girl needs her beauty rest."

Instantly, I saw the look of recognition in my brother's eyes. He touched Lola on the arm and chuckled, "Well, give me a few moments with him and then he's all yours, okay?"

"Okay. Stefan, can I wait in your office?"

"Yeah, that's fine. I'll be in in a minute."

Lola closed the door behind her and Kane roughly pulled me toward the front bar. "I think I know what's going on, but you know what this will do if Shay finds out."

All the anger and all the frustration of not finding a way out of the whole Lola-Shank mess exploded out of me. "For months, you've been telling me I have to keep her happy. Even when I understood, you kept telling me, hammering it into my brain as if I was too stupid to understand. I got it. Cash hasn't been able to find anyone to replace Shank for what we need, so I'll do what you've lectured me about over and fucking over!"

"Don't do this, Stefan. Don't listen to all those times I said to keep her happy. Listen to me now. You do this and whatever you have with Shay will be ruined, even if she doesn't find out, which she probably will from Lola herself. Don't do this."

"I don't have a choice. Do you think I haven't tried to find a way out of this? Cash and Olivia are getting married in a few months. He's finally happy. I can't let my fuckup with Lola ruin that. I can't do that to him again."

"Holy fuck! That's what this is? You think whatever you're going to do with her is going to make what you did with Rachel all better? Cash forgave you, Stefan. Let it go. You two have a thing for living in the past, but this is going to ruin you and Shay."

"I can't let this Shank problem ruin his happiness, Kane. If I could find a way out of this and still know the club would be safe, I'd be at Shay's right now, but there's nothing I can do."

I pulled my arm from his grasp and walked away as he repeated his warning about what would happen if I went into my office, but I wasn't listening anymore. As I closed the door, I heard him walk up the stairs and leave me to deal with the mess I'd made.

Seated behind my desk in my usual position when Lola and I got together, I stared at her as she sat patiently waiting for me. "What's up, Lo?"

"My father told me he came to talk to you the other day. I promise I didn't ask him to, Stefan."

I didn't know what she expected me to say. Thank you? Was I supposed to say thank you for not directly telling your father to threaten the happiness of everyone around me even though the end result was the same?

"Are you mad at me?"

Yes. No. I didn't know who to be mad at.

"I'm not mad, Lola."

Her eyes filled with fear. "Yes, you are. I can tell. You never call me by my full name. Not since the first time we were together. You've always called me Lo, but now you're calling me Lola."

"I'm not mad."

She walked around the desk and slowly turned my chair so I faced her, exactly the positions we'd been in the last time we were together. Bending over, she brushed her lips against mine. "I thought you liked me, Stefan."

I wanted to push her away into the wall to get her away from me, but even as my hands raised to do that, I knew I owed this to Cash. He deserved to be happy, and at last, I could do more than just give empty apologies for all the terrible shit I'd put him through.

"I do, Lo. I like you," I said quietly, knowing those words would be all she needed.

She dropped to her knees and looked up at me like what she was about to do would please me. Licking her lips, she slid her hands up over my thighs until they met at the top of my jeans. For a moment, everything seemed to stop and I realized I wasn't even hard. Then slowly, she opened my pants and ran her hand over my boxer briefs that still hid my unwilling cock.

"I've missed this," she cooed as she reached in and stroked me until I reached semi-hardness. My cock was even weaker than the rest of me.

Just as I began to close my eyes to push the image of her going down on me away, I saw her look up at me and smile. "You're going to love this so much you won't want to be with whoever she is ever again."

Her mouth slid over the head of my cock until she'd swallowed it all and I was nudging the back of her throat. In true Lola fashion, she went to town on me like her next breath relied on my enjoying the blow job she was giving me. Not that what I felt mattered. I just needed her to be happy so she told her father and he kept helping us.

Kane's words rang in my ears, blocking out much of the sounds Lola made as she slurped and sucked up and down my cock. At some point, I vaguely had a feeling that something in the room had changed, but with my eyes squeezed tightly closed, I didn't see the door open in time.

Lola did, though, and quickly bobbed her head up. "Shay! What are you doing here?"

Every part of my being rushed back to consciousness and my eyes flew open to see Shay standing near my desk staring at the horrible scene in front of her—the horrible scene of the man who'd just told her he loved her a day earlier now receiving a blow job from another woman.

Everything seemed to go in slow motion. Lola jumping up to explain, as if it wasn't perfectly obvious what we were doing. Me stuffing my cock back into my underwear and zipping up my pants. Throughout it all, I couldn't tear my gaze from her eyes so full of pain. I'd seen the look in them before.

In Cash's eyes that night he found me fucking his wife.

She ran out without saying a thing, and I pushed Lola out of the way to catch up with her. I didn't know what I'd say, but I had to say something.

I caught up with her just as she reached her car. As she opened the door, I grabbed her, not thinking of anything but stopping her before she left me forever.

"Shay, let me explain."

She opened her mouth to speak, but nothing came out. No words. No sounds. Nothing. I waited to hear her tell me she hated me, that I'd turned out to be the horrible fuck she always thought I'd been, but she said nothing for a long time, just staring up at me with a look that made me feel like my heart was being torn out. Then, finally, she sighed and her eyes filled with tears.

"So this is what all that stuff last night was about. You were planning to fuck Lola."

"No! No! I didn't want to. I didn't have a choice. Her father helps us keep the cops away so they don't shut us down. He threatened to stop helping us if I didn't—" I couldn't say the words, so I just let my sentence trail off.

"You always had a choice, Stefan. So now you'll have to live with that choice. I hope you're happy with her."

"Don't do this. Don't make any decisions yet. Please. I'm begging you."

"Do you think I'm going to feel any better about this once a little time goes by? Do you think the vision of Lola going down on you is something I'm ever going to forget?" she screamed.

"Please, you have to believe me. I never wanted her.

I want you. You're everything to me, Shay. Tell me what I need to do and I'll do it."

Wiping her eyes, she said, "Leave me alone. Don't call me. Don't text me. Don't look for me. Forget everything we were together."

"No, don't do this. You have to forgive me. You have to forgive me, Shay," I pleaded as she pushed me away.

"Like Cassian had to forgive you? Like every woman who cared more for you than you did her had to forgive you? No. I never want to see you again, Stefan March."

"You have to see me at work," I said, grasping at any connection left between us.

"I quit."

Shay moved to get into her car, but I held her by the arm, refusing to believe this was it. "No. I won't let you go. I can't. I love you."

Spinning toward me, she pummeled my chest with her fists as she cried, "You let me go the minute you walked into that office and let her do that! You told me you loved me last night. Were those just words to you?" A sob overtook her, and she fell back against the car and hung her head. "They meant something to me. If you hadn't been so goddamned drunk, I would have finally told you the truth. You didn't lose that bet. I did fall for you. I fell hard. I believed you were that person I hung out with at the beach, who I braved going out on the water for because I trusted you."

"Please Shay. Don't leave me. We can get past this."

"What happened to honesty and the truth thing we had, Stefan? I can't trust you. You're that guy I always knew in the back of my mind would do something like this. I let myself believe you weren't because I wanted you to be that guy I was falling for. It was a lie. You played me. Congratulations."

"You know it wasn't like that. Stop talking like that."

I felt her slipping away even as she stood there with me. I was losing her.

"I can't do this with you. Let me go."

Her words made my chest feel like something was crushing it. I reached out but she pushed me away and as I stood there watching her go, she drove away.

I walked back into the club to find Lola still in my office, but one look at her and all I wanted to do for the first time in my life was hit a woman. "What are you still doing here? You got what you wanted. Go home, Lola."

"Are you with her?" she asked with an edge in her voice that only pissed me off more.

"Get out!"

For the second time that night, a woman stared at me with tears welling in her eyes, but unlike with Shay, I didn't give a fuck if Lola felt like shit or not. As long as she got the fuck away from me.

She ran out in tears, but I didn't care.

X

I rolled over on top of a vodka bottle and pushed it off the couch, hearing it shatter as it hit the floor. Looking down through bleary eyes, I pushed the glass under the furniture. Just in case I had to eventually had to leave the couch. Not that I had any plans to do that. The bottles lined up on the coffee table would allow me to stay blasted for a few more days, and after that I'd figure something out. I did own a fucking bar, didn't I? It couldn't be that difficult to get my hands on more.

Closing my eyes again, I tried to think of anything but Shay's face as she stood there out on the street in front of the club, her beautiful green eyes filled of hurt, but it was no use. That's all my brain gave me every minute of the day and night. I wanted to remember the time when she buried me in the sand. The time we ate Mexican and on a dare she took a bite of a pepper so hot tears flowed down her face as we laughed at her stupidity. The night we rode through the streets of Tampa with her holding on so tightly I thought she'd break one of my ribs. Every minute I spent worshipping her body as we made love. Her lips. Her tongue teasing me like no other woman ever had.

Her gorgeous green eyes when she looked at me like I was the greatest guy in the world.

It always came back to the eyes.

I felt something run down my palm and opened my eyes to see a stream of blood from a cut on my fingertip. It should have hurt—it might have if I wasn't so fucking drunk. Grabbing a bottle off the table, I took a swig of whatever it was and watched the blood from my finger drip down the glass.

Lost in thought, at least I got a reprieve from thinking of what I'd done. It didn't last long, though, and a few minutes later I was back to feeling guilt so overwhelming that it felt like something was sitting on my chest and at any moment I might smother under the weight of it.

In the distance, I heard knocking. It started off soft and after a while it seemed to be close enough that I wondered if someone was trying to knock down my neighbor's door. I didn't care, but it gave me another distraction from my thoughts.

"Stefan? Stefan? Open your eyes," a voice demanded but I shut them even tighter to block it out.

"Wake up, Stefan. Why are you bleeding?"

I slowly raised my eyelids to see Cash standing over me and Kane yanking the bottle out of my hand. "Go away."

"You need to get up. Two binges in a week? What the fuck is this?" Cash asked in that mix of concern and disgust voice he often used when speaking to me.

"I'm not getting up, so go away. Kane, help me out for once, will you?"

"Stefan, you need to sit up. There's blood all over your hand," Kane said in a similar voice to Cash's.

"Neither one of you really gives a fuck about me, so you can just leave me to my life."

"Oh, Christ. We're not going to do that again, are we?" Cash asked as he sat down in a chair nearby.

"Go easy on him, Cash. I think he might have a reason for this bender."

I looked up at Kane as he pulled me up to a seated position. "You know?"

"Yeah. Let me get you something for that cut on your finger. I'll be right back."

He walked toward the kitchen as Cash waited for me to explain why I was laid out on my couch piss drunk and bleeding. Recounting all the stupid things I'd done wasn't on my list of things to do today, so I pressed my head against the cushion and closed my eyes again.

Kane returned with a wet cloth and cleaned up my hand, wrapping it around my finger to stop the blood. Taking a seat across from Cash, he said, "Stefan and Shay had a problem."

Cash looked confused. "Stefan, I get that you're dating her, but women problems have never sent you into this kind of tailspin before. What's going on?"

I licked my parched lips and tried to keep my eyes open even though they kept trying to close. "Can one of you get me a glass of water if you won't let me drink while you're here? My mouth's like a desert."

Cash hurried to the kitchen and returned with a glass of water. "Here, drink this. Your body's probably dehydrated. How long have been on this bender?"

"What day is it?"

"Sunday."

"I don't know. I don't remember much about the first couple days. Ask Kane."

"Cash, Stefan did what he could to make Lola happy. I'm not sure what happened, but Shay hasn't been back at work since that night. Stefan, did she quit?"

"Yeah. She caught me with Lola."

Neither of my brothers said anything. Good. I didn't want to talk about it.

"Stefan, we told you we didn't expect you to do that. Why would you? You had to know if Shay found out you'd lose her," Cash said as if I'd been with Lola for any reason other than to help them.

"I got a visit from Shank after we talked and he made it perfectly clear if I didn't get back to business with Lola, he'd stop helping us. I didn't want you to suffer for my fuckup again, Cash, so when she asked to meet with me in my office after the club closed, I did it. Shay walked in and found her going down on me."

Cash frowned and hung his head. "Stef, you never had to do that. I don't suffer because of your fuckups. You're my brother, and I love you. You don't have to make up for what happened anymore. I'm happy now. I don't expect you to pay forever."

"I didn't want to see your engagement party or your wedding ruined because of problems at the club. I knew Shank wouldn't keep helping us if I didn't keep Lola happy. I couldn't think of any other way."

"I'm sorry. I never wanted to see you so unhappy. I would never ask you to give up what you had with Shay for my happiness."

"Well, you were right when you said someday I'd love someone and I wouldn't be enough to keep her."

"Stefan, I didn't mean that. I never wanted this to happen to you."

I hung my head and quietly said, "I've had it coming for a long time. I deserve this."

Cash stood and patted me on the shoulder. "Take all the time you need. I can handle the club. Don't forget about the engagement party. Olivia and I want you there to share our celebration."

"I'll be there, Cash. I even promise to clean myself up."

He left me sitting with Kane, who thankfully hadn't said much yet. I could only hope he'd continue being so kind.

"Do you need anything from me? You going to be okay?"

I looked over at him and shook my head. "Nope and nope. But thanks for asking. I assume you're here to take possession of your new place."

"No," he said and then chuckled. "You can forget all about that bet. Stefan, I know it's a longshot, but maybe if you told her why you did it she might be able to forgive you."

To hear Kane try to find a way to help me seemed so out of character for him that I couldn't help but smile. "I told her. It didn't matter."

"Stefan, I meant what I said the other day. Shay is the only woman you've ever been with that didn't disgust me. She's smart and funny and somehow made you into a person who actually thought of other people's happiness before his own, no matter how stupid that was. You need to go to her and convince her to forgive you."

Obviously, Kane's kind moment had ended.

"She doesn't want to see me or hear from me ever again, Kane. What I did can't be forgiven, no matter what my intentions were. I can't blame her. Just the thought of her with another man makes me so fucking angry I want to kill someone. I can't imagine what seeing her fucking someone would feel like. No, I fucked this up just like Cash predicted I would."

"Stefan, for the first time in your life you have to fight for something you love. Don't let her get away or you'll regret it for the rest of your life. Trust me on this."

I reached forward to grab a bottle of whiskey. "You're not fucking listening. She doesn't want to even see me anymore. What the hell do you know about this anyway? I don't think I've ever even seen you with a woman."

Kane nodded. "I know how it feels to lose someone you love. I didn't do enough once, and now she's gone forever. Don't make the same mistake, Stefan. Find a way to win her back."

I shook my head. "I don't deserve her, Kane. I deserve bar sluts like Lola. No need to worry about me. I'll never be alone."

Just saying those words made me sick to my stomach, but it was the truth. I'd aimed for someone out of my league — someone I had no right to be with — and fate had made things right.

Standing, Kane did the same patting thing on my shoulder Cash had done. "Think about what I said. With Shay, even I liked you, Stefan. That's got to mean something."

I lifted the bottle to my lips and took a gulp of whiskey. With Shay, I liked me too, but that didn't matter. Nothing mattered now without her in my life.

TWENTY-THREE

🌸 SHAY

For five days, I lay in bed and cried like a baby. Carrie came over each night and held me as I sobbed and repeated every horrible moment of how I let myself fall for a player like Stefan March and how he broke my heart.

"I know, honey. I know," she whispered softly as she gently stroked my hair. "I know it hurts, but it'll get better. It just takes time."

How many times had I said that to her and thought what I was saying couldn't have been helping. *What a crock of shit it'll get better. Your heart's broken. It'll never get better. You'll never be the same again. You'll always be broken.*

I never want to feel this way.

And there I lay in her arms while she whispered words meant to soothe me, but they weren't working. I still felt as awful as I had the moment I walked into his office and saw him sitting there with his eyes closed, a look of almost pain on his face as Lola…

I couldn't finish that thought. Just thinking about that moment caused my chest to tighten. Like falling for him had put something in my heart so that every time I thought of him now, it felt like a hand was squeezing it tightly.

Taking a deep breath, I dried my eyes for the fourth time that night. "You must be asking yourself what happened to the old Shay you used to know. Imagine what Elliot would think. He'd probably have a good laugh at my expense if he saw me now."

Carrie smiled at my mention of Elliot. "He'd be so jealous it would probably eat him up inside."

"Why? Who would want to feel like this?"

Pushing my tangled and tear-dampened hair from my eyes, she said, "Not jealous because he'd want to feel like this. Jealous because he could never make you miss him this much."

"I miss those days when I didn't feel like this for anyone."

"Oh honey, this is the best stuff of life. You'll never feel more alive than you do right now. That feeling that your heart is being torn out of your chest tells you it was real. You love him. There's nothing better in the world than love. Even when it hurts, it still makes you feel."

Furrowing my brow, I shot Carrie a nasty look. "I had no idea I was best friends with a sadist."

"Shay, I'm not happy you're sad, but I am happy you finally found someone to really love. I was getting worried you'd never open up to anyone and instead choose the cold world of science over emotions, and yes, love."

"I would have been better off sticking with the cold world of science. My research never betrays me by sleeping with another woman."

"He didn't sleep with another woman. Don't make it worse than it already is. He let her go down on him. Entirely different."

My stomach felt sick when she said things like that, as if his betrayal was any less terrible because his partner-in-crime wore clothes during it. "Again with making excuses for bad men, Carrie."

Sliding off my bed, she began rummaging through my closet. "They're not excuses. A blow job isn't anywhere as bad as if you'd caught them having full blown sex in his office, or even worse, making love in a bed." She poked her head out and held up a black sweater for my approval, as if she thought I was ready to get dressed and leave my bed. "I'm not saying what he did doesn't deserve some punishment, but you did say he claimed to have to do it. You'll wear this with jeans when we go out."

"I don't think so on both accounts. I'm not ready to go out, even if you put me in mourning clothes, and a man never has to let another women go down on him. How could I ever trust him again?"

She threw the sweater on the bed and headed toward the linen cabinet to get me a towel. "I'm not saying you can. All I'm saying is there are possibly things going on outside of what you know that mitigate the circumstances and might make you feel better about never seeing him again. That's all."

As she buzzed around my apartment, I thought about never seeing Stefan again. That pain in my chest that had finally receded came back with a vengeance, making me wince and want to cry again. There was no way I could forgive him, but thinking about never seeing him again hurt as much as the memory of what he'd done.

I heard a knock on my front door and looked at Carrie, who seemed surprised. "Did you order in?"

"No. I'd planned on getting you out of this house tonight, in fact. Do you want me to tell whoever it is that you're unavailable?"

I knew she was thinking the same thing I was. Stefan had finally come to beg me to take him back. "You can tell them whatever the hell you want, just as long as they go away."

"Okay. You sure you don't want to talk?"

"I'm sure."

Hidden in my bedroom, I listened as she answered the door, but I couldn't hear what the person in the hallway was saying. Peeking my head out, I saw Olivia standing in my doorway talking to Carrie. Why was she here?

I looked a wreck, so I smoothed my hair back off my face as best as I could and brushed my clothes off from the two days I'd spent in bed in them and stepped out into my living room. "It's okay, Carrie. Let her in."

Olivia sat down and smiled the way she did that day she saw me at the hospital to visit Stefan's mother. Always sweet, she had a look of concern in her eyes. I may have looked worse than I thought.

"Why are you here, Olivia?" I asked, too curious to remember my manners.

"I wanted to see if you were okay. Cash told me what happened."

"How nice of the March brothers to share sex stories. I'm fine. You don't have to worry. Just another notch on Stefan's bedpost. You must have to devote a good portion of your days if you go to visit every woman he's hurt."

I knew I was being unfair. I didn't care. Something about the idea of her fiancé and his brother talking about what had happened made me angry. That Olivia bore the brunt of that anger couldn't be helped.

"It's not like that, Shay. Cash told me you and Stefan broke up because of what he did for the club."

"You're buying that nonsense too? Is there some kind of collective delusion that comes from being around this family?"

"I just want you to know the whole story, okay? After that, I'll leave and you can decide if you think what I said meant anything to you."

"If you're going to defend his actions, you can just go now, Olivia. The man slept with another woman."

"Not slept with," Carrie said as she walked over to sit next to me.

"Olivia, this is Carrie. She makes excuses for bad men. Carrie, this is Olivia. She's marrying Stefan's brother Cassian."

In true Carrie style, she asked, "Is he a bad man too?"

Olivia smiled and let out a little chuckle. "He used to be."

"I'm glad you were able to reform a bad man, Olivia. Unfortunately, I don't seem to have that ability," I said quietly as I curled my legs up underneath me, already missing my bed. At least there I could cry and not feel as pathetic as if I started to sob right there in front of Olivia, which very well could happen if she continued to talk about Stefan.

"Stefan very well might be a bad man. I've always had a soft spot in my heart for him, though. When I started working at Club X, it was Stefan who made me feel welcome. Not that Cash and Kane didn't, but Stefan was funny and sweet and put me at ease. I know his reputation precedes him, but I saw a change in him after he began spending time with you."

"Yeah, well that change didn't stick."

"I know you think that he cheated on you because of who he is, but that's not what happened. Yes, everything you ever heard about him was true, but this time he went with Lola to help Cash and me. You see, Lola's father is a cop. A dirty one, but a cop, all the same. Each month, Cash and his brothers pay him to make sure the police don't shut the club down. I know you know what happens in Kane's part of the club, and without Lola's father, Club X would be closed because of that."

"What does this have to do with me and the fact that Stefan chose to go with Lola instead of staying loyal to me?"

Olivia frowned and continued, "Before you, Stefan and Lola had been spending time together —"

I turned to Carrie. "What a nice way of saying fucking, isn't that?"

Carrie gave me the "you're being a bitch" face and I turned back to face Olivia. "I'm sorry. I shouldn't shoot the messenger."

"It's okay. I'd probably be just like you are now, so there's no need to apologize. Yes, Stefan and Lola were fucking each other. Nothing exclusive like the two of you. Just a workplace get-together every so often. But Stefan didn't know that Lola's father was the person they paid to keep things good at the club. When he found out and it became an obligation to spend time with her, he didn't want to. The problem is Lola still wanted to."

"So her father put the pressure on Stefan to sleep with his daughter or risk hurting the club?" Carrie asked.

"Exactly. Stefan put her off for weeks as you and he were getting close, Shay. And the pressure wasn't just coming from Lola and her father. Cash and Kane were also telling him he had to find a way to keep Lola happy so her father wouldn't stop protecting the club. They didn't know Stefan was falling for someone, so they acted like they always have. Why wouldn't they? All he had to do was what he'd always done, so why would it be a problem now?"

"Why did he decide to do it that night?" I asked, needing to know why after telling me he loved me he'd go and do something he knew would break us up.

"Because her father stopped by the club to talk to him and told him if he didn't get back to hanging out with Lola, he'd stop protecting the club. Stefan didn't want Cash to have to worry and he didn't want the club to suffer just before our engagement party and wedding, so I guess he didn't think he could find another way and still protect Cash and me."

"How honorable."

"I know it sounds pretty dirty, and in many ways the world Cash, Stefan, and Kane live in is dirty. But what Stefan felt for you was real. I admit I didn't believe it when I first heard it either. Once a man whore, always a man whore, right? But he changed because of you."

"Once a cheat, always a cheat, Olivia. I know what he did with Cassian's ex-wife. He told me."

"I know, but I think that's part of why he did this too, bizarrely enough. For years, Cash couldn't forgive his brother for what he did. It was only after he and I got together that he could finally let that go. Stefan couldn't let it go, though, and even though it didn't appear to bother him, once he began spending time with you, what he'd done to his brother seemed to really eat at him."

"I don't know what to say to all this, Olivia. I'm not sure it changes anything. He lied to me and even if he didn't sleep with Lola and even if she still had all her clothes on, he betrayed me. I don't see how I can forgive him."

Olivia looked disappointed but gave me one of her gentle smiles. "I understand. I just wanted to make sure you knew that this wasn't just him being the player he'd always been. He's crazy about you. Cash tells me he's a mess since this happened. He hasn't been to work in days, and Cash and Kane found him last night drunk and pretty much out of it on his couch."

"Why are you telling me that? So I'll feel bad for him?"

She shook her head. "No. I guess just because I'd want to hear the man I love is a mess without me."

I stood and forced a smile. "Thanks for coming by, Olivia."

As she walked toward the door, she said, "I hope you'll still come to the engagement party out at Alexandria's house. It would mean a lot to me if you'd be there."

"I don't know. It might be too soon. I'm not sure we could be civil to one another and not ruin your party."

"Please think about it, and if you need anything, call me, okay?"

"Thanks. I will. And thank you for coming by to check on me. If you decide to report any of this to Cassian or Stefan himself, would you do me a favor?" I hesitated and then quietly as the tears began to come again said, "Would you make it sound like I'm okay?"

Olivia touched my shoulder softly and smiled. "Yeah. I'll say you're doing fine."

"Thanks."

I closed the door and Carrie took me into her arms as I cried harder than I'd cried in five days. Nothing Olivia said should have made me sadder, but it did. And angrier, but I didn't know who to be angry at. Stefan? Lola? Lola's father? All I knew was what Olivia told me muddied up how neatly I'd planned on hating Stefan March for the rest of my life.

X

A uniformed man waved me forward into the line of cars waiting to be parked, and I handed him my keys as I closed my car door. "Take care of the old Taurus. She needs to get me through a few weeks more."

"Not to worry, miss. We'll take good care of her."

I turned and saw Alexandria March's home all decorated for the Christmas holiday and looking like something out of a design magazine. Its Victorian charm had been amped up about a thousand percent by the evergreen boughs draped over the top of every window and the tiny white lights that twinkled along the verandah railing. Crowds of people milled about on the large wrap-around porch, and it looked like everyone in Tampa had turned out for Cash and Olivia's party.

Dressed in a silver strapless gown Carrie had loaned me from the boutique and wearing my hair in an upsweep, I felt like an entirely different person than the Shay I'd always been in jeans or shorts and a t-shirt. Being a different person sounded like a good idea as I walked up the stairs to enter the house since the person I really was felt like she stuck out like a sore thumb.

Like everyone at the party knew what had happened between Stefan and me and were staring at me judging me for the fool I was.

The outside of the house may have looked like it belonged on the cover of a magazine, but the inside was even more breathtaking. Designed as a Victorian home, it had obviously been updated but in a way that integrated the Victorian style with modern beauty. The heaviness of the Victorian look had been replaced with the lightness of white painted walls and woodwork. By the time I made it down the main hallway and into the kitchen, I was so engrossed with admiring the décor that I'd forgotten where I was and who would be there.

"I'm glad to see you came," a deep, raspy voice I instantly recognized as Kane's said.

Turning around, I saw him leaning against the wall just inside the kitchen looking distinctly uncomfortable. Dressed in a black suit and shirt with a blue tie that nearly matched his crystal blue eyes, he cleaned up nicely.

"I almost didn't."

He gave me a smile and nodded. "Me too, but I couldn't let Cash and Olivia down."

"Same here."

"As long as I avoid Alexandria, I should be fine. She always stares at me like she's deciding if today's the day she won't hate me."

I smiled as the conversation I'd had with Stefan's mother flashed through my mind. "It's not hate. She's worried you're too alike, actually."

Kane didn't ask what I meant, and we stood in silence as the entire party seemed to pass in front of us right there in the kitchen. Something about having him near me made me feel safe, and the idea of Alexandria not approaching me because I was next to him appealed to me. Not that I didn't like her, but any discussion between us that night would invariably be awkward and end up coming to the subject of Stefan, which I so desperately wanted to avoid.

"You know he's here, right?" Kane said low in my ear.

My heart began pounding in my chest as I attempted to remain calm and scan the room for any sign of Stefan or his mother. "I assumed he would be, but it's a big house. With any luck, I'll be able to avoid him."

"I don't think so."

I turned to look at Kane and saw his eyes focused on the living room across the hallway. Following his gaze, I saw Stefan standing alone over near a large bay window. He wore a dark grey suit and deep red shirt, and even though I couldn't say I'd ever seen him look so good, something about him told me it was all a façade. He stared at me with a longing in his eyes that pinched at my heart, even now after days of my swearing that I would never let myself feel for him again.

Turning away, I smiled up at Kane. "It was nice seeing you again. Where can I find the happy couple?"

"Through that room he's standing in. They're in the room right past it."

I sighed. "Merry Christmas, Kane."

"Merry Christmas, Shay."

There was no way to avoid him now, so I mustered up all my courage, even as my legs began to shake under my dress, and walked toward where I saw Cassian and Olivia. I felt Stefan's gaze on me every step of the way, and as much as I wanted to hate him, I couldn't help but look as I walked past him. The longing I'd seen from the kitchen had changed to utter sadness in his brown eyes.

My chest hurt so much I wasn't sure I could breathe, but Olivia's smile beckoning me toward her and Cassian helped and I made it past Stefan without collapsing to the floor. I couldn't stand much more of this, though. Even when I couldn't see him, I knew he was looking at me with those eyes so sad.

"Shay, I'm so happy you came!" Olivia said as she reached out to hug me. Dressed in a gorgeous pink floor length gown that highlighted her red hair, she looked stunning. Stepping back away, she said, "I'm so glad to see you. You look beautiful!"

"Thank you. You look lovely. Congratulations to both of you."

Cassian kissed me on the cheek and handed me a glass of champagne. "Time for a toast." Addressing the room full of people, he said, "Thank you to everyone who's come tonight to celebrate with Olivia and me. I hope each of you finds the happiness we've found."

Everyone said, "Cheers!" and I raised my glass to them. "I'm very happy for the two of you. Thank you for inviting me, but I think I need to go."

Both of them looked over in Stefan's direction and then back at me. Leaning in to hug me again, Olivia whispered, "I know it was probably hard for you to come tonight, but I'm so glad you did. I hope we get to see you again soon."

Her words made my tears well up in my eyes. I didn't know why since Stefan and I had never planned on being anything permanent, but I felt like I was losing a friend as I turned away to leave. I slipped out onto the porch and took a deep breath of air, happy that I'd made it through it all.

Just as I began to believe I'd made it out emotionally unscathed, a hand touched my arm, and I looked to see Alexandria standing next to me. "It's so wonderful to see you again, Shay."

"Hello. I was just leaving. You have a lovely home."

"Are you leaving because of Stefan?"

"You're more direct than I am. I can respect that, though. Yes, I'm leaving because he's here."

Alexandria's brown eyes searched mine as she said softly, "I was sorry to hear that the two of you aren't together anymore."

I felt the tears welling up in my eyes again. Swallowing hard, I said, "I have to go. I'm sorry, but I can't be here. It's too hard. I hope you understand."

"I hope I get to see you again, Shay. I liked our time together, and I think you made my son happy."

It was all I could to push a weak smile on my face as I bid her goodbye and walked quickly toward the road. Unfortunately, I had no idea where the attendants had parked my car, and they were nowhere to be found. On the verge of tears and searching for anyone who might be able to help me without having to go back to the house, I heard footsteps coming behind me and turned to see Stefan walking toward me.

"Please don't go. I was hoping we could talk."

"There's nothing to talk about. Just leave me alone so I can find my car and drive away from here."

Stefan slid his hand over my shoulder, and just the merest touch made a yearning spike inside me. "Please stay. I know you miss me as much as I miss you."

Refusing to face him, I hung my head. "No, I don't."

He came around in front of me and cradled my face in his hands, looking down at me with pure pain in his eyes. "Yes, you do. I see it in your eyes. It's the same look I see every time I look in the mirror."

I couldn't do this with him. Closing my eyes, I willed the tears away, but they came anyway, a single one sliding down my cheek followed by the rest that wouldn't stay hidden. "Please let me go," I sobbed. "Why do you want to see me cry? So you can know I still care? Fine. I care. Now let me go."

Stefan gently slid the pads of his thumbs over my cheeks. "I can't function without you, Shay. I try, but all I can think of is you and how much I hurt you. These last two weeks have been hell. I know I fucked up huge. I know. But I'll do anything if you'd just come back to me. You're everything to me."

"I can't get the image of you with her out of my mind. It hurts so much, Stefan. Every time I think of you, I think of that night and every inch of my body aches."

Pressing his forehead to mine, he whispered in

a voice full of his own pain, "I'm sorry, Shay. I never meant to hurt you. I just couldn't let Cash suffer for me anymore, but I never wanted you to get hurt."

I stepped back, afraid of what my heart was already feeling. "How could you think I wouldn't get hurt when you did that?"

"I wasn't thinking straight. I just didn't want to fuck up Cash's happiness anymore. Shay, I'll do whatever it takes to get you back. I can't go on like this. Every day without you is killing me."

I closed my eyes and lowered my head. "Olivia told me what happened with Lola's father. Why didn't you say anything to me? We were supposed to tell each other the truth."

"I couldn't tell you. I think I knew I'd eventually have to risk everything, but I kept thinking I could push it off to the future. When he came to see me, I knew the time had come. That's why I finally told you I loved you that night."

"I wish you would have told me what you were going through. I might not have understood, but you wouldn't have been alone."

"I couldn't. I couldn't let you see me as that kind of man. I can't deny I was that man for a long time, but you made me want to be someone better."

I stared up at him as my heart broke for both of us. It was stupid and foolish and I couldn't explain it, but I loved him even now after all the times I'd sworn to hate him forever.

"Please don't go. I'll do anything, Shay. Just don't go."

"I was always going to go, Stefan. What does it matter if it's now or at the end of the year? We always had an expiration date, whether we wanted to admit it or not."

Stefan shook his head. "No. Doesn't it matter that we love each other? That's got to mean something, Shay."

"We were never going to ride off into the sunset like Cassian and Olivia. We're not that kind of people."

"Why not? Why can't people change? I did because of you."

Stefan pressed his lips against mine in a kiss that made me wish we could rewind time to before all the horrible things happened. I'd been lying to myself thinking that I could be fine if I never saw him again. I couldn't be. But I couldn't change the reality of who I was either.

Taking his hands in mine, I brought them to my lips and kissed them. "Before there was a you and me, there was just me, and I've dedicated years to my future. I have to be who I am, and who I am is someone who's leaving in a few weeks and will be gone for a whole year while you're back here with the Lolas, Mikas, and Kats of the world. How could I ever believe you'd wait for me?"

"Because I would. I could install cameras throughout the bar and in my office so you could see wherever I am and whoever I'm talking to at all times. I'd even put cameras in my condo so you could see it's just me moping around all lonely wishing you were there next to me."

"Cameras? What kind of relationship is that, Stefan? This is what happens when two people don't have honesty between them. I don't want to watch you like a hawk, worried that you'll want someone else because I'm not there. I can't do that."

I backed away from him as the reality that a year apart from each other would bring all those problems. I couldn't live like that.

"We were never meant to be forever. You and I knew

that. I love you, Stefan, but it's time to say goodbye."

"No! I can't let you go. I can't believe I'd finally fall in love and then lose you before I had a chance to show you I'm not the man you thought I was from that first day. I swear it, Shay."

I kissed him softly on the cheek. "I know, baby. I know it's not fair, but I can't spend an entire year wondering if the man I love is making another mistake. Maybe when I finish my year away if we still feel the same—"

As I tried to keep myself from crying at the thought of us never being together again, he pulled me into his body and held me against him. "You can give me a thousand reasons why we won't work. All I can give you is one answer. I love you. You're my everything. I'm lost without you. Make whatever demand you want and I'll do it. Quit the club. Move to Copenhagen with you. Leave behind the life I have here. I'll do all of them if you'll just give me a chance to show you I love you."

I looked at him, stunned by what he'd just said. "Your entire life is here. You would do those things for me?"

"I would do anything. I love you more than I ever thought I could love anyone. Being without you is killing me. Please say we can try again."

"Stefan, how can I ever trust you?"

He frowned and shook his head. "I don't know. All I can do is show you every day that I love you and hope that one day you believe me."

"What if that's not enough?" I asked, afraid of his answer.

"I made you happy once. I can do it again. I know I can. All I need is the chance."

Wrapping my arms around his neck, I pulled him close and buried my face in his chest, whispering, "I want to believe you. I've missed you so much. I've never been so unhappy in my life. I want to be like we were, but what if too much has happened?"

He hugged me tightly and said, "I can't believe that. You don't believe that either. Tell me you don't and that you believe in us."

"I love you so much I don't know what to do. Every instinct in me says to walk away, but my heart keeps saying stay."

Stefan tilted my head back and smiled. "Then listen to your heart."

"I've never listened to my heart. I'm a scientist. I listen to my head. But my head says to run away because you're that person I met that first day at Club X."

"That guy wanted you from the moment he met you. Maybe not for the right reasons, but he did. And then when he got to know you, he saw a million more reasons why he'd want to be with you. What does your heart say?"

"That being without you hurts so much all I wanted to do was lie in bed and cry. That being without you left a hole in my life nobody could fill."

"You know what my heart says? That whatever it takes I'll do it because I love you, Shay. Please. I'm begging you. Give me another chance."

"I want to, but it hurts so much to think of what you did."

"Then don't think of it. Give us the chance to create a million other memories so that one gets pushed out of your mind. I love you, Shay, and I swear I won't screw up again."

Every logical part of me said no, but for the first time, I listened to my heart and how much it hurt to go on without him. Taking me in his arms, he held me close to him and I let myself feel how incredible it was to be next to him again.

"I love you, Stefan."

"I won't let you down, Shay. I promise to be that man I became because of you. I promise."

EPILOGUE

🍾 STEFAN

For three weeks, Shay and I had spent every minute we could together. Lola quit when she realized I wouldn't keep doing her and Shank's bidding, so Shay and I ran the bar and then went home together to my condo every night. I didn't want to think about it, but every morning when I woke up, I knew we were another day closer to her leaving me again, this time for a whole year.

And then that day was here.

Shay rested her chin on my chest and stared up at me. "You look a million miles away. Where are you?"

I ran my hand over her soft hair that fell across my stomach. "Right here where I should be."

"It's only for a year, Stefan. I know it seems like a long time, but it's not. We can Skype every night before you go out into the club, and it will be over before we know it."

"I guess."

She slid up to kiss me. "Think of it as the last year you get to do whatever you want before settling down."

"I don't need a year to do anything. I'd rather be with you."

Shay remained quiet for a minute as the thought of seeing her get on that plane in a few hours made me feel like I was losing my entire world. I didn't want to let go, but I had to and it was tearing me up.

"What are you worried about, baby?"

Finally, I admitted the fear that terrified me most about her leaving me for a year. "That you'll meet some scientist who can understand what you mean when you talk about your work and you'll realize he's what you really want. One night you'll send me an email saying you can't talk that night, that you're busy, and then before I know what happened, I'll have lost you to someone smart like you."

"Oh, Stefan, that won't happen. I promise."

"Why wouldn't it happen? You're going to be surrounded by all those science guys who know exactly what you're talking about and one thing will lead to another and…"

She chuckled at me. "Have you ever seen any science guys? They're notoriously not hot. I've never met one that turned my head in the least."

"That's not helping."

Holding my face in her hands, she stopped teasing me and said quietly, "Stefan, I'm madly, crazy, out of my mind in love with you. That's why it won't happen."

"And what happens after the year is up?" I asked, knowing even after a year in Copenhagen that her work might keep her away from Tampa.

"I don't know. I've worked a long time to get where I am in my work, but there might not be any way I can stay here and still do my research."

"I've never lived anywhere else, you know that? I have all this money and I never even go on vacation to other places. Maybe it's time I should."

"Maybe."

"Maybe it's time I think about leaving Tampa."

Shay knitted her brows. "Leaving? Where would you go?"

I looked down at her and smiled. "Wherever you go."

"Could you do that? Would you?"

Nodding, I said, "Yeah, I would."

Her smile lit up her face, and she hugged me. "That means so much to me that you'd be willing to go where I could do my work."

"I already lost my house and my bike over you. Why not completely change my life up?"

Shay sat up next to me and poked me in the side. "That was your fault you made that bet. You and Kane are bad. By the way, when does he move in?"

"He doesn't want to collect on the bet. I think he likes his rooms at the club. Maybe I'll tell him if he's willing to wait a year, he can have this place when you get back since we'll either be moving to our own place here or moving to a new city."

"I like that idea." Her smiled slowly faded away. Running her fingers along my jaw, she touched my cheek. "I need to start getting ready. My flight leaves at 1:30."

Swallowing hard, I nodded. "I know." I'd thought about that flight and when she'd leave me every day since we got back together. I knew.

She leaned down and kissed me softly and whispered, "I love you, no matter where we are. Don't forget that."

We stopped at the security checkpoint for Shay's flight, and I felt the same ache in my chest as when I'd lost her just a few weeks before. I wanted to believe this wasn't goodbye, but deep down I wasn't sure, even if she seemed to be.

Shay bit her lip and wiped her tears from her eyes that had taken on a watery green look. "I promised myself I wouldn't cry, but I can't help it. Promise me every night, Stefan. Every night we'll talk, right?"

Pulling her to me, I held her close and kissed the top of her head. "Every night. I promise. I'll bore you with stories about the club and you can tell me all about your day. It will be just like we're sitting next to one another."

Stepping back, she looked up at me. "Promise me one other thing."

"Anything."

I saw the worry in her eyes and knew what she wanted to say. "If at any time you decide you can't wait for me, promise me you'll at least be honest with me. That's all I ask. Honesty."

"I can't promise that because I don't want anyone else and I won't. There's only you, Shay."

"A year's a long time, Stefan. What if…?" She didn't finish her sentence but I knew what she meant.

"I have hands," I said with a smile. "And I can always fly over to you if I just can't wait anymore."

Wiping her cheek, she smiled through her tears. "Only you would say that. Okay. We can do this, right?"

"Yeah, we can do this," I said, trying to control my emotions as I felt my last moments with her slipping away. "Go show those science nerds how smart you are, princess. I'll be here when you get back."

Shay wrapped her arms around my neck and clung to me. "I love you, Stefan. Part of me doesn't want to go, but the other part knows I have to. I have to do this."

I kissed her and wished I'd never have to let her go. "I love you. No more tears. I'll see you tomorrow night when we talk."

Watching her walk away into that security line, I wasn't sure I could take a breath my chest hurt so much. She turned to blow me a kiss and I smiled, and then she disappeared in the crowd of people like her heading to their gates to take off on planes and leave behind the people who loved them. Two hours later, I stood watching through the airport windows as Flight 3279 finally lifted off the ground taking the woman I loved with it.

I just hoped it wasn't forever.

X

Sitting in Cash's office for the weekly meeting I still didn't see the point to, my brother and I waited for Kane, who'd kept us hanging for the last twenty minutes. He strolled in like we had all the time in the world. Cash and he might, but I had a standing date with the woman I loved to video chat, and Shay would be calling in less than an hour.

Kane sat down in the chair next to mine and shrugged, like his wasting our time meant nothing to him. "Sorry. It couldn't be avoided."

"Yeah, yeah. Let's get this meeting going. I have to be out of here in a couple."

Both of them stared at me like I'd said something bizarre. Cash smiled and shook his head. "Anything important, Stef?"

"Yeah, it's important. I'm going to talk to Shay like I do every day, so let's get going."

"I still can't get used to you as a committed man, little brother," Kane teased. "And that you got that woman still amazes me."

I rolled my eyes at the same jabs he always made.

"You need some new material, Kane. Maybe if you ever spent any time with women you wouldn't be fixated on my love life."

"Okay, okay. Let's get going with this. Olivia and I have to finalize the plans for the wedding at four today," Cash said as he typed his password into his laptop. "We've got to discuss what we're going to do now that Shank isn't going to be around to help us anymore. We've been lucky for much longer than I thought we'd be, but luck runs out."

I looked at both my brothers for any sense that they blamed me. The whole Lola situation hadn't been my finest hour, and in truth, Shank gunning for us now was my fault. That Cash and Kane had forgiven me made me feel a little better about things, but the truth was that the club was in danger as long as we didn't have someone to protect us from nightly raids.

"Any progress with that councilman?" Kane asked. "He could help. He's already a member of the club. I'm sure he wants it open again."

Cash solemnly shook his head. "Maybe. I have a meeting set up with him in a few days." I saw the look of worry in my brother's eyes, but he quickly forced a smile. "He's got deep pockets and seems to be interested in adding to them, so he might be willing to. I think he might be able to help with the police if we can convince him."

I hated seeing him so stressed out. More than Kane or me, Cash bore the responsibility for the club's security and the concern he had about it was written all over his face.

"What if we kept it legal for a while?" I asked, knowing how much of Club X was outside the bounds of what was legal. Virtually everything in Kane's area could be something we'd get shut down for on any given night.

"That's going to cut into profits, Stefan. This comes as a bad time for Cash especially."

I looked at Kane and nodded. "I know, but it's got to be better than being shut down." Turning toward Cash, I said, "I'm sorry this is happening just around your big day. I didn't mean for any of this to happen."

"I know, Stef. Don't worry. We'll get through this. We handled things before we found Shank, and we'll handle it now. It's nice to hear you say you're sorry, though."

Kane elbowed me and I saw him smile. "Who would have thought you'd finally grow up on a bet between the two of us?"

"Does your girlfriend know you made a bet on her?" Cash asked.

"Yes, she does know. I told her. I'm a changed man, gentlemen. Being with Shay has transformed me."

The two of them sat staring at me as if I'd announced I planned to travel to Mars, but it didn't matter if they believed me or not. I believed in Shay and me. That's all that counted.

"Now, if I can please be excused, Mr. March, I have a date with my girlfriend I'd like to get ready for."

Cash rolled his eyes and smiled. "Go. You're no use to us when you're acting like a lovesick puppy. If you need to know anything about the week ahead, Kane or I will tell you."

I stood to leave and Kane smacked me on the arm. "Tell Shay we miss her here. The bar isn't the same without her. I miss seeing her on the fourth floor."

"Watch it, big brother. That's the woman I love you're talking about."

Positioned in front of my laptop, I sat waiting for Shay's call, nervously running my hands through my hair as I readied myself to see her again. Every night of the week we did this together, and every time it made me miss her even more than the time before. I never told her that because what would be the point? She was thousands of miles and a continent away in Copenhagen for another eight months, and there was nothing that could change that.

Sometimes late at night as I lay in bed missing her more than I thought it was possible to miss someone I thought about telling Cash and Kane I couldn't do this anymore and I had to leave. I had more than enough money to pay for a few months of living in Copenhagen, no matter how much it cost. But I couldn't do that to them after how much I'd fucked things up at the club, and Shay needed to do her work. She didn't need me hanging around her neck. We'd endured four months apart. We could handle eight more.

My laptop made that chiming noise that signaled she was calling me, and I turned to see her beautiful face in front of me again and that smile that never failed to make my day.

"Hey, baby! What's going on?" she asked as she always did at the beginning of our chat.

"Not much. How's my girl today? Doing lots of research?"

Chuckling, she shook her head. "I love that you ask me about my research, but you don't have to, Stefan. I know it's not your thing."

"It's my thing because it's your thing, Shay."

"Well, I could bore you with all the details, but I'd rather talk about other things. What have you been up to?"

"Just the club and home. Counting the days until you're back," I said, trying to sound upbeat.

"What's new at the club? I miss that place. I never

thought I'd say that about a bartending job, but I do."

"It's always the same. You know how it is."

Her smile faded just a touch, and she asked in a quiet voice, "Is something wrong, Stefan? You seem different tonight."

I forced myself to smile and shook my head. "No. Just tired."

She leaned in toward where the camera was on her laptop and blew me a kiss. "I miss you, baby. It's lonely without you."

"Me too. It's just eight months, though, right?"

Nodding, she said, "Right. We'll be seeing each other soon. Those months will go by like it's just a few minutes."

My cell phone rang and I looked over to see it was Cash calling. Silencing it, I ignored it, pissed off that he didn't remember how important these calls from Shay were to me.

"Do you have to go? I heard the phone ring."

"No, that's just Cash. I'll talk to him later."

Just then, my phone rang again. I looked over and saw it was Cash for a second time. What the fuck? Irritated, I silenced my phone again and turned back to Shay as she said, "I'll let you go. We can talk later."

"No, no. I don't need to go yet. I want to spend more time with you. Whatever Cash wants can wait, Shay."

"Are you sure? Maybe you should go see what he wants."

I leaned forward toward my laptop screen and touched my fingertip to it, wishing I was touching her. "I don't want to talk about my brother or the club anymore. I want to hear you tell me about your day, even if I don't have a clue what you're talking about. I want to close my eyes and pretend you're here instead of what feels like a million miles away."

"Oh, Stefan. Honey, you look so sad. I hate that we can't be together, but I had to do this. I couldn't just be some girl who mooched off you. You understand that, don't you?"

I hung my head. "Yeah. I understand. I just wish you were here."

A knock on my office door set me off, and I jumped out of my chair to find out who the hell couldn't figure out I was fucking busy. Throwing the door open, I saw Cash standing there with his phone in his hand.

"What do you want? You know I'm busy talking to Shay in here."

"I need you to come into my office. We've got something we need to handle right now."

"No! I'm talking to Shay now. When I'm done, I'll come back. Now get the fuck out of my face."

"Stefan, this is club business. I know you want to talk to her, but this takes priority."

From behind me, I heard Shay's voice come from my laptop. "Stefan, I can call back in a little while, if that would be better."

Storming back to my desk, I sat down. "No. We don't get much time together, so whatever my goddamned brothers want from me will have to wait."

Shay's green eyes stared out at me with a look that told me she understood. I didn't, but she did. "It's okay, baby. Remember, we can talk again tonight, and we'll see each other really soon, right? How about I give you a half hour?"

I looked up over the laptop and glared at Cash. "You have thirty minutes. Any more, and you and Kane will have to figure whatever it is out by yourselves."

"Thirty minutes. Fine."

Turning my attention back to where it belonged, I forced a smile. "I'll talk to you in a half hour, okay?

We'll pick up right where we left off."

"Okay. I love you, Stefan."

"I love you too, Shay."

My laptop screen returned to my screensaver of a picture of Shay and me at the beach, and I slammed the top closed. "Cash, what the fuck could be this important? This better be big. I mean, fucking huge."

"It is."

"Well, it better be," I grumbled as I followed him out into the club. "So what's the problem?"

"I think you'll get a better handle on the situation when we get to my office. Relax. She said she'd speak to you in a few minutes. It'll be fine."

I shot him a glare and followed him into his office. Kane was nowhere to be found, though. Looking around, I snapped, "I better not have just walked away from a chat with Shay to wait for that fucker to get his ass down here. He's as bad as I used to be these days."

Cash picked up his phone and dialed a number. "I'll get him. Just head back into the conference room and take a seat. I'm sure he'll be right down."

"Conference room? Are we having another goddamned meeting, Cash? You couldn't do this without me?"

"Just go. We'll be back in a minute."

"Fine. I swear you two would be lost without me, you know that?"

Cash was already ignoring me as he began to speak to Kane on the phone, so I headed back to the conference room and took a seat at the enormous cherry wood table that reminded me of something my father used to have in his office. Closing my eyes, I tried to calm down, knowing it would take just one or two wrong words from Kane and I'd lose it.

I heard Olivia's office door open, and I turned to see

her wearing a huge smile. At least someone was happy to be there. "Hey, Olivia. What's up? Any idea what this meeting's about?"

She stepped aside and from behind her Shay stepped into the room. Any coherent thoughts in my mind slipped away, and I stood up from the table in shock. "How? When? I was just talking to you in Copenhagen."

"The researcher I'm working with had to leave for a conference and he gave us all a week off. I wanted to surprise you, so I arranged it with Olivia to fly in last night and stay at her and Cash's place."

My body felt frozen on the spot where I stood. After all those nights alone, there she was right in front of me. Shay smiled and ran into my arms, and I was sure at that moment I'd never felt happier in my life. "I can't believe you're finally here again. I missed you so damn much, Shay."

She squeezed me tight and looked up at me. "I missed you too. It's only for a week, but it's something."

Cradling her face, I joked, "Well, if all we have is a week, we better get going. We've got a lot of time to make up for."

I took her hand and led her out into Cash's office where he, Kane, and Olivia stood. "You were all in on this, weren't you?" I asked.

"We couldn't stand your moping anymore," Kane said with a smile. "But it was Shay who came up with the idea to surprise you."

"Well, I'm glad she did, and thanks for helping her. This might be the best surprise I've ever gotten."

"What are your plans for the week?" Olivia asked.

"About that guys. I'm taking the week off. Don't call or even text me. I'm busy until next week, right?" I announced as I looked down at Shay.

"Right. See you guys!"

I figured I'd hear some complaint from Cash or Kane as she pulled me toward the door, but they just nodded as if they'd expected me to be like this. All the better. I didn't have time to argue with them today. I had one week with Shay, and I wasn't going to waste a minute of that time.

X

Shay climbed off my bike and took my hand as we walked into my building. Looking up at me, she said, "I missed that, you know that?"

"What? The bike?"

"Yeah. Silly, right? But I missed that feeling of holding on as you fly through the city."

We entered the elevator and as the doors closed, I pulled her into my arms. "I missed this. Getting to feel you next to me when I come home."

"Well, for the next six days, you can have that to your heart's content," she said smiling up at me.

"I'm not sure six days is going to be enough. This time apart is harder than I thought it would be, princess."

"I know, Stefan. It is for me too, but this is important to me."

I kissed her forehead. "I know. Epimenics and all that."

She chuckled as I mispronounced her field for the four thousandth time. "Epigenetics. I don't want to talk about that while I'm here, though. All I want to do is focus on you, my gorgeous, incredible boyfriend who I haven't seen for four long months."

"I'm all for that," I said as I pressed the button for the fifteenth floor.

Shay gave me a wink and pushed the STOP button

so the elevator came to a halt just as it began to rise. As she slowly lowered herself to her knees, she smiled. "Do you know in all the time we've been together I've never made up for that night I left you high and dry in your office? Do you remember?"

She unzipped my jeans and took my cock out to playfully flick the head with her tongue, nearly driving me crazy.

"I remember," I said nearly breathless in anticipation of her going down on me right there in the elevator.

"Well, I think it's about time to remedy that oversight, don't you?"

She slid the first few inches of my cock into her mouth, sending my body into near hyper drive. It had been four long months since anything but my own hand had touched me, but the wait had been worth it. The feel of her lips and tongue gliding up and down my shaft made my legs go weak, and I reached back to grab the bar on the wall for balance.

Shay popped my cock out of her mouth and smiled up at me. "You okay up there?"

"Yeah," I answered in more a groan than a word.

She slid her mouth back over the head of my cock and all the way down to the base, taking me into her so far I had to be nearly gagging her. Then she slowly came back up, her tongue teasing the underneath as my cock retreated from her mouth.

"Baby, it's not going to take long. Four months of just my hand isn't the same as you. I'm close."

"Good."

I stuffed my hands into her hair and tightened their hold to direct her as she proceeded to give me a blow job that nearly took the top of my head off with it when I came. I flooded her mouth as my knees buckled, and she took every last drop I gave her.

When she was finished, she stood up and kissed me. "I think that makes up for that night, don't you?"

Opening my eyes, I said with smile, "It might require a few more to really make up for that heinous thing you did."

"Well, how about I give you time to recuperate and I'll do more making up later. Deal?"

I pressed the STOP button again to make the elevator continue up to my floor and nodded. "Deal."

Lying in bed watching the sun set on our first day together made me miss her already and she'd just come back to me. My heart felt like someone had it in a vice. How was I going to live without her for eight months more?

I squeezed her against me, and Shay gently pushed my chin so I had to look at her. "Hey, what's wrong? No sad faces. We have a week together we didn't expect."

"I know."

"Then what's wrong, Stefan?"

"I miss you so much, Shay. Everything I thought meant something in my life doesn't anymore without you here. The club, my life, none of it means anything now that you're not here with me."

"I know, baby, but it's just for eight months more."

"What's Copenhagen like?"

"Cold. Snowy. Pretty much the opposite of Tampa. I work all the time and look forward to talking to you every night. That's about all I do."

"Then not somewhere we want to go, right?"

She smiled and shook her head. "No. I don't think I want to live in Copenhagen after my time there is up. But I have a surprise for you."

I looked down at her to see her grinning from ear to ear. "What's that?"

"While I'm here, I'm talking to Dr. Taduch about

a position at the university for when I get back. He emailed me a week or so ago and told me about it, so I sent all my materials in to apply already."

"So after the year is up you might be back here to stay?" I asked, my heart filling with joy at her news.

"Yeah. It might just be for a year, but that could give us some time to figure out what we want to do when we grow up."

"Will you be able to come back for Cash and Olivia's wedding?"

Shay shook her head. "I don't think so. The soonest I could come back for a visit would probably be August. I think we all have a week off then."

"That's only four months," I said quietly, trying to convince myself it wasn't that long.

Snuggling up against me, she pressed her lips against my neck and nuzzled my skin. "And then four months later I'll be back."

"I know. Not too long."

Not very convincing.

She whispered, "But then I'll be back and we can spend every night together like this. Deal?"

"This isn't as good as the last time you offered me a deal a few hours ago," I said, trying to find the humor in what made me feel like shit.

Shay sat up next to me and drummed her fingers on my stomach. "What if I told you something I think will make you smile?"

I crossed my arms behind my head and nodded. "You don't have to go back and you'll stay here with me forever?"

She gave me a look that told me I was being difficult and shook her head. "No, but I think this will still make you smile."

"Okay. Shoot."

"Do you remember the first day we met—the day you and Kane made that infamous bet?"

"Yeah…"

I wondered if she was about to tell me Kane had said something to her about our bet now that she and the rest of my family were close enough to keep secrets from me.

"Well, I made a little bet of my own that day."

I was intrigued. "A bet? About what?"

"I was so furious with you after how you acted that I bet Carrie I could make you, one of Tampa's biggest players, fall for me."

I knew there was a reason I couldn't resist her from the minute we met. Few women had confidence like she did, and even fewer could back it up. Shay sat there looking at me with a playful expression that made me want to take her in my arms and never let her go.

"So you bet you could get me, and I bet I could get you? I guess we're not so different after all, Shay Callahan."

Leaning down, she kissed me sweetly and snuggled up against me again. "Who'd have thought it, Stefan March?"

She was right. In many ways, we were as different as night and day, but that feeling I'd had the moment I met her hadn't been just physical. I'd been with more women than I cared to remember, but even though I didn't know it that day, I'd met the one who could beat me at my own game.

Maybe winning wasn't the most important thing after all.

THE END

SURRENDER EXTRAS

Visit Pinterest to check out the **Club X board** to see Stefan's Ducati, Cassian's Maserati, Kane's Mustang, and other great pics related to the Club X series!

Turn the page for a sneak peek at:

POSSESSION (CLUB X #3)
COMING EARLY 2015!

POSSESSION

CLUB X #3

Kane Jackson, the ruler of the fantasy section of Club X, has always been different from his brothers. The bastard son of Cassian March III, he grew up without the money and privilege Cassian and Stefan enjoyed from the March name, instead only knowing his father as the man who abandoned him and seeing himself as unloved and unwanted. He let love in once and like everything else in his life, all that came from it was pain. His heart hidden behind the walls he's built since then, Kane is now just the dark figure who rules over the fantasies of others but has none himself.

Abbi Linde can't seem to get a break. Too many bad men and bad choices have left her bruised and broken, but the opportunity to dance at Club X could change everything. For the first time, she might be able to make a life for herself and find the happiness she longs for. After what feels like a lifetime of heartbreak, Abbi still believes one day her dreams will come true and she'll find the love that's eluded her.

Even the darkest heart craves the light, but will the darkness be too much for love to overcome with these two souls?

ADD POSSESSION (CLUB X #3) TO YOUR GOODREADS SHELF TODAY!

ABOUT THE AUTHOR

K.M. Scott writes sexy contemporary romance with characters her readers love. A New York Times and USA Today bestselling author, she's been in love with romance since reading her first romance novel in junior high (she was a very curious girl!). She lives in Pennsylvania with her teenage son and a herd of animals and when she's not writing can be found reading or feeding her TV addiction.

Be sure to visit K.M.'s Facebook page at **https:// www.facebook.com/kmscottauthor** for all the latest on her books, along with giveaways and other goodies and her website at **www.kmscottbooks.com**! And to hear about Advanced Review Copy opportunities and all the news on K.M. Scott books first, sign up for her newsletter at **http://mad.ly/signups/91132/join**

BOOKS BY K.M. SCOTT

Heart of Stone Series
Crash Into Me **(Heart of Stone #1)**
Fall Into Me **(Heart of Stone #2)**
Give In To Me **(Heart of Stone #3)**
The Heart of Stone Trilogy Box Set
Ever After **(A Heart of Stone Novella)**

Club X Series
Temptation **(Club X #1)**
Possession **(Club X #3) Coming Early 2015**

Add them to your Goodreads shelf today!

Love sexy paranormal romance? K.M. writes
under the name Gabrielle Bisset too! Visit Gabrielle's
Facebook page and her website at **http://www.
gabriellebisset.com/** to find out about her books.

BOOKS BY GABRIELLE BISSET

Vampire Dreams Revamped **(Sons of Navarus Prequel)**
Blood Avenged **(Sons of Navarus #1)**
Blood Betrayed **(Sons of Navarus #2)**
Longing **(A Sons of Navarus Short Story)**
Blood Spirit **(Sons of Navarus #3)**
The Deepest Cut **(A Sons of Navarus Short Story)**
Blood Prophecy **(Sons of Navarus #4)**
Blood & Dreams Sons of Navarus Box Set

Love's Master
Masquerade
The Victorian Erotic Romance Trilogy

This paperback interior was designed and formatted by

www.emtippettsbookdesigns.com

Artisan interiors for discerning authors and publishers.

19894297R00190

Made in the USA
Middletown, DE
07 May 2015